The Good Life
Part 3:
A New Generation

The Good Life

Part 3:

A New Generation

Dorian Sykes

www.urbanbooks.net

Urban Books, LLC
300 Farmingdale Road, NY-Route 109
Farmingdale, NY 11735

The Good Life Part 3: A New Generation

ISBN 13: 978-1-64556-435-5
ISBN 10: 1-64556-435-5

First Mass Market Printing May 2023
First Trade Paperback Printing January 2022
Printed in the United States of America

10 9 8 7 6 5 4 3 2 1

Distributed by Kensington Publishing Corp.
Submit Orders to:
Customer Service
400 Hahn Road
Westminster, MD 21157-4627
Phone: 1-800-733-3000
Fax: 1-800-659-2436

Acknowledgments

All praises are due to Allah, without any association of partners. If you've read *Part One,* in the acknowledgments you see that I had been released from prison and had just inked my first deal with Urban Books. However, there was so much going on in my life at the time that I put one foot back into the streets until I found myself waist-deep again in the very things that I vowed never to touch again. Needless to say, my writing career took a back seat, and as I pen these acknowledgments today, I regret to inform you that I am on my way back to prison. I was given this talent of crafting stories and sharing them with the world by the Creator, Allah. And I realize now that I am where I sit today because I wasn't using the gifts He had bestowed upon me. Allah has a way of reminding us that He is the best of all planners . . . and that it is His plan alone that shall prevail. And those of us who refuse His plan will be punished. It is Allah's plan to sit me here to remind me of the gift He gave me, which is to pen these tales my fans have come to love.

Acknowledgments

Beyond that, I must thank my ol' Bird, Ms. Leslie K. Sykes, for always being consistent like a heartbeat. Ms. Michel Moore-White for adopting me as her "Dorian" and for being a real person outside of this book ish. To all the fine folks at Genesee County Jail who took good care of me: Lt. Lanning, Lt. Skinner, Nurse Lori (Boss Lady), Nurse Janell, Nurse Taquana, and Sara.

My dude Richard Jeanty for still taking my calls from where I'm at and giving me the advice you've given me. Thanks for not giving up on me. My ol' head Gerald "J-Bo" Johnson, you tried to keep me from going back to prison the few times we bumped into each other, and, man, I just wanted to let you know that I heard you then and I really wish I had listened to you. My Big Homie, Arthur "Plex" Pless, man, I know that I fumbled the ball. All I can do now is get back up and try harder next go-round. Big Meech and my nigga B. Gizzle (SMH), both y'all boys gave me a million-dollar blueprint. I'm sitting on them until I touch down again, ya feel me?

Kevin Chiles (Don Diva), man, thank you for always taking my calls and for just being a good dude. DJ Kay Slay, the same goes for you, my dude. I'ma get you those promos soon. To every person who's ever read one of my books and told me how much you really enjoyed it, no lie, y'all inspire me to keep writing. I thank y'all, and I hope you enjoy this one here. I'ma keep 'em coming.

—Dorian Sykes

Prologue

The sign above the one-way-in slate gray building read: FATT MARK'S BARBER SHOP. The inside was
packed to standing room only with regulars all
hoping to get their fresh blend by one of the four
master barbers. It was a Saturday morning, so
SportsCenter played vaguely on the plasma TV
mounted high above the seating area, but street
politics, wisecracks, and talk about the night before made up the vibe.

The only windows to the shop were blocked
windows, so there was no seeing outside or inside.
A lone camera faced the entrance, so the barbers
could see anyone approaching on the shop's monitor. Everyone had to be buzzed in. But there were
the times people would catch the door opening as
others headed out. And that was the case on this
early Saturday morning.

As an older black guy dressed in his GM work
clothes exited the shop with his young son in front
of him, two masked figures closed their path. The
man's eyes shone with fear as he instinctively put
his arm over his son's chest, drawing him close.

The little boy's eyes rose with two AK-47s that were ushering them back inside the shop. There was a yelp of screams and panic, and suddenly two shots rang out. Baka! Baka!

The second barber, Toni, had gone for his .380, which he kept on his hip, and fired in the direction of the masked men. He'd struck one in the arm, but it proved to be a grave mistake, because the two men returned fire. Lakaa! Lakaa! Lakaa!

The little boy and his dad were the first to feel the flames of the hot, burning rounds being rapidly thrown aimlessly around the shop as the two gunmen sprayed side to side with all intent to kill. It was complete mayhem and a bloodbath. The shots seemed as if they would never cease.

The 200 rounds between the two drums were enough to kill everyone inside along with anyone else who may have wanted to join them.

But not everyone was killed when the shots ceased. All of a sudden, the two men had vanished from the shop just as quick as they'd come. Screeching tires signaled their getaway.

The shop reeked of gunpowder and the smell of blood as a cloud of smog hung over a slew of bodies lying around the floor. When the smoke cleared, a total of seven people had lost their lives, including the young boy who looked to be around 8 years old and his father, who lay soaked in blood with his arm wrapped over his son. Toni had been killed.

His brain dripped from his barber mirror behind him. The two customers getting their hair cut were slaughtered in their chairs, one of them being 7 Mile Slim. His silk designer shirt was torn open by the wrath of the gunfire. His chest looked as if a tiger had attacked him in the wild. Slim's head was dramatically thrown back with blood oozing down the diamond 7 Mile pendant on his chain.

Others lay dead about the shop while many clung to hope that help was on the way and they'd prayerfully survive their own injuries.

Chapter One

The massacre up at Fatt Mark's didn't even make the news. There had been so many murders in Detroit since the summer started that it was almost expected somebody would be killed as the summer rolled on. Everyday someone was getting gunned down. It used to be a nighttime thing, when killers would stalk their prey to a location, then get their man. But that was a thing of the past. This new and upcoming generation had taken to murdering their opts, as they called their enemies, in broad daylight. They wanted the kill to be grand and talked about.

Although the local news hadn't covered the shooting at the barber shop, the streets had. There were so many theories as to why the shop got shot up, but the one that made the most sense was 7 Mile Slim being the intended target. It was common knowledge that he had $50,000 on his head, contracted, from what the streets were saying, by Saw.

Supposedly, all the murders around the city were attributed to an ongoing feud between Slim and Saw, which wasn't even about drugs, territory, or money. It all started behind Karmesha, a sack-chaser who had sunk her claws into both Slim and Saw and many other ballers before them. The beef turned into an all-out war because both men had their pride, neither wanting to be the one to back down.

On the corner of 7 Mile Road and Syracuse sat an old pub that used to be called Sheeba's. It had been painted completely black now and bore no official name, and it was closed to the public. A line of old schools sitting on rims lined the front of the building, while three bulletproof S600 Benzes black with tint hugged the curb along 7 Mile. The spot was a fortress for Saw and his team.

Close to fifty niggas stood posted outside, kicking it by their cars and just hanging out. Chicks were stopping through, drawn to all the ballers known to be from Syracuse. They had the grill burning, blunts in rotation, plenty of liquor, and the music pumping. But them having a good time wasn't to be mistaken for them slipping, because every one of them was strapped. The ones who hadn't any felonies, Saw made them go get their gun license so that they could legally carry, so many of them had AR-15s hanging around their necks as if it were nothing.

Saw wanted everybody together at all times, at least until the war was over. Both sides had lost some good men, and Saw was determined not to lose any more on his account.

The sound of dominoes being mixed up against the table filled the club along with Lano's high-pitched voice. "I'm whooping y'all ass," bragged Lano as he leaned over to check his score scribbled on the paper Hood was keeping.

"See, this is why I don't like letting this nigga win. Always talking shit," said Hood as he snatched his bones from the yard to start a new game.

"It ain't how you start but how you finish," said Saw as he took a swig from the MGD deuce-deuce and peered at the bones he pulled.

"Ah, here you go with this philosophical shit. I'm beating yo' ass," said Lano, jamming his finger into the score on the paper.

Saw pulled back a cheap smile and made his play on the board. "Knock, nigga, 'cause I know you ain't got none," Saw told Lano.

Lano's face tightened as he studied his hand and the board, and then he reluctantly knocked on the table, to which Hood enjoyed a laugh. "Told him, keep runnin' that mouth," said Saw.

It was a friendly game but still competitive because they were all men of pride who liked the idea of winning at everything that they did. The bar inside was empty with the exception of Saw, Hood, and Lano. They sat at one of the center tables, slapping dominoes and talking shit and drinking cold beer. The classic movie *Belly* played silently on the flat screen behind the bar, while "Too Far Gone" by Street-Lord Juan played in the background. The song was the best way to describe Saw and his niggas. They were all too far gone. They were waist-deep in the game, and there wasn't no turning back from what was ahead.

There was a slight knock at the door, and then it opened slightly. Bull stuck his massive head inside the crack of the door. He met eyes with Saw.

"Ya li'l manz out here," Bull informed him.

"Let 'em in," said Saw.

The game ceased as Thugga and Maine entered the club. Bull shut the door behind them. Saw pushed back his chair and got to his feet. He rounded the table to meet Thugga and Maine at the bar. He gave them both plays, then headed behind the bar.

"Y'all want somethin' to drink?"

"I'ma fuck with some Henny," said Maine as he and Thugga bellied up to the bar on stools.

"Same," ordered Thugga.

Saw set two shot glasses in front of them along with a fifth of Hennessy. "Y'all can pour your own drinks." Saw reached into the icebox for a fresh MGD and cracked it.

"Dawg up outta here," Thugga informed him, then took a shot to the head.

"I know," replied Saw, setting his beer down. "What's understood need not be said."

Saw grabbed his beer and walked to the back of the bar into his office area. He came back with a black gym bag and tossed it onto the bar between Thugga and Maine. They both nodded in gratitude.

Thugga downed another shot, then snatched the bag off the bar. He knew it was all there, the whole $50,000, so he wouldn't insult Saw by counting the money in front of him. He and Maine were two of Saw's shooters on payroll, so the money was always straight.

"Let us know if you need us, big bruh," said Maine as he slid off the stool.

"I'm sure something will come up," Saw assured them as he walked them to the door and let them out.

Something always came up when you were getting major money, especially in a city like Detroit. The war between Slim and Saw had ended, with Saw as the victor, but he was certain many more wars would follow.

Saw took a seat back at the dominoes table and resumed playing. The murder of Slim was just a drop in the bucket, and those slain in the process were only casualties of war. Just like the game of bones, Saw and his team were playing to win.

Chapter Two

Saw was a small man in stature, only standing at five foot six and weighing 150 pounds, but in the streets he was considered a giant because of his ruthless reputation for murder. He paid his dues to the game and made his bones by putting niggas in the dirt whenever they tried him on his size. Before he had shooters, Saw was putting in his own work. He was only 20 years old, but he had a graveyard of niggas he'd personally put there. Saw was able to excel in the game mainly because people respected violence, and they trusted he wouldn't hesitate to bring it their way if need be.

His baby face would put one at ease until they caught the murderous glint embedded in his hazel-brown eyes. His high yellow skin was covered with tattoos from the neck down. Saw had an addiction to power, beautiful women, and tattoos.

Saw's crew was into every aspect of the drug trade, everything from pills to exotic weed, but Saw kept all the money from the heroin spots he had around the city and his O.T. (out of town).

Not too many niggas in the city could match his bag because heroin money had always been on another level from cocaine and weed. Saw was a millionaire by the time he was 17, and he made sure that his two best friends, Hood and Lano, were millionaires as well. They had grown up on Syracuse together and had been through the trenches together. Hood was a goon and a loyal nigga since day one, while Lano was a jokester and a money-getting nigga. Lano could flip anything, and he was a people person. If he could avoid a war in the streets, that was what Lano was about, because wars only made it hard on business. But when Saw and Hood vetoed Lano's peace-making attempts, he knew to fall back because he knew they were about to fuck the city up.

The war between Slim and Saw seemed to be over, but Saw knew not to fall asleep, because although Slim was gone, he was a real nigga, and a lot of people loved him. Slim was a west-side nigga from off Dexter, and his team were known to bust their guns, too, so Saw still had a few loose ends to tie up. A lot of niggas were in hiding somewhere out of town, but the city was like a moth to a flame: they always had to come back. If niggas could just stay away from Detroit, then maybe they would live, but in so many cases they had a destiny to die in the streets that they loved so much.

Saw owned houses all around the city, but he never laid his head down in a single one of them. He had three luxury spots stashed on the outskirts that only Hood and Lano knew about as far as men. If Saw had any one weakness, it had to be for beautiful women. He couldn't close his eyes at night without having something beautiful lying beside him. His preference was dark chocolate women, but they had to be pretty and thick. He liked them dark probably because he was high yellow.

He lay in bed with Karmesha, his third baby momma. Today she was his favorite because he had won the war against Slim. Karmesha was the whole reason behind their fuel. She had babies by Slim and Saw. She had a 6-year-old son by Slim, and a 2-year-old daughter by Saw.

Saw had gotten with Karmesha while Slim was doing a one-year stretch in the county jail. And Slim took it as disrespect that Saw had pursued his baby momma while he was on lock, so when he got out, he tried confronting Saw when they bumped into each other in ATL at King of Diamonds. But what Slim got was a rosé bottle cracked over his head by Hood. A full-fledged brawl ensued between both sides, and the beef continued once they got back to Detroit.

Karmesha was ten years older than Saw, and she was seasoned when it came to sinking her huffs into a baller. She came from a long line of sack-chasers, starting with her mom, aunts, cousins, and sisters. So working a nigga came natural to her. She knew how to make any man feel like a king.

And that was exactly how she was making Saw feel as she blessed his game with some head. He felt like a king as he ran his fingers through her hair. Saw lay on his back with Karmesha looking up at him with those pretty green eyes. She'd deep throat him then pull his dick out and jack it.

They lay up in his mansion in Grosse Pointe Farms. The estate was on Jefferson Avenue facing the Detroit River. It was by far Saw's favorite crib because he loved the water. Besides that, before he started seeing real money, he used to always drive through Grosse Pointe Farms and imagine himself owning one of the sprawling estates. He'd see old white people walking their dogs and jogging, and he'd tell himself that the only difference between himself and those white folks was that he'd have his mansion in his twenties.

There's something in your eyes, baby.
It's telling me you want me, baby.
Tonight is your night.

R. Kelly's "Honey Love" poured from the state-of-the-art sound system as Karmesha straddled Saw and began riding him to the music. She'd always try to make love to Saw, when really all he wanted was some head and to fuck. Karmesha wanted Saw to love her. That was her trip—making niggas fall in love with her and not just her pussy. But she had her work cut out for her, because Saw was heartless. The only time he showed any signs of love was with his three kids. He had two boys, ages 2 and 3, and then his little girl. With everyone else it was business.

Saw suddenly pushed Karmesha off of him and rolled out of bed. She watched his ink-cloaked back as he padded toward his walk-in closet.

He was done with her.

He could be cold like that.

Saw returned, carrying a fresh outfit and a pair of Jordans. He tossed a roll of money with a rubber band around it to Karmesha, then headed for the master bath.

"I'ma take a shower, so get yourself together," he said, which really meant, "Don't still be here when I'm done."

Karmesha sucked her teeth, but nevertheless she broke the rubber band free from the wad of cash. Her manicured nails fanned through the blue faces. She rolled out of bed and got dressed. She wasn't used to a nigga treating her like she wasn't really that deal, when in fact she knew that she was. At first it turned her on when Saw played her to the left, because it was the thrill of the chase, and it was something different. But that shit had gotten old.

Karmesha was beginning to think that she'd never get Saw to love her, and that she couldn't stomach. Slim had loved her, but now he was gone. Karmesha had heard about Saw and Slim's beef, but she refused to believe that they would go so far as to kill one another. When she asked Saw about it, he looked her in the face and told her that, no, he wasn't responsible. It was like the scene from *The Godfather* when Michael lied to his wife about not killing his sister's husband.

Karmesha had to reason that Slim was in the streets, and Saw wasn't his only enemy, so it was fair to say that anybody could've killed him.

When Saw got out of the shower, Karmesha was already gone. He knew that she wanted more, but he wasn't certain nor convinced that she was worthy. She reminded him of his own mother, Denise, which was what he called her to her face whenever addressing her. Saw never called her Ma because she never acted like one. She showed him love growing up, but it was with gifts and Jordans she'd gotten with money from niggas in the street. To put it simply, Denise was a sack-chaser. Never worked a day in her life, yet had three kids: Saw and his two older sisters.

Saw wasn't ready to slow down yet, but if he were to ever settle with just one woman, she'd have to be able to give him something that she'd never given to another man before, preferably her heart as well as her body.

In the meantime, Saw was in the streets having his way. He loved the power that having money brought him, but it was a turn-off for a woman to be moved by money alone. That meant one thing in Saw's eyes—she couldn't be trusted.

His first baby momma was cool though. Sherise worked as a medical assistant and was still in nursing school part-time. Sherise had his oldest son, Demarcus. And Tammy had little Marco. Tammy refused to work because she figured, why would she break her neck busting down a nine-to-five when she had a millionaire for a baby daddy? Between Tammy and Karmesha, they stayed with their hands out. One was determined not to let the other two baby mommas receive more. Karmesha had Saw's daughter, Lovey.

Saw finished getting dressed and was out of the house. He always rode behind tint, and he had all his vehicles outfitted with bulletproof armor. He knew that niggas were dying to catch him slipping, some out of revenge, others out of jealousy and envy, and some out trying to make a name for themselves. Either way, Saw wasn't ready to be put on the front of an RIP T-shirt. That was why he stayed strapped with a baby fully automatic AR-15 he had specially made. And whenever he was in the city limits, two cars full of shooters rode close by.

Saw pulled out of his estate in a triple-black BMW 750 and headed for the city. He enjoyed the slow drive along the water each time. It made him think about things like, would he ever live a peaceful life? Saw already knew the answer, which was no. He was in too deep and had put too much negativity out there for it not to come back. The good life he'd grown accustomed to was merely borrowed time before he had to pay it all back.

Until then he was going to stack up.

Whatever happened after that . . . *It is what it is.*

Chapter Three

Droves of people dressed in fine white linen moved about the dance floor underneath the white canopy out by the river. They were ballroom dancing to the classic R&B jams being played. It was Detroit's annual All-White Party. The venue was Chene Park. Every summer it was a must do for those getting money and for those who just liked the scene of a good party. People would take weeks preparing for the part, most having their linens tailor-made so they'd not only stand out but also show their status.

Saw's crew had reserved tables all around the park. Lano was the partygoer because it gave him a chance to politick the game with other like-minded hustlas. He had reserved the crew's tables months before the war kicked between Saw and Slim. And now that it was over, Lano wanted to get back in the field because he'd been holed up at the bar with Hood and Saw while the street war played itself out.

Let's pretend for one night, I'm the man in your life,
And we do the things that lovers do.

Musiq Soulchild crooned out one of his early
hits, prompting more ladies to the dance floor. If
there was only one word to describe the party, it
was "sexy." The All-White Party always brought
out the baddest women Detroit and the surrounding areas had to offer. There was only one
drawback though: everybody knew about the party,
so a nigga who was juggling multiple women was
likely to get caught up this day, because there was
a good chance at least two of his women would be
there.

Such was the case with Saw. All three of his baby
mommas had shown their faces at the party. They
were still young and sexy and loved the party, so it
wasn't out of the norm for them to be there.

Karmesha was killing the white miniskirt and
red bottoms. Her long black weave gave her
an exotic look, like a dark-skinned Cuban or a
Dominican. She'd come to the party with her best
friend, Neisha. They were in attendance at all the
fly parties and couldn't miss this one for anything
in the world. Karmesha had her own section reserved with bottle service. She grooved to the
music in her seat while her head was on a swivel in
search of Saw.

Tammy was looking good as hell herself. Her thick chocolate frame was showcased in a white catsuit, leaving nothing to the imagination. Her camel toe was on the menu, as were her nipples. Everything about her screamed "sexy," from her body to her short Halle Berry do. She was also there to look good and keep tabs on Saw's ass.

Sherise was there just to unwind and have a good time. She and a few coworkers had come together. They were out on the dance floor doing the hustle with drinks in their hands and smiles on their faces.

Saw was dressed in a linen shirt and matching shorts he had made at Broadway's, along with a pair of all-white Gucci gym shoes from back in the day. His bust-down platinum Rolex and diamond pinky ring shone under the lights as he took a swallow from his bottle of Louis 13. He was seated at his reserved table, with two of his goons standing at his sides.

Saw wasn't really a partier. He'd go because niggas needed to see his face from time to time. It was more of an appearance then having a good time for him. He would always show up late and leave early. That way he'd make both a grand entrance and a grand exit. He knew people were gawking his way, wishing to borrow his ear, but Saw wasn't the type of nigga to just let people cut into him. That's what he had Lano for, to talk to niggas.

Saw never moved from his table. He watched the party as if everyone were there for his entertainment. He made a couple of mental notes of some fine asses he'd hit in the near future. He caught the eyes of Karmesha and Tammy, both vying for his attention, both wanting to go home with him for the night. He spotted Sherise out on the dance floor smiling as she danced against some guy. She was looking more than good. And Saw had made his mind up. It was Sherise he was taking home with him.

His murderous eyes were always on high alert, not out of fear but caution. He'd done so much dirt that being constantly on point was a prerequisite if he wanted to stay alive. None of the faces looked out of place, but again there just wasn't no telling. He couldn't account for all of his enemies' shooters. In the game they were playing it was best to stay ready so that you didn't have to get ready.

Lano was moving about the party, politicking like he was the mayor trying to get reelected. He was back in his element, greeting almost everyone with a smile and handshake. Meanwhile, Hood was waylaid over by the bar between two redbones with long, pretty legs and banging bodies. Hood knew who he was going to the room with after the party.

Hood stood at a solid six foot six and weighed 240 pounds of all muscle. He had fair brown skin but hardened features from a life of crime. His strong aura, deep voice, and shoulder-length dreads were what the ladies liked about him. Everything about him was, in fact, hood.

Lano stood at six feet even and had a thin build. He had a million-dollar smile that made it bearable to look him in his shit black ugly face. What put him on were his confidence and good conversation.

The party had lived up to the buildup. It had been a beautiful turnout. A few people were starting to leave, so Saw checked his Roly. *Yeah, it's about that time.* He whispered a word to his goon standing on his right, and the man nodded and made his way through the sea of bodies.

Saw locked eyes with this short, petite, honey beige chick from across the park. She was standing bow-legged, which Saw was liking very much. She saw the lust in his eyes and flashed a devilish smirk. Their eyes were dancing like the party around them.

Damn, shorty bad.

Ol' girl, flanked by her equally bad friend, made their way over toward Saw's table. His goon stepped out in front of the two women though just as they reached Saw's table. "Nah, they straight," said Saw. He wanted to see what was up with baby girl and hopefully her friend. The man stepped aside, and ol' girl stepped forward, still smiling.

"How y'all ladies enjoying the party?" asked Saw.

"Oh, I really had a good time," said ol' girl.

"Me too. It was a lot better than last year's," added the friend.

"Well, I'm Saw. And who might y'all be?"

"I'm Taquana, and this is my friend April," said ol' girl.

"Okay. What y'all doing after y'all leave here?"

"We was probably gon' go to the casino, but I don't know," said Taquana.

Saw's other goon had cleared a path and was waving for them to come on. Saw stood up and opened his phone.

"Well, let me get ya number. That's why you came over here, ain't it?"

"I'll tell you what—I'ma give you my business card," said Taquana.

"Your card?" This amused Saw as he watched her dig into her clutch.

But what she dug out wasn't a card at all. It was a baby .380 Taurus. Before Saw could register what was really happening, she opened fire. Boom! Boom! Boom!

Her friend had pulled her Ruger from her clutch and opened fire on the goon who had stepped in front of them. Boom! Boom!

Screams erupted throughout the park, causing a stampede for all exits. Lano and Hood fought through the crowds in search of Saw. Neither had seen him since the shots rang out. Hood found Saw stretched out on his back behind his table. His white linen shirt was patched with red holes that were filling with blood. He'd been hit in the side of the head as well.

Damn, my nigga, thought Hood as he kneeled down. He put his hand on Saw's forehead, and his eyes rolled to the back of his head. "Stay with me, my nigga. You gon' make it," said Hood as he carefully scooped Saw up into his arms.

Saw groaned from the pain as he slipped in and out of consciousness. Hood made his way through the frantic crowd with Saw in his arms. Lano spotted them and raced to get his G-Wagen. They put Saw in the back seat and rushed him to Henry Ford Hospital nearby.

Chapter Four

On the corner of Dexter and Monterey sat a liquor store owned by some Arabs, but the block was owned by the niggas who sold heroin out there. The block had been infamous since the YBI era with Butch Jones and his counterparts. The rights to the land had changed hands a few times over the years with the major players such as Brick. But with Butch and Brick both back in the Feds, the new generation was out there keeping the legend of Monterey alive.

Slim was now dead, so until his void was filled, the block was fair game to anyone who had birth rights to the hood. Monterey was still a $50,000-a-day dope stroll, so there were plenty of niggas out there hustling, exercising their birth rights to get rich.

Lookouts stood posted on the corner outside the liquor store, while all hand-to-hand transactions were done from cars at the middle of the block, where pack workers stood taking turns serving cars. It was a cop operation. The block was open for shop twice a day: once in the morning then again around nightfall.

The night rush had begun, and cars lined the block. Thugga and Maine both cradled Chinese AK-47s across their laps as they sat behind the tinted windows of the midnight blue supercharged Durango, inching to the front of the line where niggas were serving bundles.

Thugga was driving while Maine sat behind him. As Thugga made it to the front of the line, a young nigga dressed in a Nike short set approached the car in the street. Thugga let all the windows down at the same time. The look in ol' boy's eyes was that of a dead man as he stared into the barrel of Thugga's AK. Laaka! Laaka! Laaka!

Thugga and Maine opened fire simultaneously. Thugga killed the young nigga instantly, then took aim on the crowd of niggas posted against one of the vacant houses. Niggas were dropping from the barrage of bullets, but some of them were throwing shots back, as was to be expected. It sounded like rocks hitting against the metal, which was Thugga's cue to get them out of there.

Maine kept shooting though until he bent the corner and got to safety. Word had gotten back that Taquana was really Slim's baby sister, and that was why she took a shot at Saw, for revenge on her brother.

Hood was infuriated that the bitch was able to get that close to Saw. Out of all the niggas they had on payroll, nobody knew who Taquana was until it was too late. If she could take a shot at a nigga like Saw, then what was that really saying about their security? Hood was going to address the situation, but first he had to send a message to their adversaries via murder. He had unleashed his shooters with orders to kill on sight any nigga or bitch in opposition to them. Nothing was off-limits.

Thugga and Maine switched cars and jumped into an all-black Hellcat. They weren't finished for the night. Hood had told them to go dick hard, so that was exactly what they were going to do. Thugga and Maine were natural-born killers. They were put on earth to kill. There was no other way to put it. Some niggas were good at hustling. Well, they were great at killing shit. If there was a ticket on a nigga's head, best believe they were out to collect it.

Thugga and Maine were both 18. They'd been slumping niggas since they were about 15. Thugga was an ugly nigga with nappy hair who looked like Ol' Dirty Bastard. He had this wild look in his eyes that said, "Try me!"

Maine was more laidback and spoke with a slow drawl. He was stout and grim faced with a razor wound down his left jaw. He kept his head under a black du-rag and he chain-smoked Newports.

Maine brought the Hellcat to a slow creep, but its beast of an engine grumbled the dual exhaust. They were still on the west side on Petosky and Glendale. They rode past the crib known to be owned by Taquana. People could be seen moving about inside the house, but neither of them saw Taquana in sight.

"What you wanna do?" asked Maine.

Thugga looked at the old man who had come outside onto the porch with a cigarette in his mouth. Then he thought about Saw lying in the ICU at the hospital. "Pull back around," said Thugga as he readied his AK-47. When Maine pulled back around the corner, he parked in the middle of the street, leaving the car running. The old man flicked his cigarette butt to the wind as he locked eyes on the two masked men rushing toward him. He turned for the screen door, but a single shot to his back knocked him to the porch.

Screams yelped from inside the house as Thugga snatched the screen open and announced himself with a barrage of gunfire. Laaka! Laaka! Laaka!

He struck an older woman in the chest as she sat watching TV from the loveseat. Two men jolted from the sofa, making a run for it, but Maine chewed their backs out with a hail of bullets. Laaka! Laaka!

They split up to search the house. Thugga hit the basement while Maine checked the bathroom, back bedrooms, and then upstairs. He found a little boy about 5 years old crying in the closet. Maine had a mind to kill the little nigga as he raised his AK to the boy's face, but something inside of him made him lower his rifle.

"Bruh, bruh!" called Thugga from the bottom of the steps. Maine closed the door on the little boy and jogged down the stairs in a hurry.

"Was anybody up there?" asked Thugga.

"Nah, we good," lied Maine as he led the way out of the house. He knew Thugga wouldn't have hesitated to kill the little boy, only because he'd seen him kill others in the past.

For Thugga, the murder game spared no one. There was no such thing as the wrong place at the wrong time with him. If your ass was on the scene when he pulled up, then that meant it was your time to die. In that order.

Chapter Five

After five days of being in a medically induced coma, and two surgeries later, Saw had opened his eyes and was recovering in the ICU. He was hooked up to an IV and had tubes running through his nostrils. The hospital room was heavily guarded by his henchmen posted outside. The only ones allowed to see him were Hood, Lano, and his moms. Even the doctors and nurses were frisked before going into check on Saw. Hood was kicking himself in the ass for allowing this to happen, and he wasn't taking any chances. He knew that for the right paper a nigga would try to down Saw again, even as he lay in the hospital. They all knew the legendary story of how Maserati Rick was killed in his hospital bed by a hitman dressed as a doctor. True story.

"I keep tellin' you, ya ass gon' end up either dead or in a cell right there beside ya damn daddy and grandfather," snapped Denise, Saw's mother. She was standing at his bedside with a scowl on her yellow face. "And where was y'all asses at? Shit, why

is my son the only one in here laid up half dead?"
Her question was directed to Lano and Hood.

They both paced the floor. They hadn't a good
answer to Denise's question, so they allowed
her to vent. She went on for a bit, then snatched
up her purse and kissed Saw's forehead. "You get
some rest, and I'll see you tomorrow," she said.

Saw didn't respond, not because he couldn't
talk, but because he didn't want to feed Denise
any more fuel for her bitchin'. He was glad when
she shut the door behind her. He sat up with pain
shooting everywhere in his body, but he managed
to snatch the tubes from his nose.

"Bruh, what'chu doin'?" asked Lano.

"Fuck it look like? I'm getting the fuck outta
here," said Saw. He hated hospitals with a passion.

He snatched the IV from his hand and searched
the room with his eyes for something to put on besides the gown he wore.

Hood stepped forward with concern. "Saw, why
don't you at least wait 'til the doctors release you?"

"You see all these balloons and bears?" said Saw
of all the "get well" sentiments that crowded the
room. "How many people know I'm here?"

"Bruh, we got twenty of our men right outside
that door around the clock. You good," Lano assured him.

But Saw didn't feel good. His paranoia was
kicking in. "Get me some clothes," he told Lano
firmly.

Lano drew in a deep breath and exhaled out of frustration. He reluctantly turned for the door and stepped out, leaving Hood and Saw alone.

"Who was it?" asked Saw. He remembered the bitch shooting him, but he wanted to know who sent her.

"Come to find out the bitch who shot you was Slim's little sister."

Saw was heated more so with himself because he hadn't seen the play coming. He allowed the bitch to get the drop on him, and it nearly cost him his life. Taquana had only grazed his temple, but she made her mark with five shots to the chest.

Hood knew Saw better than anyone else, so he'd known that his best friend had a weak spot for beautiful women. He didn't want to be burying his best friend because of it.

"That was a close one," said Hood.

"Close only counts in horseshoes," spat Saw.

Hood knew that Saw was as stubborn as a bull, so he didn't press the issue. Lano came back in with some clothes and shoes. "Here, this is just until we get you outta here," said Lano.

Saw stashed himself away at his mansion on Orchard Lake. The only people who knew where he was were Hood, Lano, and his baby momma Sherise.

Sherise was to help nurse Saw back to good health, given her background in nursing. Saw always enjoyed her company because she didn't have a negative bone in her body. Sherise always kept a positive outlook on life, and besides that, she was a sweetheart who had a loving spirit.

Saw loved seeing her in those tight, sexy scrubs she wore to work. She had on a powder blue set this day as she tended to Saw's every need. He loved the way her booty rolled against the fabric of her pants. He watched Sherise move about the bedroom as he lay in bed, propped up by large pillows with the remote in his hand.

Goodfellas was playing on the massive screen atop the wood-burning fireplace of the master suite. Saw was vaguely watching the movie. It was one of his favorite mob films.

Sherise had made Saw a hearty breakfast of scrambled cheese eggs, links, hash browns, and wheat toast, with a glass of orange juice. She carried in a tray meant for serving in bed, and she set it in front of Saw.

"I want you to try to eat something," she said, putting the back of her hand to his forehead. "You're warm."

"I'm good," lied Saw. He was always supposed to be tough in other people's eyes. It was part of his persona. Truth be told, he felt like shit, and he looked it. Sherise knew him all too well. They were high school sweethearts, and Saw had taken her virginity. He had a soft spot in his heart, but sometimes it was hard to find it.

Sherise kicked off her shoes and crawled into bed beside Saw. She reached for the fork that Saw had yet to touch, and she scooped food up. "Here, if I have to feed you myself, you're going to eat something."

Saw gave in and allowed Sherise to feed him. Low-key he liked having Sherise pamper and spoil him. She had a sensual aura that Saw loved about her. Besides that, she was a nurturer. Saw could tell by the way she tended to their son that she was the best mother of his three baby mommas. She wasn't the argumentative type either like Karmesha and Tammy. They were both drama queens.

Saw finished eating, and Sherise gave him his orange juice to drink. "Thank you," said Saw. He had gratitude for Sherise being there because he knew deep down that she wanted to be there.

"You know how you can thank me?" asked Sherise as she took the tray over to the sitting area by the balcony.

"How's that?"

Sherise had his undivided attention because she never asked for anything. Saw always just provided. She nestled back into bed and lay next to Saw, their eyes searching each other's faces. "I want you not to leave me to raise Demarcus by myself. He needs his father in his life."

Saw drew a deep breath and exhaled while rolling onto his back. His eyes were to the ceiling. Sherise's request wasn't coming from a bad place. She was all right. His son needed him. All his kids did.

"What'chu thinking about, what I said?" asked Sherise in a small voice. She hadn't meant to make him shut down.

"Yeah," admitted Saw.

He was also thinking about his mom, Denise, and what she said about him ending up like his father. His whole life his mom had been convinced that Wink was his father, but Saw didn't know one way or another.

Chapter Six

The massive stone walls that surrounded the United States Penitentiary, Lewisburg made it impossible for the 2,500-plus souls condemned to serve time there to see anything of the free world. When the convicts were out in the yard lifting weights and playing handball and basketball, if they were to look up, the only thing they'd see was the sky. The seven gun towers situated at every angle of the prison served as a constant reminder that whatever sentences their judges had handed down would in fact be served out. Many of the men doing time at Lewisburg, or the Big House as the guards called it, were doing life bids.

There was always tension throughout the prison mainly because of all the time the men were serving. The least little sign of disrespect and there was sure to be a bloodbath, because respect was about the only thing left that the Feds hadn't taken from the men, so the convicts treated their respect and others' as if it were tangible.

Every day it was the same routine. Most spent their days in the prison Unicor Factory, where they made furniture. While others stayed outside on the yard engaged in prison politics, only a few went to the law library to work on their appeals.

Wink could always be found with his nose crammed in one of the new law books or on LexisNexis in hopes of finding any new decisions that would substantially help his appeals. He only had one shot left, and he was saving it. Wink's hair was starting to gray at his temples, but other than that he still had a youthfulness to him. At least he thought so anyway. When he looked into the mirror after getting a fresh cut every Friday, he didn't see the "Ol' School," as the younger guys from Detroit had taken to calling him.

Wink had walked down twenty-plus years. When he first fell, he was sent to the same prison as his father, but a few years back Wink had been simply transferred without warning. He and the old man still kept in touch through kites, and they mostly shared news about the new laws and cases coming down. Over the years the mail had slowed down from the piles Wink used to receive when he first blew trial. Life had moved on. And he was among the land of the forgotten.

"Count time! Stand up! Comin' down!" yelled one of the guards from the end of the hall.

Every day at 4:00 p.m. the entire federal prison system did stand-up counts to make sure everyone was alive and no one had escaped. Wink shared a tiny cell with a youngster from Detroit by the name of Sharky. They both stood up long enough to watch the two white faces of the guards peer in at them then pass. Count time usually lasted thirty minutes unless they screwed up and had to do a recount.

"I better get a letter from my bitch today," said Sharky as he stood posted by the steel door. Wink chuckled to himself as he lay down across the bottom bunk. Every day Sharky would hold the door up after count time in hopes that a letter from his baby momma would slide underneath the door. Wink had tried schooling Sharky not to sweat nothing that was beyond his control. But the young'un was one of those who did their bids worrying about their old lady twenty-four seven. As soon as Sharky got some money on his account, he was burning through it chasing up behind his baby momma. He didn't realize that he was only making his time harder.

"Mail call!" shouted an officer.

Moments later a lone white envelope came under the door, hitting Sharky's foot. He picked up the envelope in a blur, but his anticipation was short-lived as he tossed the piece of mail onto Wink's stomach.

"It's for you, big homie."

Wink had dozed off for a minute. He sat up and swung his feet to the floor and into his shower shoes. He eyed the name of the sender: Denise Manning. The name sounded familiar, and the address was right there in the hood. *Denise?* thought Wink as he pulled the folded letter from its envelope. A small picture from back in the day fell to the floor, and when Wink picked it up he recognized Denise immediately. She stayed around the corner from him growing up. They hadn't even been on serious terms. Denise was more like weekend pussy or late-night action. Wink remembered her being pretty, but Denise was also a sack-chaser out looking for a sponsor. He unfolded the letter, interested to see what she wanted.

> *Dear Wink,*
> *I know that it's been a long time and that you probably don't even remember me, so hopefully the pic will jog your memory. While I hope you're doing well, this is not a social call. I never told you this because of so many different reasons, but we have a son together. His name is Cortez, but he goes by Saw. He's 20 now, and I swear he's your twin in not just looks, but in y'all ways. Look, I know this comes out of the blue, and I know you've got many other bitches claiming to*

*have mothered your kids. But that's not
my case. Wink, I'm not sending you this to
ask you for money. Our son is grown. I'm
asking that you try to reach him because he's
headed down that same path you were once
on, and we both see where that got you. I
don't want to lose my son, Wink. But I can't
reach him. Maybe you can. I'm hoping this
letter finds you well. You have my address,
so please let me know if there's anything you
can think of to get through to him.*

    Take care now,
    Denise XoXo

Wink folded the letter and picked up the pic of
Denise. A frown took over his face. He didn't know
what to make of Denise's letter and her claims of
them having a son together. She made it clear that
she wasn't asking him for money, but he still
felt she was working some sort of angle.

Wink let out a sigh of frustration. The CO could
be heard unlocking the doors. Count had cleared.
Sharky was by the door mumbling to himself how
he was about to get on the phone and cuss "this
bitch out" for lying about sending his letter and
pics.

"Young dawg, you ever heard of a nigga named
Saw?"

"Yeah. He out there chewing. He a eastside nigga from yo' hood, matter of fact. Why, what's up with him? He on his way here?"

"Nah, I was just asking."

The CO opened their cell and Sharky raced out to the phones, leaving Wink to his thoughts. He'd decided to at least look into whether Saw was his son. He felt that everyone involved deserved that much.

Chapter Seven

If there was any question as to who would fill the void of Slim's absence on the west side, Taquana had one simple answer for all of those asking. She was running shit effectively immediately. The way she saw it, none of her brother's underlings had the balls to win the war against Saw and his people. Saw's shooters were terrorizing all of their dope strolls, and they'd even killed her two aunts and her father, so the way Taquana saw it was that she had lost too much to this war not to see it through.

She thought that her bold move of shooting Saw at the All-White Party would've won the war, except Saw survived. Taquana wanted to make a clear statement by killing Saw in broad daylight because he was out celebrating while her grieving family made funeral arrangements for Slim.

Taquana's only mistake, she realized, was that she didn't finish him. She was supposed to stand over a nigga like Saw until she was certain he was dead. But she vowed to get a second chance, and this time she wouldn't miss.

Taquana had called a meeting on Dexter and Monterey. She wanted everybody who hustled on the block in attendance. A gathering was held outside the liquor store while Taquana stood in the center circle addressing the listeners. "Shit's about to change 'round here, starting with the bundles y'all been moving," said Taquana.

"And what's wrong with the bundles we got now?" one guy asked.

"Yeah, it's the same dope Slim had us pushing," another nigga added.

"The problem is it ain't my dope that's being sold out here. From now on y'all gon' be working for me, understand?" asked Taquana. She was dressed in all-black block-wear, with her hands inside of her hoodie.

A group of niggas all busted out laughing in Taquana's face. One nigga from the back dared to say, "I ain't working for no bitch."

"Who said that? Why don't you come up here?" said Taquana.

A muscle-bound nigga emerged from the crowd with his face screwed up into a murder mask.

"Now, what'chu say, nigga?" asked Taquana, biting her bottom lip.

"I said, I ain't working for no—"

Boom!

Taquana had pulled the .40-cal from her hoodie and issued ol' boy a single dome shot between his eyes. She stood over him with two additional face shots. Boom! Boom! Then she turned to the niggas who were brave enough not to flee. "Now anybody else got a problem working for a bitch? 'Cause we can take care of that right now." She searched their faces, but all stood silent.

Taquana had officially taken hold of the block. A nigga would have to drop her casket before she ever let it go. She was all in. Taquana had plans to take over all of Slim's spots and strolls. If any nigga bucked her program, they'd be scraped from the sidewalk like the rest of them.

Slim had inadvertently taught Taquana the dope game when he was first blowing up. He didn't trust a lot of people to package his dope, so he taught Taquana how to step on the heroin and how to store it once she'd packaged it. She also knew Slim's Chinese connect directly because he had sent her to cop in New York a few times.

Taquana had all the pieces of the puzzle to run her game down. She just needed to win the war against Saw because there had been too much bloodshed to call a truce now. There would be only one victor. And Taquana was as sure as hell was hot that Saw was somewhere plotting her demise as well. She had heard he left the hospital early and was stashed somewhere until he healed.

Taquana was sure Saw would come back with a vengeance, which was why she needed to take advantage of his downtime to get her operation going like a well-oiled machine. She knew that it cost money to fight a war, especially if she wanted to come out on top. Her goons had to be fed. Guns had to be bought. Palms had to be greased. And most importantly, the streets had to want to see her win.

Chapter Eight

For two weeks Saw stayed at his mansion in Orchard Lake, healing up. Sherise had taken a leave of absence from her job so that she could be there with Saw. He had made a full recovery, even putting on a few extra pounds from all the good cooking Sherise was feeding him three times a day.

His heart was there at home with Sherise. Being with her felt right, and it made all the sense in the world for them to be together, but Saw's heart was still in the streets at the same time. He was grateful that Sherise had been there by his side, but he was itching to get back to his throne in the game.

Sherise was quiet as she gathered her things and packed them into her bags. Saw was getting dressed, and from the look in his eyes, he was gearing up to go run the streets. That was why their young relationship hadn't lasted, because Saw loved the streets far more than anything or anyone else. Sherise couldn't understand for the life of her just what was in those damn streets that Saw loved them so much.

She just hoped that all their talks over the past couple of weeks hadn't gone in one ear and out the other one, because their son deserved to have his father in his life. Sherise threw her bags over her shoulder and started for the door. "Call me if you need me," she said.

"Hold up for a minute," said Saw, darting inside of the closet. He returned with a wad of cash and handed it to Sherise. She gave him a look that said, "You just don't get it, do you?"

"What?"

"Saw, I didn't do this for a payday."

"I know that. But I still want you to have it. Buy yourself something nice, and take my li'l man shopping."

Sherise wasn't going to start an argument, so she just accepted the money. But what she really wanted to tell Saw was, "Why don't you spend some time with your son and take him shopping?"

He kissed her forehead and she pulled back a weak smile.

"Be careful," she pleaded.

"A'ight."

Sherise let herself out while Saw continued to get ready. He stood in the mirror examining the scar on his temple. His blood ran hot as he flashed back to the day Taquana had tried to end his life. "You missed, bitch," he said through clenched teeth. It was time to even the score and find Taquana's ass so he could kill her. Hood and Lano had been briefing him about the streets as he healed, and they'd informed him that Taquana was now running Slim's operation and that she was quickly building an army of shooters.

This pissed Saw off because he wasn't about beefing with no bitch. First she had shot him, and now he was getting word that she was expanding her heroin operations around Detroit.

When Saw emerged from the cockpit of his bulletproof Benz, all his niggas standing outside the club on Syracuse flocked to him, each showing him signs of love. Saw was receptive, but what he needed at the moment was loyalty. Most of his niggas had been tried and tested, but some hadn't. And it was time to start weeding out any weak link. Saw knew that his team could only be as strong as the weakest link.

Lano and Hood stepped outside the club, and they ushered Saw inside the club, leaving everyone else out. Saw had called the meeting. He wanted an explanation as to why that bitch Taquana wasn't in the morgue yet. But neither Hood nor Lano had the answer. And neither bothered offering up any excuses. It was simple. Taquana was on top of her game. There had been plenty of boss bitches in the game before her, but what set her apart was that she busted her own gun. Niggas had no choice but to respect her mind.

Saw pulled an ice-cold MGD from the icebox and walked over to the dominoes table. But they weren't playing bones today. Hood and Lano were there to listen. "I want everything shut down today. I don't give a fuck about clientele. None of that shit matters right now," said Saw.

Lano frowned because this didn't sit too well with him. He had put in a lot of work to help build up their operations, and now Saw wanted to shut everything down.

"And why would we shut everything down?" asked Lano.

"Because I want all our focus to be on finding and killing that bitch who shot me," said Saw.

"We don't have to shut down to do that," said Lano.

"I'm not askin' you, Lano. I'm telling you to shut it down," said Saw as he glared across the table into Lano's shifty eyes.

Hood was going to back whatever play Saw called, so he had no gripes about them shutting down their drug operations. He was pretty sure Saw had a good reason for his decision, because Saw loved making money more than anyone of them.

Lano broke off their stare. He reached into his pack of Newports and fired up a square. He had enough money to hold him over, but he feared their workers would jump ship if they weren't being fed. But little did Lano know, that was precisely the reason behind Saw's decision. He wanted to test the hearts and loyalty of his men. Those who traded sides would be slain in the process. And those who stayed down would be greatly rewarded.

Saw had deep pockets and could take any nigga to war if they wanted one. By closing down shop they could focus on one thing—murder.

Chapter Nine

Just as Saw anticipated, it took less than a week before niggas on his team either jumped ship to Taquana's side or elected to go hustle out of town until the beef settled. Saw had taken account of all traders, and he promptly marked them for death. For the ones who fled to hustle OT thinking they'd return home after the war, Saw would be there waiting with unwelcoming arms.

The difference between Saw and Taquana was that Saw would never embrace a trader to the fold of his empire. With him, you were to stand in the paint when the beef came. Taquana was thirsty, however, and it would prove to be a deadly mistake.

Word on the street was that Taquana put $250,000 on Saw's head and $100,000 on both Hood's and Lano's domes. But Saw wasn't worried about getting caught slipping, because in order to get caught slipping, first you had to be ducking the drama. And Saw was out in full force bringing the drama to niggas' doorsteps until Taquana turned up.

When all was said and done, there were only twenty-five members left in Saw's crime family. But they were all solid and about that murder game. As Saw liked to put it, less was more. He broke his team up into factions of five. They each had a daily assignment to terrorize certain areas of the city.

Doom! Doom! Doom! Doom!

The chrome Desert Eagle .44-cal went off like a cannon as Saw shot through the peephole of apartment 9A of Jeffersonian Apartments. When he first knocked on the door, a man's voice called out, "Who is it?" Saw could see the shadow of a man's feet at the bottom of the door, and he knew he was looking through the peephole, which was already covered by the barrel of Saw's gun.

As soon as Saw let off those first shots, Hood kicked the door off the hinges, and they stormed the apartment. A man seated at the kitchen table counting money piled high reached for his assault rifle beside him, but Hood drilled his chest with seven quick shots from his Glock .40 equipped with a switch that made it fully automatic.

Saw chased a female toward the back rooms, gunning her down in her tracks. He dumped two rounds into her skull and stepped over the mess he'd made. When he opened the second bedroom door, he spotted a nigga in nothing but his boxers out on the balcony debating whether to jump. This brought a wicked smile to Saw's face. He barked a single shot in the man's direction, intentionally missing him. It was enough to grab the man's attention.

The man looked at the demon Saw was closing in on him with, then looked back down at the parking lot. It was a long drop, but he took his chances and closed his eyes as he leaped over the rail. He belted out a soul-wrenching scream going down, but the sound of bones cracking against the pavement silenced him for eternity.

The rest of the apartment was empty. A couple of million dollars was sprawled across the kitchen table along with blood spatter and brain matter. But neither Saw or Hood touched the money. That wasn't why they'd come. The apartment belonged to Taquana, but apparently she was holed up someplace else. It was okay though. She'd get Saw's message loud and clear that he was on her ass. And sooner or later he was going to find her, and there'd be nowhere to hide.

Meanwhile, Thugga and Maine were having a meeting with a nigga by the name of Aaron, who belonged to Taquana's team of hitters. Aaron was a bug-eyed nigga with shit breath and a reputation for being one of the grimiest niggas from Detroit. Everything was some type of cross with him, but

Thugga and Maine fucked with Aaron because they were all cut from the same cloth.

Aaron set up the meeting at Taquana's request. She wanted them to off Saw, along with Hood and Lano if they could. But if they couldn't get all three, she most definitely wanted Saw out of the way. The meeting was held at Starter's Lounge on the west side. Thugga and Maine were both strapped and wore vests, but they weren't concerned. Aaron was to come alone, which he did. He also was to bring the $100,000 down payment for Thugga and Maine taking the hits.

It was midday lunch hour, so the lounge had mostly pickups with a few sit-ins. Thugga and Maine found Aaron seated at the rear of the eatery. He pulled back a cheap grin with a toothpick at the side of his mouth. "Glad y'all could make it."

Thugga and Maine slid into the booth opposite Aaron but in view of the front door.

"You got the money?" asked Maine.

"Right here," said Aaron, setting a black duffle bag on the table.

"But do we have an understanding?" asked Aaron.

"Yeah," said Thugga. He shoved the table hard into Aaron's stomach, pressing him against the back of his seat.

Thugga and Maine both came out their waists with Glocks.

"Tell that bitch no deal," said Thugga.

Boom! Boom! Boom! Boom!

They filled Aaron's chest and face with dum-dums, then snatched the duffle bag up and made a calm exit amid the frantic patrons and employees.

Thugga and Maine were grimy indeed. But when they really fucked with somebody like Saw, they were loyal to the grave.

Chapter Ten

Taquana hadn't been in hiding as Saw thought. She'd been in Chi-Town to see her cousins Snake and Womp, who were Mickey Cobras, one of Chicago's most violent gangs. Snake and Womp were certified killers. It was sport for them to catch their opts slipping and perform a drill in broad daylight. Taquana wasn't looking to bring any new gangs to Detroit, but she felt that her cousins could help her side of the war, mainly because they'd be fresh faces in the city and could essentially go anywhere undetected.

Snake and Womp had one mission, and that was to kill Saw. She didn't want them taking shots at anyone else, no one except Saw. She decided that Hood and Lano could wait. It was Saw who deserved her undivided attention. Since her plan through Aaron hadn't worked, Taquana knew she needed fresh guns.

She was back in Detroit and had brought Snake and Womp back with her. They cruised the streets of Detroit in a tinted black Yukon. Taquana was pointing out all the probable places they might spot Saw. She'd even given them a Don Diva containing pictures of Saw at the different events around the city.

Taquana gave them everything that they needed to get settled, including a rental house down the street from Saw's club on Syracuse Street. Snake and Womp were to blend in like everyday, regular folks, Taquana had told them. They were from Indiana if anybody were to ask. She even bought them work outfits and a truck so they'd be seen leaving and coming. One would leave for the day while the other stayed and watched the club. They were trying to narrow down Saw's comings and goings like they did with their opts back in Chicago.

Taquana had the exterior of the house equipped with a camera system that was facing the intersection of 7 Mile and Syracuse. The zoom feature was of such quality that Snake and Womp could read the green Newport writing across Lano's cigarette as he stood outside the club talking on his cell phone. A host of others were posted up, but there was no sign of Saw.

Snake was a short brown-skinned nigga with brush waves. When he cracked a smile, you'd instantly recognize that it didn't match his handshake. He was a bottom-feeder for sure, always lurking in the shadows to do some dirt. His name matched him perfectly. Womp was just as grimy and dangerous. He got his nickname because of his size. He was as wide as a Mack Truck, and he had a mean one-hitter knockout game.

The pair was a deadly combination. They'd just beaten a body after sitting in the Cook County Jail for nearly two summers. For them it came with the game, having to sit down. It wasn't their first run-in with homicide and sure wouldn't be their last.

Snake and Womp were both eager to get Saw as soon as possible, because for them Detroit wasn't live enough. They needed constant warfare like in Chi-raq, where their whole city was at war.

Meanwhile, the word on the streets was that Saw and his people were winning the war. Every day and all day, shots rang out in any part of the city where Taquana was known to have her dope being sold. It was getting to the point where the innocent neighbors were flooding police head-quarters and the city council meetings, demanding action be taken. The mayor of Detroit was called out on the spike of violence during a press confer-ence, and he vowed to bring an end to what he'd learned to be an ongoing drug war.

A joint task force between the Detroit Police Department and federal agencies was formed fol-lowing the murders at the Jeffersonian. One name kept coming up during the task force's daily brief-ings: Saw. The ATF and DEA already had working files on Saw, but now the FBI wanted to open their own investigation. If the Feds could prove that the murders were connected to a drug war, then they could go after Saw's organization on RICO charges.

The Feds just needed to somehow get inside the ranks of Saw's syndicate. Because Saw had downsized his organization, and all who remained were solid members, the Feds had their work cut out for them if they intended to penetrate the ranks of Saw's men. It wasn't going to be easy like other federal conspiracies, where they build cases based on the words of low-level snitches. If the Feds wanted Saw, then they knew it would be real investigative work in the field. And no agents liked doing real fieldwork, because they'd been spoiled by snitches handing them their convictions.

But it was different when they were up against some-one as savvy as Saw, who'd shielded himself with top federal and state attorneys. Margaret Sind Raben was his best mouthpiece, while he kept Martin J. Beres on retainer for any would-be appeal. The Feds had this of course in their files, so the first thing they'd try to use were intimidation tactics on Saw's lawyers. They'd pay them a visit, demanding legal documentation on how Saw was legally paying them. But the Feds came up empty because he'd been laced by Ms. Raben that he needed legal sources of income, and that it would protect them both.

So Saw had invested in a dealer's license and opened a used-car lot. He'd also bought up over 200 houses around the city for next to nothing. He rehabbed them and rented them mostly to Section 8 tenants.

The Feds had wasted their time really. And in the process they'd tipped their hands, because it was Ms. Raben and Mr. Beres's duty to their client to inform Saw of the Feds opening their investigation.

Chapter Eleven

The news from Ms. Raben about the Feds opening an investigation didn't sit well with Saw. He knew that the Feds were out there every day, but just like every other major nigga before him, Saw didn't want to believe that they were on to him. Ms. Raben told Saw that he needed to stop doing whatever it was he was suspected of doing, because it wasn't going to be the last visit from the Feds, she warned.

It pissed Saw off that with everything going on, he still hadn't slain that bitch Taquana. He wasn't ready to call off the war because it would signal defeat on his end. But at the same time, he knew that moving with total disregard was dangerous to his health.

Saw was faced with the dilemmas of knowing that the Feds were most likely watching his every move and losing the war in the streets. He called a meeting with Hood and Lano. They met at Saw's ranch out in Port Huron. The property consisted of thirty acres and had horses, cows, pigs, and a chicken farm. A man-made pond filled with catfish welcomed you to the six-bedroom estate. This was Saw's best kept secret. He had bought the ranch because he liked the independence it represented. He could live off the land if need be. He had a staff of workers who took care of the property and animals while he was away.

Saw stood out by the pond with a fishing pole, his line cast into the water. Hood and Lano pulled into the estate in Hood's black Audi A8.

"What up doe?" they said, approaching the pond.

"It's some cold ones in the cooler," said Saw, motioning to the small red Igloo on the ground.

Hood and Lano both retrieved MGDs from the cooler and joined Saw by the pond.

"Catch anything yet?" asked Hood.

"Nah," said Saw. His bucket was empty. "Grab a line," he said.

Lano looked about the property. "It's been a minute since we all been up here."

Hood grabbed a pole and cast his line to the center of the pond. "So what's up? I know you ain't call us out here to fish," said Hood.

Saw's line jumped, and he set his beer down, then began reeling in what was on the line. He brought up a healthy catfish and held it like a prize before dropping it into the bucket. "I called y'all out here because I got word from my lawyers that the Feds done opened up an investigation on me," said Saw.

"Word?" asked Lano.

"Yeah," replied Saw. "So if they're on to me, you gotta know that they're watching y'all too."

Hood and Lano both understood that much. They all knew the heat from the war was the reason for the Feds' probe.

"So what we gon' do?" asked Lano.

"I know y'all both holding on to some millions," said Saw.

Hood and Lano both nodded. They were situated and comfortable.

"Talk to me," said Hood.

"I need y'all both to put up a mill ticket, and I'ma put up a mill. We can't afford to stop the war, but at the same time, we can't afford for our good men to go unfed either. We gon' use the three million to put some money in our men's pockets to keep 'em going," said Saw.

"Say less," said Hood.

Lano nodded in agreement.

"Since the Feds is watchin' us now, I only want our men putting in work after hours, when ain't no Feds on surveillance. They asses got wives they go home to every day, so tell everybody not to make any moves until after midnight," instructed Saw.

They all agreed that for the time being this was their best plan of action. They couldn't quit the war, but at the same time, they had to feed their army of shooters. It was a small price to pay. Saw could've funded the war by himself for the next two years, but he needed to test his closest men to see if their loyalty was still intact, because if there was one thing that the game had taught him, it was that no one was above suspicion.

They spent the rest of the afternoon fishing, then Lano filleted the catfish and deep-fried them. It made for some good eating and a day away from the bloodthirsty streets of Detroit. The ills of the game awaited them, but for the day they would enjoy the serenity the ranch provided.

Chapter Twelve

Karmesha was feeling slighted that Saw picked Sherise to look after him while he healed from his gunshot wounds. Those were two weeks Karmesha felt belonged to her and that should've been used for her and Saw to grow closer. It hadn't crossed her mind that perhaps Sherise was the one who Saw picked to help him get back on his feet simply because she had a background in nursing. In Karmesha's mind, the bitch was trying to steal her man.

Karmesha was getting to the point of jealousy, which she had never done with any other man in her life as a sack-chaser. She was the pursued. Her jealousy was starting to fuel her anger and would soon become scorn if Saw didn't wake up and realize that she was the best woman for him. She hadn't physically laid eyes on Saw since the All-White Party, and she was starting to think that he was done with her.

Karmesha told herself just to give it some time. So she enjoyed a night out with her homegirls.

They were enjoying the bottle service at Club Liv downtown. It was the newest club, so all the city's ballers were in the spot showing off their wealth while looking for their new baby mommas. The sack-chasers were in full attendance, each looking for their next sponsorship.

This well-groomed bald black nigga kept making eyes with Karmesha from across the club. He was draped with beautiful women standing over his shoulders, but his eyes were only on Karmesha. This made her blush because she loved the attention. Plus he was fine.

Karmesha wasn't blushing simply from the attention though. It was an invitation, which he accepted. The man excused himself from his party and made his way over to Karmesha's section. He was well-built and had swag from the way he was dressed in cream linen and Gators.

"Girl, who is that fine-ass nigga comin' over here?" asked Kim, leaning over to Karmesha.

"He is fine," agreed Cookie.

All three of their hearts skipped a beat when the man stopped at their table and pulled back a smile.

"Ladies," he said. His voice was deep and sexy. His eyes arrested Karmesha's. "I came to borrow your girlfriend."

"Karmesha," offered up Cookie. "And yes, you certainly can."

Karmesha played coy as the man stood with his hand out awaiting hers. "Let's dance," he said.

Kim was kicking Karmesha underneath the table, egging her on.

"Okay. But just one dance," said Karmesha as she stood up, accepting his manicured hand.

"That's all I need," he said, leading them out to the dance floor. The DJ had the perfect song playing as they stepped out on the floor.

Step back; you're dancing kinda close.
I feel a little poke coming through
On you
Now, girl, I know you felt it.
Boo, you know I can't help it.

The sounds of Next had the party going. Karmesha was grinding sexily into the beautiful man who still hadn't told her his name. But as if reading her mind, he whispered into her ear over the music, "I'm Gerald."

Gerald was a smooth brother. He had dreamy yet serious eyes that captivated Karmesha each time their eyes met. She was drawn to him. What was supposed to be only one dance turned into five songs as the DJ kept the R&B hits from the early 2000s rolling. Neither wanted to end their embrace because their touches were bliss. It had been a long time since Karmesha had been held like that.

They came off the dance floor only when the DJ changed his set to today's rap. Gerald escorted Karmesha back to her table, then waved their waitress over.

"Put whatever they're having on my bill," said Gerald.

"I'm likin' him already," said Cookie.

"Okay," said Kim.

"You ladies enjoy the rest of your night." Gerald turned to Karmesha and said, "And thank you for the dance."

With that Gerald turned and left. Karmesha was certain he had forgotten something, like her number. But Gerald didn't turn around until he reached his own table, where he was engulfed by beautiful women.

Karmesha was hot and bothered that he had romanced her and not even asked for her digits. He wanted her. She knew from the eye contact they shared that Gerald yearned to be lost between her thighs. What bothered her was that she didn't know what his game was.

Chapter Thirteen

Candles flickered around the master suite of the luxurious mansion tucked in the gated community of Auburn Hills. The glow of the candles cast two moving shadows making passionate love underneath the drawn canopy of the king-size bed.

Taquana dug her nails deep into the back of her lover as he slid in and out of her balls deep. His stroke was matched to the soft music of Maxwell playing around them.

"Yes. Fuck me!" pleaded Taquana, raking her claws down the man's back. Her eyes were closed, and her mouth was gaped in her sheer ecstasy. Her lover had Taquana on the verge of exploding, but he wanted to make the night last much longer. He rolled her over onto her stomach, placing a pillow under her stomach for arch, then he started digging her back out with long, powerful strokes. She wanted to be fucked, so he'd kindly oblige her request.

Taquana's mouth opened to a wide O. Her pleasure wouldn't allow a moan or scream to escape her. She was paralyzed from his manhood filling her up and touching her G-spot with every thrust. She dug into the sheets and looked back at her lover with her eyes closed. Her thick and soft ass cheeks slapped violently against the man's well-defined six-pack. His ink black muscles gleamed from a growing sweat.

He slapped Taquana's ass hard while he kept his pound game coming. "You like that?" he growled as he slapped her ass again.

"Yes," she cried. "I'm 'bout to come," she announced.

Her lover pulled out of her, leaving Taquana begging, "Put it back in me." Her voice was small and sexy.

But her lover wasn't ready for her to cum just yet. He kept his ten-inch dick primed by jacking it with her pussy juice as he climbed in bed and lay back big-dick style.

"Come here," he ordered.

Taquana was weak getting there, but he hoisted her pretty frame onto his manhood. "Oh, my God. Ah!" screamed Taquana as he filled her up with every inch. He slammed her up and down two successive times, allowing the pain to turn into pleasure, and then he began sliding her up and down at a steady rhythm.

He spread her ass cheeks apart and looked Taquana deep in her eyes as he watched her climax claim her. His stare was just as intense as the dick he'd been slinging. He could brew a nut inside of Taquana just by looking at her.

She loved and hated him at the same time, because she hated letting any man have that much power over her. Taquana took a final lap around and cried out as she became undone. She came so hard that she fell limp beside her lover, panting.

He stroked her hair softly. He was always so attentive.

"I hate you," said Taquana in a small voice.

The man chuckled in a deep voice. "You know I'll never believe that," he said.

"You make me sick," said Taquana, hiding her face in a pillow. Taquana didn't have any kids nor a steady man in her life. She was too focused on running her bag. Loving a man would only cause her problems, she told herself. But the fine brother she had been keeping company for the past few months had her head gone. She'd had good dick before in her life, but then there was good dick! She couldn't stand him because he knew what he was doing to her.

It was crazy that Taquana was finding it hard to keep her head around him. When he wasn't fucking her brains out, he was mind fucking her with good, stimulating conversation. He spoke with purpose and had drive. Taquana had never met a man like him before. She'd been searching for any flaws in his character, but over the past few months he'd shown none. He was who he por-

trayed himself to be, which was rarely the case
with niggas.

Taquana curled up on his massive chest and
made circles around his nipples while he ran his
strong fingers through her hair. His touch was
intoxicating.

"Can I trust you?" asked Taquana.

"Have I given you any reason not to?"

"No," admitted Taquana. She sat up and looked
into his deep brown eyes. And what she saw was all
man. "I have kinda a favor to ask you."

"Anything." He hadn't hesitated.

Taquana had use for everyone around her, and
today it was time to put him to use for something
other than just his good dick game. Taquana knew
just what she'd have him do. She smiled wickedly
inside as she broke down her plan.

Her homie, lover, friend was game on what
Taquana requested of him. It would be his pleasure to complete her assignment. It was all business
at the end of the day, because Taquana offered to
bring him to the table of her operation once he'd
taken care of his end of things.

Taquana could've used anyone else to accom-
plish her latest plot, but by using him, she told
herself that it would define their relationship as
being about business and loosen the hold he'd
taken on her. Taquana needed to be in control
of her emotions at all times as well as anyone
around her.

Chapter Fourteen

On the ninth floor of the Theodore Levin United States Courthouse in downtown Detroit sat a host of field agents who'd been assigned to Saw's investigation. The lights in the conference room were off so that the projector screen illuminated the slides being shown to the agents. Special Agent Hopskins from the DEA stood beside the white rolled-down screen with his sleeves rolled up, his tie loose, and a pointer in his hand. He had a picture of Saw on the screen.

"This is our guy. He's the reason we're all gathered here today and not at home with our families. I want you to all get a good look at Saw, because there's going to be a lot of long nights until we've got enough for an indictment," said Agent Hopskins.

He clicked the remote, and a picture of Hood came on the screen. "He's our number two guy. Meet Mr. Hood." Hopskins clicked again and a photo of Lano showed. "And Lano is our number three guy."

The agents all scribbled onto notepads while Hopskins kept going through the hierarchy of Saw's crime family. The Feds were getting good intel, because they had photos of Thugga and Maine and even had them listed as shooters. The Feds were slowly building their case. It all started with first being able to put faces with names and knowing what roles everyone played.

The rest would come together. In the federal system, there is a common saying that they can indict a ham sandwich. Saw hadn't any idea what he was up against.

The agents had turned their attention to Taquana's crime family. A photo of Slim came up on the screen. Slim had been under investigation before he was killed, so the Feds had a thick file on him and his operation. Slim was close to being indicted and would've been had he not been slain. A second picture of Slim's dead body slumped in the barber chair showed on the screen.

Agent Hopskins explained how Saw and Slim were at war and that Saw was highly suspected to be responsible for Slim's murder. Taquana's photo came up next. Hopskins explained how she'd taken over Slim's heroin operations and how she tried to avenge her brother's death by shooting Saw at a recent party.

"I say we go after her first while we work on building our case against the Saw organization," said Agent Hopskins.

Hopskins felt that, because Taquana had more people in her growing organization, it would be easier to penetrate her ranks versus Saw's. Once they could get inside and flip some of the lower-level members into informants, they'd be able to get an indictment rolling against Taquana.

So far she had been careful not to ever talk on the phones, but her mistake of accepting anyone into her circle, for the sake of having numbers on her side, would prove to be a grave mistake.

Chapter Fifteen

The sign in front of the hair salon said TOP-NOTCH.
It was a testament to how the women patrons
and stylists of the salon felt about themselves.
They each believed that they were top-notch boss
bitches. The salon belonged to Denise. It was one
of the two things that Saw had done for his moms
from all his hustling in the streets. He'd bought her
a nice home in Eastpointe and had the salon built
from the ground up. It sat off Gratiot Avenue close
to downtown Detroit.

Denise wasn't a stylist herself, but the shop gave
her something to do every day. It gave her a sense
of ownership, and it allowed her to stay young
and fly as she'd done her best to keep in tune with
today's generation. Denise didn't look her 40 years
of age. She could easily pass for 30, and a very sexy
30 at that. She hung out with her stylists after work
and had little boy toys half her age stashed about
the city.

It was nearing midday on this Tuesday, and the
shop was buzzing with gossip. The sound of hair

dryers and the clicking of curlers blended into the laughter of the hens sitting around sharing tea.

The salon for these women was what the barber shop is to men. It was their sanctuary, the one place where they could be themselves without any real judgment being passed. The majority of the women had been customers of the shop since it opened. Most of them were sack-chasers, sharing valuable info on the ballers they'd worked and the ones they sought to work. There was a file on damn near every hustla from east to west. The women shared everything about their prospects from their dick size down to their bankroll.

"Girl, I heard that nigga got the Hemalayah!" said one of the stylists, Terresa. She was a big-chested, brown-skinned chick with a crazy sense of humor who was stingy in the ass department. Terresa always said what was on her mind, which was always something funny because she was also animated.

The women around the shop threw their heads back in laughter as Terresa demonstrated how he be long-dicking bitches from the back. Not that she had personally had the pleasure of him blowing her back out, but she didn't allow that to stop her from fantasizing about it.

The nigga they were discussing danced at Henry's Palace, the legendary male strip joint. While niggas were throwing bands inside the strip clubs, their wives, side bitches, and baby mommas were up in Henry's Palace making it rain on the men they had fantasies about.

Denise shook her head at Terresa as she stood at the receptionist's desk, sorting through the day's mail. There was a letter from Wink in the stack. A smile formed at the corners of her mouth as she admired his nice penmanship.

"What you cheesin' about?" asked Sonay, her receptionist.

"Non' ya." Denise smiled as she cuffed the letter and rushed off to her back office.

She tore into the envelope as she rounded her desk and took a seat. Denise frowned at the letter because it wasn't she Wink had written to, but to Saw. She pursed her lips and read the brief letter anyway.

She would have liked at least a "hello, Denise, how are you doing?" It had been over twenty years. Denise told herself that at least he wrote back, and hopefully he'd be able to get through to Saw, because she wasn't ready to bury her son. Denise looked at the pictures of Saw and her grandkids that adorned her desk, and she smiled. There was a picture of her and Saw cutting the ribbon together the day the salon had opened. It was one of the only times she'd seen her son that happy.

Denise touched the picture with her nails, wishing they could all go back to that day. She sighed and tucked Wink's letter into her purse. She'd make sure Saw got it, but she'd have to track him down because she hadn't seen him since he went AWOL from the hospital.

Laughter erupted from the floor of the shop, bringing Denise back to the present. She headed out front to see what gossip she was missing out on.

Chapter Sixteen

The parking lot of Henry's Palace was packed with luxury cars as the women filled the club in droves. It was a Tuesday, which was ladies' night, so the place was especially jammed tight this night.

Karmesha whipped her silver Infiniti truck up to the valet post, and she emerged from the driver side as if to say, "I have arrived." She was flanked by Kim and Cookie. They were all eager to get inside the club because it had been a while since they last hit Henry's. The bass could be heard from the parking lot, which let them know they were missing the action.

Women screaming with fists full of bills came into view as Karmesha led the way inside the club. Four beefy niggas with third legs were on stage. Their bare chests were oiled and inviting to the host of women throwing bills at their feet.

The club anthem thrummed as the women chanted the lyrics. "'Work that mothafucka! Work that mothafucka!'"

Karmesha, Kim, and Cookie found an empty table near the back of the club. Cookie had come with her singles ready. She pulled wads of cash from her purse, which was bait money for whatever nigga she zeroed in on.

"Girl, gimmie some," said Kim.

"Bitch, you knew we was comin'. You betta tell her you want some singles," said Cookie as a waitress came to take their order. Kim smacked her lips and dug into her bag for some money.

"Can I take your order?" asked the waitress.

"Yeah, bring us a couple bottles of Moët," said Karmesha.

"I need some liquor, girl. So bring me a bottle of Patrón, and please bring this bitch some singles," said Cookie.

"Okay," said the waitress.

All the men wore masquerade masks. It was the theme for the night. It provided a little mystery to everything. The women seemed to be loving the theme, because they were out of their seats throwing money and smacking asses, demanding that the strippers, "Work that mothafucka!"

The waitress came back with their drinks and Kim's $500 worth of singles.

"Karmesha, why you ain't get no singles?" asked Cookie.

"'Cause all I throw is twenties, bitch," said Karmesha as she unearthed a wad of cash from her purse.

Cookie twisted her mouth because Karmesha was always trying to outshine her and Kim. Everything was a competition with her. But Cookie wasn't about to let something that petty spoil her mood. There were way too many reasons a bitch should be smiling walking around, each blessed with big dicks and bulging muscles.

Cookie stopped this fine yellow nigga with an eight-pack as he was passing their table. "How you doing, baby?" the man asked, revealing a million-dollar smile.

"I was hoping you'd dance for me," said Cookie, tucking a handful of bills into the man's white Speedos.

"I got you," said the man as he broke into a lap dance.

Kim locked her eyes on a sexy stripper and summoned him over with a promising wave of cash. The guy came over and started grinding to the beat inches away from Kim's face.

Cookie and Kim looked at each other like, *yes, bitch,* then looked back at the bulging dicks on display.

Karmesha sipped her flute of champagne while watching the men up on stage. She had a thing for men's backs, so she was enjoying the ripped backside of this fine chocolate nigga as he turned around so the women could view his tight ass.

Karmesha ran her tongue around her lips because, damn, he was fine as hell. The man turned around facing the crowd, and as he looked out into the crowd, he smiled straight at Karmesha. There wasn't any doubt that he was looking at her, but the mask concealed his face. They held each other's gaze until his set on stage was over. Then he made his way over to Karmesha's table.

"Would you like me to dance for you?" asked the man.

Karmesha reached for a few twenties to get him started. Her eyes traveled up his defined abs and to his wide chest. He was a masterpiece. When she looked up into his eyes, he pulled back a familiar smile.

"I didn't know if I'd ever see you again," he said.

Karmesha's eyes grew wide as she searched his face.

"Here, let me help you out," said the man, lifting up his mask.

Gerald. She knew his eyes were familiar. Karmesha didn't know what to do with herself. She hadn't expected to see him again either, let alone there of all places. It became awkward and Gerald sensed it, and he stopped dancing. That was precisely the reason he rarely gave his number to women, even if they interested him, because none of them could ever look past what he did for a living.

True, he was every woman's fantasy, but that had proven to be a gift and a curse. He could never hold down a relationship because the women would all have jealousy issues. Things would always start off well, but then they'd try to change him, wanting him to stop dancing at the clubs.

Gerald reached for Karmehsa's hand and led her to the VIP room, where they could have some privacy. He sat her down on one of the sofas and sat beside her.

"So this is what you do?" said Karmesha.

"Yeah, this is what I do. Been dancing for about seven years now."

"I'm not judging you or anything, but don't you think you could've done something different?"

"Like what?"

"I don't know. Like, you could be a model or something."

Gerald smiled. "This is what I'm good at, Karmesha. And it's what I enjoy doing."

He remembered my name. Karmesha relaxed a little. Who was she to be telling him what else he could've been in life? It wasn't as if she'd exactly graduated at the top of her class, not unless she considered sack-chasing a profession. But in her case it was. Her whole life had been dedicated to trapping ballers and living the good life.

It was just that she hadn't met anyone as special as Gerald in a long time, and now she was finding out he was a stripper. It didn't make him a bad person because of his occupation. The thing was Karmesha didn't like to share. Her whole life she had to share the men in her life. She was currently sharing Saw's trifling self with Tammy and Sherise, and whatever else side chicks he was fucking. Karmesha just wanted a man of her own. But being a prolific sack-chaser guaranteed that she'd always share a man's affection.

Gerald and Karmesha sat and kicked it for the rest of the night. She came to find out he had more depth to him than what met the eye. He made good conversation and had a sense of humor that made Karmesha want more of him. So what, he was a stripper? It wasn't like she was looking to marry him. Just like all the other men in her life, she'd have to settle for a piece of him.

When the night ended, Karmesha gave Gerald a healthy tip for his time and company. But this time he didn't let her get away without getting her number.

Chapter Seventeen

Saw checked his rearview mirror for the hundredth time as he drove along Moross. He was sure that navy blue Cherokee was following him. The two white men inside the Jeep were Feds, Saw told himself. *You bitches wanna follow me, huh?* thought Saw as he put on his blinker and eased into the turning lane for the service drive off I-94. He watched the Jeep put on its blinker and turn onto the interstate behind him. Saw was driving his new Corvette. He had a fleet of cars, most of them triple black like the Stingray he was handling. He stabbed the pedal to the floor, and the beast of an engine responded with a pretty growl, then roared into the merging traffic.

Saw smiled as he watched the white man in the Cherokee banging his hands on his wheel. There was no catching Saw in that Vette. Saw weaved in and out of the lanes, then came up the exit ramp to Van Dyke Avenue. He let the top down as he made the right onto Van Dyke. It was a beautiful day without a cloud in the sky, all the more reason for him to floss with the roof in the trunk. He had rapper Blade Icewood pumping out of the speakers: "You niggas wanna ride on me."

It was one of Saw's favorite tracks by Blade because that was how he'd been feeling, like niggas wanted to ride on him and end his life. He had let the top down so niggas could have a sighting of him, and so the streets would know he wasn't the one hiding.

Little did Saw know though, the Feds weren't the only ones clocking his moves. He had two other sets of eyes watching him on the daily as he made his stops at his club. In the cut watching were Snake and Womp from their rental crib on Syracuse. For the past couple of weeks they'd been holed up watching the club's activity from the monitors set up inside the living room. Every day around two o'clock Saw would pull up to the club and be greeted by his men standing post. Snake and Womp had his schedule down, but the only problem was that they didn't know what car he'd pull up in from day to day because Saw had so many different whips that he would be in a different one every day.

Snake was on post watching the monitor while Womp rolled them two blunts at the dining room table.

"Here that bitch go right there," said Snake as he watched Saw emerge from the black Vette.

Saw had made one slipup, and that was he always parked in the same spot, Snake noticed. His men always kept the space open for Saw. It sat right outside the club entrance.

"I got'chu," said Snake to the monitor.

He and Womp were tired of waiting to kill this nigga Saw. They were used to riding around on the hunt like they were in the Hunger Games. They just wanted to kill this nigga so that they could get back to Chi-raq.

Snake had figured out just how they were going to catch Saw down bad. "I got'chu," Snake promised again as he watched Saw slip inside the club. Womp passed him one of the lit blunts, and they lay back chiefing. "When we gon' hit 'im?" asked Womp.

"Soon," said Snake as he took a long pull from the Kush blunt. *Real soon,* thought Snake.

Chapter Eighteen

The next day, around two o'clock in the afternoon, Saw pulled up to the club in a black tinted-out Escalade sitting high on blades. He dapped up his men on the way in but stopped in his tracks at the sight of his mom, Denise. She was exiting the club, talking to Lano.

Saw gave Lano a questionable look, to which he shrugged. It was Saw's mom. *What does he want me to do, turn her away?* thought Lano.

Immediately Denise started with her bitching as soon as she spotted Saw. "Why don't you answer ya damn phone? Shit. Somebody could be callin' to let you know my ass is laid up in the damn morgue, but then again you done lost ya damn mind out here runnin' these streets," snapped Denise.

"Denise, I've been busy. And I know that you're fine because I got eyes on you at all times," said Saw.

"I hope you don't treat your mother the way he treats me." Denise looked at Lano, who stood silent.

"I know you ain't came 'round here just to cuss me out, so what's up?" asked Saw.

Denise dug around inside her large designer bag. "I came to give you this," she said, handing him an envelope. "It's from your father."

Saw looked at the return name and prisoner number on the envelope. "This nigga ain't my daddy," said Saw.

"And why ain't he?" said Denise, shifting her weight to one leg.

Saw had to hold back his true thoughts. "He just ain't, all right?" said Saw.

"Let me tell yo' ass one thing. I know goddamn—"

Everybody's attention was arrested by the growling sound of an engine and tires screeching to a stop. The front doors flew open on a wine-colored Charger 392, and two masked gunmen emerged, opening fire with fully automatic AK-47s. Laaka! Laaka! Laaka!

Saw instinctively snatched the .40-cal Glock from his waist and returned their fire, as did most of his men. Boom! Boom! Boom!

The element of surprise cost four of Saw's men their lives, because as soon as the gunmen exited the car, their assault rifles were unleashing a hail of bullets.

The sound of bullets bouncing off the brick of the building caused Saw to backpedal. He was trying to make it inside the club so he could grab his AR-15. But the bullets kept coming, causing him to take cover behind a Denali parked at the curb. The two gunmen were obviously gunning at Saw from the way the SUV was rocked with bullets.

Glass burst from every window of the SUV, causing Saw to cower farther to the ground. He could see the gunmen's feet as they stood in the street emptying their drums. He watched as one man made his way toward the truck.

Saw wasn't about to die hiding like a bitch, so he came up blazing as the man rounded the hood of the Denali. Saw filled the man's chest with all he had, but the gunman wore vests, so the impact was minimal.

Damn, this nigga about to down me, thought Saw as the gunman closed in on him with his AK-47 pointed for his face. Two shots erupted. The gunman stiffened, then collapsed to his knees and fell over onto his stomach.

A swarm of federal agents were pulling up with their guns drawn. The second gunman fired on the agents, killing two instantly, but as he inched toward his getaway car, more agents fired everything they had on him. His wide frame jerked violently as he fought to stay on his feet. But the bullets were endless, and the gunman lost his fight. He folded to the pavement and went into shock.

Saw got to his mom, Denise, who had been struck in her midsection somewhere. He cradled

her head in his hands while not wanting to believe
that she had been shot. She was bleeding badly.
Her eyes were wide with fear.

"I'm not ready to die, baby," said Denise.

"You're not gonna die," said Saw as he looked
around. "Let me get some fuckin' help over here!"
he yelled.

An agent rushed over and kneeled beside Saw.
She sprung into lifesaving action by snatching off
her FBI jacket and wrapping it around Denise's
stomach as tight as she could.

Denise cried out in pain. "It burns! Oh, God."

"Ma'am, I'm going to need you to keep your eyes
open, okay? Help is on the way. Can you do that?"
asked the agent.

"Yes," responded Denise in a weak voice.

More agents rushed over to aid with Denise
while others tended to the others who'd been
wounded. The grass and sidewalk were painted
with blood, and bodies lay sprawled out. Lano had
been hit in the shoulder and in the leg. He groaned
in pain as two agents worked to stop the bleeding.

Things suddenly took a turn for the worse as
Saw stood by helplessly watching his mom's eyes.
Agents stormed toward Saw with guns drawn and
handcuffed him.

"Get down on your knees!" ordered one DEA
agent.

Saw felt as though he were in a bad dream.

"Do it now!" ordered a second black agent.

Saw could see the itch in the black agent's eyes to kill him, so he slowly got down to his knees. Agents took a hold of Saw, manhandling him as they cuffed and frisked him. They snatched him to his feet, and Special Agent Hopskins stood inches away from Saw's face. Saw ice grilled the cracker.

"Get him outta here," ordered Agent Hopskins.

Two agents shoved Saw toward an awaiting black van. They put him inside the back dog cage and shut the door. Complete darkness enveloped Saw in the back. There was a tap on the van, and then it shifted into gear and started moving. Its destination was unknown to Saw.

"What the fuck?" Saw yelled out. He was furious not only because he was on his way to God knows where, but because so much had happened in the blink of an eye. His thoughts went to Denise. Saw didn't want their last conversation to have been an argument.

Back at the club, a team of medics loaded Denise onto a gurney and placed her in the back of an ambulance. The female agent rode with Denise to the hospital, not because she was genuinely concerned, but because she wanted to keep Denise talking and get as much incriminating information she could about Saw's operation and the street war. But Denise was a seasoned vet in the game. She knew not to say a word.

Special Agent Hopskins was canvassing the scene when he kneeled down for the white envelope Saw had dropped when the gunshots rang out. Hopskins studied the return sender and the prison information. This piqued his interest, so he cuffed the envelope into his khakis and made his way for his unmarked Lincoln. Hopskins peeled away from the scene and used his smartphone to Google the prisoner's name written on the envelope.

A photo of Wink showed up as a result of the search. DETROIT KINGPIN CONVICTED AFTER FEDERAL TRIAL, SENTENCED TO LIFE. So read the headline from the *Detroit Free Press*.

Hopskins opened the letter to see what the connection was to Saw's mother and why Wink was writing to her from the penitentiary.

The black van dipped inside the tunnel garage of the federal courthouse downtown on Lafayette Boulevard. The van parked and the engine died. A moment later the back doors of the van opened, and Saw squinted from the lights of the garage.

"Out," ordered the young white DEA agent.

Saw scooted out the van into the garage area. He was shuffled to an ajar elevator by two agents. The passenger pushed the button for the ninth floor, and the doors closed. The quick ride up made Saw's head spin a bit. He was pissed because he had yet to be told why he was being locked up.

"Why am I under arrest?" asked Saw as the doors opened.

"Off," ordered the driver. "To your right."

Saw was led to an empty interrogation room. He was uncuffed then left alone. He rubbed at his wrists from the tightness of the cuffs as he paced the small carpeted room. He looked up at the black bubble concealing an eye in the sky, realizing that he was being watched.

The door opened and in came the same cracker he'd mean mugged back at the bar. The agent wore a tight-fitting black T-shirt and tan khakis. He had a manila envelope in his hand that he tossed on the desk.

"Have a seat," said the agent.

"This won't take long," said Saw. "I just want to call my lawyer."

Agent Hopskins turned beet red in the face, because Saw had lawyered up on him immediately, which meant he couldn't lawfully question him without the presence of his lawyer.

Hopskins stood up and snatched the folder up from the desk. He needed to have the last word. "You're gonna wish one day that you talked to me."

Saw didn't even dignify him with a response. He just kept pacing the floor.

Hopskins turned for the door, then stopped. He dug out the envelope from Wink and tossed it onto the desk. "I believe that's yours," said Hopskins. He left the room, and Saw stopped to look at the envelope. He picked it up, realizing that the agent had read it.

Chapter Nineteen

Dear Saw,

I know this kite may come as a surprise to you. It was a surprise having gotten a letter from your moms telling me that I'm your father. I'm not disputing I could be, but I think that everyone involved at least deserves to know, you feel me? I, myself, didn't meet my father until I was about your age, and when we finally met he was already sitting where I am today writing you this letter.

Saw, your mom is worried about you ending up in here beside me. And I must say that that thought bothers me whether you're my son or not. I want you to know something, okay? Everything that I did out there counts for nothin' inside these walls, and you know why that is? Because there's thousands of niggas in here with a story, you feel me? But I'm here to tell you that there ain't no glory in my story.

*I'm not going to write you a book here. I
was hoping that you'd be open to a DNA test.
We could get it set up and put everyone's
mind at ease. Because if you're mine, I don't
want another twenty years to slip by us. I'd
like to be in your life as much as you'll let
me. I'ma cut the cord on this kite so it can fly
your way. Hope to hear from you soon.*
W/Respect,
Wink

Saw folded the letter back into its envelope and
sighed deeply. His thoughts were interrupted by a
slight knock at the door. Then in came his lawyer,
Ms. Raben. She was a short, feisty, all-business,
gray-haired legal genius with a sharp mind and
tongue.

"How are you?" she asked.

"I'm good. What are they charging me with?"

"Nothing today. You're leaving with me in a few
minutes. They were hoping to get you on felon in
possession of a firearm until I showed them that
all your priors had been reduced to misdemean-
ors." Ms. Raben looked Saw over. His shirt was
soaked in blood. "Do we need to get you to the ER?"

"Nah, but I'd like to go check on my moms. Is she
gonna be all right?"

"I haven't heard anything from the hospital. But
let's get you outta here, and I'll drive you there. I
believe she's at St. John's." Ms. Raben stepped into

the hallway and said something to the agents. They were trying to stall her, at least until they got word from their boss. But Ms. Raben wasn't having it. She threatened to go downstairs to see one of the magistrates who'd certainly order Saw's release.

"We're leaving now!" she yelled at the agents.

Ms. Raben may have been in her 70s, but her piercing blue eyes and shrill voice sent chills through the agents. They didn't dare try to stop her as she ushered Saw out of the room and down to the elevators. They exited the federal courthouse and walked across the street to paid parking. Ms. Raben drove a new Buick SUV. They piled into the sleek pearl blue SUV, and Ms. Raben got them into the midst of rush-hour traffic. "Anything you want to listen to? The radio's all yours."

"This fine right here."

Smooth jazz played at an even volume.

"I don't have my piece with me. Nobody's gonna try to kill us, are they?" asked Ms. Raben. She looked over at Saw and had a smile in her eyes. "I'm just kidding. You know I never leave home without it." She pulled a stainless-steel .45 from under her seat and placed it on her lap.

That was why Saw fucked with her, because she was fearless. She had told Saw a time or two that there was nothing wrong with being fearless so long as he was on the right side of things. He was still working on figuring that out for himself.

Ms. Raben never tried to preach to Saw about his doings in the street, but she'd always tell him to be careful and, more so, mindful.

"I need you to check something out for me," said Saw.

"What'chu got?" asked Ms. Raben, her eyes keen to the road.

Saw pulled the letter from his pocket. "You ever heard of an old kingpin they call Wink?"

"Yes. One of my good friends I went to law school with represented him at trial. Why, you know him?"

Saw turned to the window and stared out at the passing people on the streets.

"Do you know him?" repeated Ms. Raben.

"Nah," admitted Saw. He really didn't know Wink personally. "But I want you to dig up everything about his investigation leading up to him being indicted."

"Okay. I'll have my assistant Kathleen see what all she can dig up. Is there anything else?"

"Just thank you," said Saw.

Ms. Raben reached over and patted Saw's leg and gave him a closed, assuring smile. He was grateful to have her as his attorney. She was always thorough, unlike most paid lawyers who were hard to get on the phone once they'd gotten your money situated in their bank accounts.

***

When Saw walked into the hospital his entire family were all there in the waiting room. His two boys bolted toward him.

"Daddy! Daddy!" screamed Demarcus and Marco.

Saw kneeled down and embraced his sons and kissed their foreheads. When he stood up, his aunt Shawn was standing over him. Her eyes were bloodshot from crying. They hugged. His aunt Shawn was just thankful that he was alive.

"How is she?" asked Saw.

"She just came outta surgery. But the doctors say that she's gonna pull through. We are all just waiting to go see her," said Aunt Shawn.

Saw looked around at all the faces. All his aunts and uncles sat around the lobby. Sherise offered him a weak and worried smile. Tammy's face was screwed up as she just shook her head at Saw.

"Do you need me to stay?" asked Ms. Raben.

"I'm good, Ms. Raben. And thanks again," said Saw.

Ms. Raben touched Saw's arm for reassurance as she turned to leave. "Call me if anything else comes up," she said.

Hood and ten of their men rushed inside the sliding doors of the hospital. They had made a scene coming in that had everyone in the lobby with nervous eyes.

"My nigga, you straight?" asked Hood as he looked Saw over. With all the blood on his clothes, he couldn't tell if Saw had been shot again.

"I'm good. But they hit up Mom Dukes and Lano," said Saw. He and Hood had taken up a corner in the lobby and talked in hushed tones.

"They gon' make it?" asked Hood.

"My OG just came outta surgery, and they say she gon' be good. But I ain't heard nothin' about Lano."

"Damn!" growled Hood, jamming his fists into the wall.

Hood had been late getting to the club. He couldn't believe niggas had the balls to come through Syracuse and take shots the way they had. Them niggas Taquana had were on a suicide mission if they thought they'd make it away from the club alive. But still they had dropped their nuts and tried anyway, which really concerned Hood because it made him wonder just how many more niggas Taquana had who would go on missions knowing that they'd die in the process. She had some suicide bombers on her team, so to speak.

"I'ma find that bitch myself," said Hood through clenched teeth.

"Remember what we talked about out at the ranch," Saw reminded him.

"Fuck the Feds, my nigga. I'd rather be judged by twelve than to be carried by six. That dirty bitch is killing us, and I'ma put an end to all of it," said Hood.

Hood left Saw to his family. He ordered eight men to stay posted with Saw at the hospital while he left with two of his best goons, Thugga and Maine.

Saw had seen that look in Hood's eyes many times before. It was the look of murder. When Hood got like that, there was no talking him down or reasoning with him. Hood was going to do exactly what he said he would because he was a solid nigga who always stood on his word as a man. He was going to find Taquana and kill her at any cost, even if it cost him his own life.

The charge nurse came out to let the family know that Denise was still in recovery and was awake and that she was asking to see her family.

"When can we see her?" asked Aunt Shawn.

The nurse looked at her pink watch. "Visiting hours are over, but I can let you guys see her for a little while if it'll help her spirits."

"Thank you so much," said Aunt Shawn.

The family carried their get-well bears and balloons down to Denise's room. She lay in bed with an IV hooked up to her hand. A bright smile enveloped her yellow face when her family walked into the room. Her sister, Shawn, was the first at her bedside, along with her brother, Squirt.

Denise was tired and weak, but having her loved ones there gave her spirit a boost. Her eyes found Saw. He was standing behind everyone else. His two sons climbed in bed with their grandmother. Saw couldn't bring himself to move any closer, knowing that he was the sole reason his ol' bird was lying there with tired, sunken eyes. He had put Denise through a lot. He never thought that she really worried about him as she said she did, but he could see it in her eyes now. Saw turned and left the room. It was too much for him.

"Where are you going?" Sherise called after Saw.

He stopped and slowly turned around. Sherise closed the space between them and took Saw's hand into hers. She looked deep into his eyes, and for the first time she saw something in him that she had never seen before—fear.

"You know I'm here for you, don't you?" said Sherise.

Tammy was standing outside the room. She smacked her lips and grunted. But Sherise was too classy to entertain Tammy's petty ass. Her only concern was the well-being of Denise, her son, and Saw.

"If you're leaving, then I'm coming with you," said Sherise. It wasn't a suggestion, but a certainty. She laced her fingers into Saw's and peeked back into the room. She asked Aunt Shawn to keep an eye on Demarcus while she took Saw home to clean up.

Saw ordered a group of his men to stand guard outside his mom's room, and he sent two men to post up outside of Lano's room. Two of his men insisted that they at least follow him until he made it onto the interstate. Hood had left them with strict instructions, and there'd be hell to pay if something were to happen to Saw again.

Sherise drove them out to Saw's Port Huron ranch. For her it was the most beautiful property of Saw's estates. She secretly imagined them living on the ranch raising a family together.

Sherise got Saw undressed and stepped into the marble shower behind him. He stood underneath the showerhead with his head down and eyes closed as the blood stained into his skin rinsed down into the drain at his feet. Sherise poured a healthy squirt of Gucci men's body wash onto a white sponge and worked it into a thick lather, then started washing Saw's back and shoulders.

She washed him all over until he was anew. Her small hands ran up and down his back as they stood under the soothing hot water. Sherise wrapped her arms around Saw's waist and leaned the side of her face against his back. She prayed that he'd wake up and realize how much his family loved him. How much she loved him.

Chapter Twenty

Every time I'm with you,
Never want it to come to an end.

Gerald was cruising along Jefferson Avenue with the top down on his silver Mercedes. He was lip-synching the sounds of 112, while smiling over at Karmesha in the passenger seat. She was tickled pink and blushing as she tried concealing her smile behind her hand. Gerald was making her heart melt away, because the lyrics of the song were exactly how she felt at that moment in time. There was no other place in the world that she would have rather been except right there beside him.

They had spent the weekend in Cincinnati at the Jazz Festival. Gerald had put them up in a presidential suite at the Hyatt, and he'd showered the room with scented candles and rose petals. Even though he was a male stripper, he still knew how to wine and dine a woman.

They had just made it back to Detroit and were
on cloud nine as they enjoyed each other's company. Karmesha reached over and massaged
Gerald's bald head, which she'd fallen in love
with over the weekend. She'd been palming it two
nights in a row as he made love to her treasures
with his strong and knowing tongue.

Karmesha's hair blew in the wind, and her face
was cloaked by dark designer shades, and she wore
a beautiful peach sundress. She was feeling as
special as a little girl on her birthday.

Gerald drove toward the west side. They'd come
up on Fenkell Avenue, which was unfamiliar territory for Karmesha, but she was at ease being with
Gerald. She had not a worry in the world, and her
face showed it, because she couldn't stop smiling.

Gerald turned down a residential street and
slowed because there were kids lying bare chested
in the fire hydrant's spray. He drove to the middle
of the block and whipped into the driveway of a
nice brick home.

"Is this where you live?" asked Karmesha as the
garage door went up and Gerald pulled in.

"It's one of my spots," said Gerald, smiling.

He killed the engine and popped the locks.
"Come on," he said, getting out. The garage door
descended as Karmesha got out. She stopped and
folded her arms across her chest. Gerald turned
from the entrance to the house and looked at her.
She had a scowl on her pretty face.

"What'd I do?" asked Gerald.

"Why are you bringing me to one of your spots? What, am I just another one of your bitches you bring to your flophouse?" said Karmesha as she waved her hand about the garage.

Gerald pulled back his patented cool smile.

"I don't think it's funny."

"I'm not laughing at you, baby. I just think it's sexy that you're a little bit jealous."

"I'm not jealous," lied Karmesha.

"Anyhow, I only stopped by here because I needed to pick up some things before I take you to my real house."

Karmesha was at a loss for words. She shook her head and smiled because she had embarrassed herself. "You make me sick."

"Can we please go inside now?" Gerald smiled. He opened the door leading into the kitchen and waved for her to enter.

The smell of fresh paint was in the air, and Karmesha could see that the house had been under renovation. The flooring and the cabinets were all new. But there were no appliances. There was no table in the kitchen, and as she made her way to the living room, she found nothing but plastic covering the floor. She wondered just what Gerald could've needed out of the house, because it was bare.

As she turned around, all she saw was Gerald's fist coming at her in a blur. He'd punched her so hard that he broke her jaw on contact. Karmesha folded to the floor against the plastic. She was out cold, unable to feel the cold chains being bound around her wrists and ankles. Gerald used padlocks to secure the chains, which were bone tight and cutting off her circulation.

Gerald had the look of a coldhearted killer in his eyes as he gagged Karmesha's mouth with a scarf. He had completely transformed from the Mr. Lover Boy persona into Karmesha's worst nightmare. He snatched her up from the floor and slung her limp body over his shoulder as if she were a sack of potatoes. He clicked on the light that led down into the damp basement.

In the center of the floor underneath a single light bulb sat an old kitchen chair. Gerald put Karmesha in the chair and used another long, skinny chain to bound her to the back of the chair. When he was finished, he slammed her hard across the face, so as to wake her up.

Karmesha's eyes fluttered and then opened. She wasn't dead. He needed her alive, so were his orders from Taquana. Karmesha's head was twirling with sharp pain. Her jaw hurt so bad that it went numb. She was trying her best to wake up from the bad dream she was certain that she was having, but the demonic man standing before her was as real as day. Her eyes watered. *Why are you doing this to me?* she asked with her eyes. She groaned from behind the scarf. "Mmmh!"

But Gerald simply turned and left her alone. He got to the top of the steps and cut off the light, then locked the basement door. His end had been taken care of. Taquana and Gerald had been lovers for months. She hadn't wanted to fall in love with Gerald, so she found a more suitable purpose for him. Taquana wanted Gerald to prove his worth to her, and by doing so, she would invest the money into opening Gerald's own male strip club. And she'd also supply him with all the drugs he needed to keep his high-end clientele happy as they partied away at his new club.

Karmesha was just a sacrificial lamb on the chopping block. Taquana had sicced Gerald on Karmesha because she'd done her homework on all three of Saw's baby mommas and she knew Karmesha would be easy to lure because she was a sack-chaser.

Now that Taquana had something that belonged to Saw, she'd see just how much he would do to get it back.

Chapter Twenty-one

The sound of the light switch clicking on arrested Karmesha's undivided attention as she raised her head and looked toward the basement steps. A woman's heels clicked coming down.

Taquana came into Karmesha's squinted view as she and Gerald reached the floor of the basement. Taquana was all dolled up and draped in gold jewelry. She smiled back at Gerald for having done such a good job. "Awww, look at you. Did he hurt you?" asked Taquana as she soothed Karmesha's swollen jaw with the back of her hand.

Karmesha jerked away as she groaned and moved around, trying to fight the clenching chains bounding her to the chair.

"Oh, my name? That's not important. What's important is that you know I'm the bitch who's gonna decide if you live or die," said Taquana. She pulled a throw-away phone from her clutch and opened up the photo feature. She aimed the phone at Karmesha. "Smile now," she teased while taking several pictures.

"That should be enough," said Taquana as she set the phone to forward the pictures.

Karmesha glared at Gerald, who had this cold look in his eyes. She couldn't bring herself to fathom Gerald doing something like that to her. It was just inconceivable to think that the man she had just spent the weekend loving on was even capable of harming her. And what Karmesha wanted to know was, *who's this bitch?* None of this was making any sense. Why were they holding her there? Had she been kidnapped and held for ransom? What were the pictures about?

A thousand questions raced through Karmesha's mind, and she began to have a panic attack because she just knew that they were going to kill her. She sobbed and moaned from behind the scarf, and her eyes were filled with fright and running tears.

"Shut her the fuck up while I do this," snapped Taquana. She was still sending out the pictures.

Gerald reached his fist back to his shoulder and delivered a knockout blow to Karmesha's temple. Her head jerked violently on impact, and then her neck rolled to the side where she sat slumped.

Silhouette of a perfect frame,
Shadows of your smile, will always remain,
Beginners love, soon fades away.

"My First Love," by Avant & Keke Wyatt, was pouring through the master suite while Saw lay on his stomach across the bed with his eyes closed. He was enjoying the sensual touch of Sherise as she treated him to a full-body massage. She was working his shoulders as she sat over his lower back. She used Hot Six Oil to relax Saw's muscles, because he was tense all over.

Sherise secretly wished that catering to Saw every day as his wifey could be more than her fantasy. She had never stopped loving him. As the song's title boasted, they were each other's first love. She looked down at Saw's closed eyes and wondered if they'd ever be together.

Saw's cell phone vibrated against the pillow beside him. His eyes opened, and he reached for his phone. Sherise stopped massaging him because his taking the phone message had ruined her mood. She rolled off him and reached for the remote, turning off the music then turning on the TV. Saw jolted into an upright position, startling her.

"What's the matter?" she asked with concern.

"They got Karmesha," answered Saw as he scrolled through the pictures of Karmesha chained up to a chair with her mouth gagged.

"Who's got Karmesha?" Sherise didn't understand.

Saw dropped his phone on the bed and shot into the closet, snatching at anything to wear. Sherise flipped through the pictures with her hand over her mouth in disbelief.

Saw quickly dressed and snatched his keys off the dresser inside the closet. He grabbed his twin gold-plated .45s and stuffed them in the back of his pants.

"Where are you going, Saw?" asked Sherise as he came back into the bedroom. Her voice was demanding of an answer.

But Saw wasn't listening. His eyes were searching for something. Sherise held up his phone, snapping him back to her. He took the phone from her and shoved it in his pants pocket. Sherise was off the bed now, and she raced to the door to block Saw's path.

"Sherise, move out of the way."

"Not until you tell me what's going on. Who has Karmesha and why?"

Saw flashed. "To get to me! They want me, okay?"

There was a brief silence.

"Don't you think we should let the police take care of this?"

Saw laughed at this. "The police? Sherise, I ain't never call the police a day in my life. In the streets—"

"Damn them streets, Saw. What about your family? What about me?"

"Look, I gotta fix this. If it were you, I'd be doing the same thing."

That wasn't what Sherise needed to hear. She didn't know how much more her heart could afford. "I don't know if I'll be here when you get back."

"Well, I hope you will be." Saw meant just that.

He didn't want to leave at that point in time. Being alone with Sherise was always special, and he knew how she felt about them. But at the same time he was balls deep in the game and in the middle of a war that he was losing. He couldn't just leave Karmesha to the wolves. After all, she was his daughter's mother.

As Saw slipped behind the wheel of his Benz S600, a text came through on his phone, which read: If u ever wanna see this bitch alive again, you'll do exactly as I say. Wait for my call.

Chapter Twenty-two

Saw always had been good at thinking on his toes, so even though the pressure was on to get Karmesha back alive, he knew not to panic as most would in that situation. He texted Hood and told him to meet him at Fugi's ASAP.

Fugi was Saw's younger cousin by a couple of years. He wasn't a street nigga though. He'd grown up with both his parents together, and they lived in the suburbs most of his life. Fugi had gone to school for IT and owned his own firm, which Saw helped with. There wasn't anything Fugi wouldn't do when it came to a computer in front of him. He was so cold that even the Feds wanted him to come work for them after school.

Saw pulled into the parking lot of Fugi's Clinton Township office. He was relieved to see his cousin's black Lambo parked. Saw parked and rushed inside, where he found Fugi standing over his secretary's desk explaining something.

"Cuz, I need you!" said Saw.

Fugi looked up into Saw's face and saw that he was distraught. There had to be something really wrong, because this wasn't the Saw he knew. "Follow me," said Fugi, leading them to his back office.

Workers moved about the floor of the firm, so Fugi shut the door behind them. He shoved his stubby fingers into the pockets of his slacks as he leaned against the front of the desk. Saw was going through his phone when Hood came in.

"What up doe? I got ya text," said Hood. He was dressed in all-black war gear with a hoodie and Tims.

Saw pulled up the pictures of Karmesha and handed the phone to Fugi. Hood was leaning over Fugi's shoulder as he scrolled through the pics.

"That bitch. She's got her," said Saw, slapping his hands together.

"How long ago did you get these?" asked Fugi.

"'Bout twenty minutes ago," answered Saw.

Fugi rounded his desk and took a seat. His fingers stabbed at the keyboard of his computer. "One thing about GPS, if whoever took these pictures sent them from the same place they're holding her at, I'll be able to give you that exact location."

"We gon' get her back, my nigga," said Hood, putting both hands on Saw's shoulders.

"We got to," said Saw, thinking about his little girl.

"Got it," said Fugi as he scribbled the address onto a yellow sticky.

Saw took the paper and read the address aloud. "19195 Cherrylawn."

"West side, over there near Fenkell," said Hood.

Saw's wheels were turning.

"Did they say what they wanted in exchange for her?" asked Fugi.

"Nah, I got that last text telling me to wait on a call," said Saw.

Just then Saw's phone rang. He had switched from vibration mode because he didn't want to chance missing the call.

"Put it on speaker," said Hood.

Saw set the phone on the desk and answered the call. "Who this?"

Taquana's sinister laugh came through the phone. "Let's not play any games. You know exactly who this is. I'm the bitch who gave you ya face lift."

Saw's jaw clenched, and his knuckles were balled into a fist. He kept his composure for the sake of Karmesha. "How much you want?"

"This isn't about money. See, I'm sure you've got a lot of money, so that's not gonna hurt you any."

"Then what do you want to get her back?"

"I'm assuming you mean alive? And for that to happen you're gonna have to meet me at Zoro's on—"

"I know where it's at," said Saw.

"Good. And you are to come alone."

Hood was shaking his head no. There was no way he was sending Saw by himself. It was a death trap.

"And then what?" asked Saw.

"Then you and I will talk. That's all. I just want to look the man in the eyes who took my brother from me," said Taquana.

"Well, you gonna have to give me a minute."

"All you've got is a minute. Twenty to be exact."

"Let me talk to Karmesha."

The sound of the call ending chimed. Taquana had hung up. Saw had his orders. If he wanted to get Karmesha back, then he would do exactly as Taquana told him to do.

"It's a trap, my nigga," said Hood.

"You don't think I know that? But we can't waste time on that. What I need you to do is take some niggas with you to this address and grab Karmesha," said Saw.

"Let's just hope they haven't moved her," said Fugi.

It was a gamble. Saw's whole plan at the moment was a gamble, but the dice were in his hand. He just was praying for a seven and not craps.

"What about you?" asked Hood.

"Nigga, I'm me," said Saw. For a second he had that look in his eyes that said, "I will not lose!"

Hood reluctantly went along with it. He dipped off to go snatch up some of his men while Saw headed in the opposite direction. Both Saw and Hood looked to their rearview mirrors at each other's taillights, wondering if that would be the last time they'd ever see each other alive.

Chapter Twenty-three

Karmesha had come back since Gerald's second knockout blow to her temple. Her vision was blurred, and her head was drumming with pain that she wouldn't have wished on her worst enemy. She was wet for some reason. Her mind began to wonder if she had used the bathroom on herself while she was unconscious, but then the undeniable smell of gasoline hit her.

She began to get hysterical at the realization that they were going to set her on fire. *Why?* she screamed inside as her tears betrayed her. She couldn't understand why Gerald and that bitch were doing this to her. Had she wronged them in any way? Karmesha told herself that she wasn't a bad person and that she didn't have any enemies. Haters, yes. But no enemies who would want her dead. She tried jogging her memory to see if she could remember the ol' girl. Had she fucked her man or husband? Then it came to her.

Karmesha flashed back to the All-White Party. *That's the bitch who shot Saw.* More tears welled in her eyes as she realized that she was caught up in the middle of Saw's shit. *All the people who lost their lives because of him . . .* Karmesha was certain that she wouldn't be any exception.

The sound of the side door being kicked in commanded Karmesha's attention. The kicking continued until the door crashed open against the wall. Gunshots erupted seconds later. Boom! Boom! Boom!

There was a foot chase through the house. Then there were more gunshots, but this time they were from a fully automatic. Kaa! Kaa! Kaa! Kaa!

The gunfire ceased, and a man's voice Karmesha recognized was barking orders. "Search the house. She's in here somewhere!"

Karmesha smiled inside because the voice belonged to Hood. They had found her. She moaned as best she could from behind the gag, hoping they'd hear her. *I'm down here!* she wanted to scream.

Someone clicked the basement light on and started down the stairs. It was Maine. He yelled up the stairs at the sight of Karmesha. "She's down here!" Maine rushed to Karmesha's side and fingered the padlocks on the chains. "It's okay, ma, we got'chu."

Hood and Thugga rushed down to the basement while their other shooters posted up outside the house with AR-15s ready.

Tears streamed down Karmesha's face as Hood kneeled down beside her. She could tell from the way he'd looked at her that her face was messed up. Hood sighed in frustration because of the locks.

"Fuck it. Just carry her up like this. We'll get the chains off later."

Hood pulled the scarf from Karmesha's mouth, and she went to speak but couldn't because her jaw was sitting to the right side, broken.

"Get her outta here," said Hood.

He was itching to catch Saw if he hadn't already walked into Taquana's death trap. Hood tried calling Saw's cell, but he got the voicemail.

Chapter Twenty-four

Saw slowed down as he approached Zoro's Coney Island on Livernois and 7 Mile. He was caught by a red light, but he could see the restaurant from the intersection. It was like being summoned to a mob meeting, knowing that you'd be killed at the meeting.

The parking lot was half filled with customers doing carryout while the drive-through was empty. The light turned green, and Saw inched toward the entrance of Zoro's. He pulled into the lot, scanning for anything that looked out of place. His phone rang in his lap, and he stopped in the middle of the parking lot to answer it.

"Are you ready to die?" It was Taquana. Her voice was low and deadly.

Saw's eyes danced in his side mirrors and then to the rearview. A black Suburban bent up into the lot behind him. Another Suburban swung around the alley and blocked Saw's Benz in.

"Get out of the car," ordered Taquana.

"Where's Karmesha?"

"Oh, I'm sure you two will be seeing each other soon. Now get out."

Saw clutched the door handle, knowing that he was walking into a death trap. He thought about Karmesha, but self-preservation kicked in. There was no sense in both of them dying.

Taquana stepped out of the passenger side of the Suburban in front of Saw's Benz. She had this victorious smirk on her face as she awaited Saw to meet his fate. But Saw stepped on the gas, causing the Benz to roar forward. Taquana's eyes grew to the size of golf balls as she tried reaching for her door. But Saw had struck her leg as he intended to. Taquana's men emerged from the trucks, blazing at the Benz as Saw made his getaway. Bullets bounced off the armored Benz as if it were nothing.

Saw dipped down a couple of littered alleys before turning down a residential street. He had felt the car make impact with Taquana. He hoped that he'd crippled the bitch at least. But then his thoughts went back to Karmesha. He would have to look his daughter in the eyes knowing that her mother was dead because of him. It was a hard pill to swallow.

Saw gunned the Benz up to 8 Mile and headed back to the east side. He blew past an Oak Park police car sitting in a median, and he just hoped the cop wouldn't pull out behind him. He had two guns on him that he knew the Feds would've just loved to add to their case that they were building against him. Luckily, though, the cop didn't budge.

Saw's cell phone blared in his lap, signaling a text from Hood: We got her, read the text.

Saw couldn't believe it. They had found Karmesha.

"Is she alive?" was the first thing Saw asked when Hood answered. "A'ight, I'm on my way," said Saw after learning what hospital they'd taken Karmesha to.

Karmesha had been rushed to Beaumont Hospital. The doctors had just finished wiring her broken jaw shut, and they expected she would be fine, but because of the head trauma, they still wanted to monitor her for a couple of days. Her face was swollen on both sides, and her jawline looked deformed.

Tears streamed down her face when she held up a small mirror that one of the nurses had given her. *Look at my face,* she cried on the inside. She was afraid that she'd look like that for the rest of her life. She let the mirror slip out of her hand and broke into a shoulder-shaking sob.

Hood was standing at the window looking over the parking structure when Saw rushed through the door. He slowed at the sight of Karmesha's face. She hadn't deserved this. Not his mom either. They were both casualties of a senseless war.

Hood came over and put his hand on Saw's shoulder. Karmesha looked up at Saw with hate in her eyes. *You did this to me!* She so badly wanted to scream the words. The nurse looked back at Saw and realized that he was the cause of Karmesha becoming hysterical. She had gone from crying to kicking and fighting to get out of bed.

"Sir, I'm gonna have to ask you all to leave," said the older black nurse. It really wasn't a question as she ushered Saw and Hood to the door.

More nurses came into the room to help assist in calming Karmesha down while Saw and Hood were left out in the hallway. Saw punched the wall hard with his fist. It killed him to see her like that.

"Dawg, we gotta end this shit," said Saw, because it was tearing his family apart.

Beefing in the streets was one thing, but when it was brought to your doorstep and started affecting your family, that was when the beef took on a whole different level. Saw had been through his share of beefs, but it had never cost him any of his family members who had nothing to do with the streets.

"What happened when you got to Zoro's?"

"When I pulled in, two Burbans tried to box me in. Ol' girl got out of the truck in front of me, and she wanted me to get out too, but I peeped the play, so I smashed the gas and hit the bitch. They let off some shots, but I was in the six."

"Did you kill the bitch?"

"I doubt it, but I know she's somewhere fucked up right now."

Hood ran a hand over his face then through his dreads.

"Did she say how they grabbed her?" asked Saw.

"She can't talk because her jaw is wired. But I can see if she'll write it down once she calms down," said Hood.

"Yeah, from the look she gave me, I don't think she fuckin' with me right now."

"She almost died, my nigga. She still frantic right now. Just let her calm down."

Saw nodded in agreement. Hood was right. She needed time. Saw had put her through a lot. All three of his baby mommas for that matter. He couldn't help but think about Sherise. He wondered if she was still at the ranch. If she'd left, Saw told himself that he couldn't blame her. He had too much shit going on, and Sherise most definitely deserved to have a good man in her life.

"You gon' post here for a minute?" Saw asked Hood.

"Yeah, you need to shoot a move?"

"Just for a minute."

"Go handle ya business. I'll be here," Hood assured him.

Saw and Hood dapped up, and Saw headed for the elevators while Hood gave a light knock on Karmesha's door before stepping inside.

The nurses had calmed Karmesha down, and she was lying back with her eyes nervously studying the ceiling tiles above her. Hood stepped to her bedside as the nurse exited the room. He touched Karmesha's hand gently, then laced his strong fingers into hers. She turned her head and looked up into his eyes. She wanted to say, "Thank you for saving me."

They held each other's stare, neither wanting to be the first to look away. Hood raised the back of her hand to his lips and kissed it. "Get some rest. I'll be right here with you."

Hood released her hand and walked over to the window, where he stood with his back to Karmesha. She still hadn't taken her eyes off him.

Chapter Twenty-five

When Saw made it back to the ranch, the property was crawling with federal agents. The double wooden doors had been smashed in, and glass from the stained window framing the door lay in shards in the entrance.

Saw wasn't about to try to run from the Feds. If they wanted him, then he'd meet them head-on. He parked his bullet-riddled Benz and got out. The first person he cast eyes on was Agent Hopskins. He was standing with a stack of papers in his hand and yelling orders at his field agents.

"What the fuck are y'all doing?" asked Saw.

"Federal search warrant. Signed this afternoon by Judge Borman," said Agent Hopskins. He slapped the search warrant into Saw's hand. "Don't worry, you're not under arrest. At least not today," said Agent Hopskins, stepping away from Saw.

Saw scanned the warrant, then looked up at the house. Sherise was coming out of the house with her belongings. Saw raced to her.

"Baby, you okay? They didn't put their hands on you—"

"Saw, I can't do this anymore," said Sherise as she headed for her car.

Saw followed Sherise to the trunk of her white Lexus. She tossed the bags inside the trunk and closed it. She chirped the alarm, causing the locks to pop. Saw stepped in front of her.

"Sherise, I need you right now."

"I need me right now. And our son needs me. The only time you seem to ever need me is to help pick up the pieces."

"That's not true."

"Why ain't it? Sure in the hell seems that way to me. You don't love me, Saw. And you never will. I'm done with this." Sherise moved around Saw and opened her door and got in. She started the car, and Saw watched as she backed out then drove around the pond toward the exit of the ranch.

Damn. He breathed heavily at the sight of the agents carrying out boxes of his belongings. The items they carried were replaceable. But Sherise wasn't. Saw didn't know why he couldn't just tell her that he loved her. Saw figured that if he told her that he loved her, then he'd have to start showing her as well.

Saw's world was crumbling around him. The search warrants that he held weren't only for the ranch but for his other estates as well as the club. The Feds were combing through everything from his boxers to his finances. Anything that didn't add up they were seizing.

Chapter Twenty-six

Saw drove to the office of his second attorney, Mr. Beres. He needed his perspective at the moment, because Mr. Beres always had the right words of wisdom whenever Saw happened to need to hear them. Mr. Beres was a bright older gentleman, very kind and well versed in both state and federal law. He didn't have any partners at his small firm because he preferred working alone.

Saw would go sit and watch Mr. Beres in action as he defended other clients in court. Mr. Beres was one of the best trial lawyers in Michigan. What made him sought-after was the fact that he listened to his clients. And he delivered nothing short of whatever he'd told his clients he would upon accepting their money.

Mr. Beres was at his desk preparing an appeal when Saw walked into his office. "And to what do I owe the pleasure?"

"How are you doing, Mr. Beres?"

"Have a seat. I was just going over some things. What can I do for you?" Mr. Beres sat back with his fingers laced across his chest.

"I feel like everything that I've grinded for my whole life is being taken right from under me."

"Is this about the Feds and their investigation on you?"

"Yeah, that and some other things."

"You know what your problem is? You don't know when to quit. None of my clients do. I look at you, and I don't understand." Mr. Beres had a tone like a grandfather talking to his grandson. "You don't even realize that you've won whatever game it is that you're playing out there. Look at me. I'm sixty-five, been a lawyer for over forty years, and you're far wealthier than I am. You're what, twenty? I don't want you to look back twenty years from now in some federal penitentiary and realize that you could've done a lot more with your life."

"Do you think that it's too late?" asked Saw. "I ask that because that's what it feels like. Like it's too late."

Mr. Beres sat up and studied Saw for a moment. "If you want to get out of that life, then I can help you."

"What do you mean, like work for the Feds? You know I can't ever do nothin' like that."

Mr. Beres waved his hand no. "Not everything is about cooperating, or snitchin' as you guys call it. There's a law dealing with conspiracy that says if a person walks away from an ongoing conspiracy and asserts that they're no longer a part of the common scheme, then no indictment for conspiracy may be charged against that person."

Saw had caught only about half of it. "Run that by me one mo' time."

"Look, it's simple. If you want out of the conspiracy charges the Feds are building against you, then you have to let your associates know that you're done with everything. And then you must not receive any profits from any illegal activities they're still involved in. You can only be charged with conspiracy if you're a willing participant and the illicit activities are ongoing."

Saw nodded. Mr. Beres knew the law through and through.

"Question is, are you ready to realize that you've already won and that anything else is fool's gold?" asked Mr. Beres.

He was right. That was the million-dollar question that only Saw had the answer to. It wasn't as if the war in the streets was going to simply vanish. Saw didn't know if he could simply walk away like that. But then there was the Feds. It wasn't like they were going to stop building their case against Saw either. Time was not on his side. Saw needed to make up his mind, and fast, before it was too late.

Mr. Beres had given him the blueprint, but then again, that was like leading a horse to water.

Chapter Twenty-seven

When Taquana looked up from her hospital bed, two federal agents with FBI jackets entered the room. Her family were all taken aback, because the two white agents were carrying shackles and cuffs.

"Taquana James?" asked one of the agents as he stood over her bed.

"Yes, that's me." Taquana's eyes were wide with fear.

"You're under arrest," the agent informed her.

"For what?" demanded Taquana and all her family.

"The government has just unsealed an indictment against you," said the agent as he and his partner began shackling Taquana to the bed.

The agents had already spoken with Taquana's doctor, and she would be discharged in the morning, the doctor had informed them. She had suffered a broken hip and bruised ribs, but other than that, Taquana was not suffering from any condition that would keep her from tasting the county jail.

Until she was released from the hospital, the two agents had been assigned to watch Taquana. Her family was told to leave, and after they cleared out, the agents wheeled Taquana's bed into a different room for safety precautions, just in case someone was maybe thinking about trying to set her free.

"What exactly am I being charged with?" asked Taquana.

The agents sat close to the door with their jackets off, revealing the bulletproof vests they wore.

"Mostly conspiracy right now," said one agent.

"But charges are like the stock market. They can go up and down," the other agent chipped in.

"You have the power to decide if your charges go up or down," said the first agent. They were tag teaming her to see if Taquana had any snitch in her blood.

"How do I do that?" she asked.

"By being the first one to help yourself. It's called gettin' down first," said the first agent.

These crackers want me to snitch. She looked the two young agents over and could tell that neither was in any position to help her. She was a boss, and therefore, she only dealt with other bosses. Anything she said to those agents would've surely been used against her in court. That much

Taquana knew. She wasn't about to entertain their funky asses any further.

"I want to call my lawyer," said Taquana.

The two agents stopped talking and stared at her with the shit face.

"You did place me under arrest, right? Which means I have the right to call my attorney," Taquana assured them.

The agents didn't like this one bit, but she was right. She was legally due a call to her attorney.

Chapter Twenty-eight

Hood owned a five-bedroom house out in Taylor, Michigan. His home was situated in a wealthy community of doctors and business owners. He was only the second black homeowner on his street, but the neighbors had made him feel welcome since the day he'd closed on the property. All of his neighbors were up there in age, many of them past their retirement but still working. The word was that he played for the Pistons. Hood hadn't birthed the lie himself, but he figured if that's what they all needed to believe for them not to go prying into who he really was, then it was fine by him.

Hood lived alone. Karmesha was expecting to see at least some evidence of a woman part-time living at Hood's crib, but she found none over the past few days that she'd been staying there. Hood had stayed with Karmesha at the hospital until the doctors released her to go home, but instead of driving her to her own place, Hood kept driving until they pulled into the black granite circular drive of Hood's home. It wasn't a mansion, but it had "wealthy" written all over it.

Karmesha's jaw was still wired shut, so she asked with her eyes as Hood parked the Escalade against the garage, "What are we doing here?"

"Just for a little while," said Hood.

He was an authoritative man. No asking. Only doing. That was Hood's style, and Karmesha liked it.

The decor of Hood's home was modern and sleek. Every piece of furniture was like a piece of art. Much to Karmesha's surprise, Hood was into collecting art. He loved to paint and even had a studio set up inside his home. He'd shown Karmesha his work, and it blew her away how talented he was. Her favorite painting of his was of a young black boy wiping the tears from his mother's eyes as he looked up at her. The setting was a tattered kitchen table with the stove open. The little boy and his mom were both bundled in winter coats.

Karmesha wondered if Hood was the little boy in the painting, only because he had a sense that he had to be strong for others, much like he was doing by taking care of her. Hood made Karmesha feel at home and like a queen as he waited on her hand and foot. He prepared her liquid diets and ran her baths with Epsom salts.

He was doing everything that a man would do for his sick woman. There was a mutual attraction, no doubt, and had been since the day Hood had met Karmesha. Saw had been dating Karmesha for a few months when Saw finally brought her out to a club in Atlantic City. When Hood first saw Karmesha, it was one of those times when your best friend has a bad chick, and you're happy for them, but really you're like, *damn, why I ain't meet her first?* That was what went through Hood's mind when their eyes met.

Saw was his right hand and his heart, but the opportunity was there for Hood to see if Karmesha was feeling him as much as he was feeling her. Hood had really stopped thinking about what Saw would think, because none of that mattered.

What Karmesha liked about Hood was that he lived in the moment and was attentive. The first thing that she noticed about Hood that stood out was that he turned off his phone and tossed it into the dresser. That got him major points because Saw's phone was a constant distraction. He didn't know how to fully relax and just to be in the moment. It was like he was always anticipating something.

Karmesha kept trying to tell herself not to compare Saw and Hood, but it was hard not to because they were best friends. She wasn't going to try to fool herself into thinking that Hood didn't have plenty of bitches, but it seemed that if he ever found the right woman, then she would at least have the peace of mind knowing that she was the queen of his life and that all those bitches in the street were just side pussy.

Hood was just fun to be around. Really he was this big and gentle giant with a heart of gold and an infectious smile. Hood had really boosted Karmesha's spirits after going through what she did on account of Saw's street war. Hood had saved her life, and because he had done so, he was her knight in shining armor.

They played board games and watched their favorite old movies from Hood's home theatre. Whenever Karmesha wanted to communicate something to Hood, she'd write it down and give it to him.

As they were watching the classic movie *Blow*, Karmesha scribbled onto her notepad that Hood had given her. She finished writing, then gave the pad to Hood.

Do you think I'm still pretty?

Hood reached for the pen and jotted down something on the pad, and then he handed it back to Karmesha for her to read.

You will always be the most beautiful woman I have ever met in my entire life. No cap!

The "no cap" part made Karmesha's eyes smile. Even when he was being gentle, he was still Hood.

Chapter Twenty-nine

Lano was home from the hospital, but he was on crutches from the shot he took to the leg. The bullet had knocked a chunk of meat off and had torn through some nerves, so the doctors were skeptical about Lano ever being able to fully use his leg again. In the meantime, they had set him up in physical therapy sessions four times a week with biweekly follow-ups at the hospital. His shoulder was wrapped in gauze, but he had full use of his arm, which he'd had surgery on because the bullet tore straight through his rotator cuff.

Lano looked like 2Pac being wheeled out of the hospital by a male nurse. A caravan of black armored vehicles lined the curb. Lano's bodyguards loaded him into the middle truck along with his crutches, and set off to a remote location in Adrian, Michigan, where Lano owned some land.

As Lano rode alone in the back seat of the divided Navigator, he stared out at the pasture of the countryside of southern Michigan. His mind was stuck on one thing, and that was breaking off from Saw and Hood so he could do his own thing. Lano told himself that their way of handling things would be the death of them all. Their way of doing things was the reason he might not ever walk again. Neither Saw nor Hood had any diplomacy skills. There was always a war with them.

But Lano had had enough. He was the one out in the streets making the needed connections to sell their drugs. And for what, just so Saw could inevitably fall out with his people and start a war?

Saw didn't want anyone else to eat if they weren't on his team. That was the real problem. Saw was on this power trip of needing to be the top nigga in the city. But what he didn't realize was that Detroit had always been a city where any man could make a run in the game and become his or her own boss. No permission needed. It wasn't like Chicago or New York, where niggas had to work under others. In the D, that was a choice. But Saw had other ideas. He was a shrewd businessman, but a people person he was not.

I don't need them niggas. I'm the one, Lano told himself. He had cooked up a master plan as he lay recovering in the hospital. Lano had been trimming money off the top since day one. He handled all the drugs as they came in, so it gave him a window of time to step on the dope more than he should've. With the extras, Lano used those drugs to fuel his own out-of-town operations, which neither Saw nor Hood knew anything about. They were too busy playing the role of dons to notice all the millions Lano had been squirreling away.

Lano had been planning his departure for some time, and there was no better time than the present to make his move.

Chapter Thirty

The Feds followed three cars behind Saw as he crossed the Ambassador Bridge into Windsor, Canada. They feared that he was trying to flee the U.S. because of the indictment that was brewing against him. Agent Hopskins was furious when he got the call, because the Feds had no legal authority to stop him from entering Canada. Saw wasn't a felon either, so the Canadians didn't refuse him at the border when he presented his license and passport.

"Don't lose him!" was Agent Hopskins's only order to his two young FBI field agents.

They followed Saw to the Caesars Windsor hotel and casino, where he checked into a suite overlooking the river facing Detroit. Saw had only brought one bag of clothes and some legal papers he'd gotten from Mr. Beres and a package Ms. Raben had given to him. He tossed the bag onto the center of the queen-size bed and stepped to the vaulted windows. The view was crazy. Saw watched cars inch along the same bridge he had just crossed and the traffic moving through downtown Detroit.

Detroit and Windsor are only separated by a small body of water, and yet they are two completely different worlds altogether. Windsor is a peaceful place while Detroit is murderous.

The reason Saw had gone to Canada wasn't to flee from the Feds. It was to think about what Mr. Beres had told him. Saw needed to step outside of everything for a moment to try to gain some perspective. He flopped down on the bed and reached for the room's phone atop the nightstand. He ordered up some room service, then began reading the legal materials Mr. Beres had given him.

He was holding the statutes of what constitutes a federal conspiracy and what the government must prove beyond a reasonable doubt at trial should they indict someone on conspiracy charges. Mr. Beres had given Saw what the Feds didn't want in the hands of any criminal. He'd given him the real rules of the game along with the cheat codes on how to beat the Feds at their own game.

The only thing that was keeping Saw from winning the game was the fact that he loved playing it. He questioned, *what else am I gonna do?* The game was the one thing in life that he was great at, and it drove him. Saw just didn't know if he was ready to give all that up. He set the reading material aside and lay back on the bed.

Getting money was an addiction for Saw. The same high that a dopefiend feels from the rush of heroin hitting their bloodstream was the high Saw felt whenever millions of dollars in profits were being counted before him. There was no better feeling. What could Saw use to fill that void?

His mind filled with thoughts of Sherise. He hadn't spoken to her since the Feds raided the ranch. He wished that they were in Windsor together, away from everything. Saw told himself that he'd give her the space she needed while he sorted through what he had before him.

He sat up at the sound of knocking at the door. It was his room service. He tipped the young lady, then carried his corned beef sandwich back over to the bed. He dug into the sandwich while opening the package from Ms. Raben. It was everything her assistant was able to pull up about Wink, mostly old court transcripts and newspaper articles covering Wink's trial back in the day. But there were also the Feds' field notes that were handwritten by agents, detailing how they'd built a strong case against Wink and his counterparts.

Saw couldn't set the paper down, because it was like reading a good book for the first time. Growing up he'd heard all the legendary stories of how Wink was getting major money, but Saw was looking at it with his own eyes. Wink was jumping on and off private jets and was plugged in with the Cuban Mafia. The Feds had estimated Wink to have raked in over $200 million.

When Saw had finished reading everything about Wink, it left him wanting to know more. *Damn,* thought Saw of the way Wink had taken the fall because of his best friend. It made Saw think of Hood and Lano. He couldn't see either of them ever trading their lives in exchange for his. And it was unthinkable that he would ever do such a thing either.

Saw couldn't stop thinking about Wink and the possibility of him being his father. What if Denise was right? From everything Wink had read, Wink was a stand-up nigga's gangsta, whether he was his father or not.

Saw found a pen and a piece of paper, and he sat down at the table next to the window. He thought about how he should start his letter to Wink. *Just be real,* he told himself. Then he started writing.

Chapter Thirty-one

"Suck my whole dick!" yelled ol' Coop from behind the steel door of his cell.

"Suck ya own dick, fuck nigga!" yelled Mike Bell.

Their voices echoed down the hall of D block of the USP, Lewisburg. The prison was on complete lockdown status following the bloody knife fight between St. Louis and Florida. Two people had been killed in the riot, while several others had to be flown by Life Flight helicopters.

Coop was an old-school con from St. Louis serving four life bids, while Mike Bell was the shot caller for the Florida car. Sharky stood at the cell door, enjoying the bar fighting between the two men as they sold each other death. They were both heated, having both lost one of their homies in the riot.

Wink lay in bed with his feet crossed at the ankles while listening to his MP3 player. He was listening to Biggie's *Life After Death* LP. The lockdown didn't bother Wink anymore because he'd learned that they would happen anyway. It was the penitentiary.

Wink kept a survival kit of food, starting with the hundred ramen noodle soups. Lockdowns were known to last for months at a time, and Wink wasn't a fan of being hungry. He tried schooling his cellie, Sharky. But all his money went to the phone so he could chase his baby momma.

The one thing the cons had to look forward to during a lockdown was the mail. Sharky was holding the door up as he hoped for a letter from the crib. A lone letter, along with the new *Straight Stuntin'* magazine, came under the door at mail call. Both were addressed to Wink. Sharky nudged Wink's foot, then passed him his mail. The fine chicks on the cover of the magazine held Wink's attention for a brief moment, but then he focused on the small white envelope. The postmark was from Canada, but the return address was a lawyer's office in Detroit. Wink pulled the folded letter from its envelope, hoping to make sense of it all.

> *What up doe?*
> *I don't know whether to call you big homie or Pops, you feel me? So right now I'm just gonna call you Wink. I got the kite you sent to my OG, and I'd be lying to say I haven't been thinking about you since. You's a real nigga on a lot of levels, so I appreciate you writing back. You said some things in your kite that I needed to hear at the time. I did*

a thorough check on you and read your investigative notes on how ya manz was an informant way before your case. That's fucked up that they can use a nigga against you who they know lied in another case. I'm doing a lot of research on conspiracy right now because these bitches trying to get at me, you feel me? The address on the envelope is my lawyer's. She's good people and will make sure that I get anything you send for me. And as far as the situation my OG keeps stressing about you being my father, I mean, I'm open to whatever we need to do so that we can clear that up. Just let me know, you feel me? Hold it down and stay up.

    Saw

Wink was happy that Saw had taken the time to get at him. He most certainly had every intention to start the DNA testing process on his end at the prison. But then he thought about the lockdown. That could be months. Wink wanted to perhaps build a bond with Saw and deter him from the road to the penitentiary before it was too late. He knew that if it were proven that he was in fact his father, he'd have a better chance reaching him.

Wink also needed the investigative notes Saw spoke about, because he had never seen them. Wink had boxes of discovery papers from his case and appeals, all of which he'd internalized over the years. If Wink had these investigative notes, then that meant that the Feds had withheld evidence from the defense at trial. And there was only one remedy for this, which would be to set aside Wink's convictions.

Wink knew not to geek himself up. First, he needed copies of what Saw said he had in his possession.

Chapter Thirty-two

The courtroom was packed with different family members of the defendants being arraigned in front of Federal Magistrate Grand for the afternoon. Taquana was dressed in dark green jail clothes from the Wayne County Jail, where she'd spent the past seventy-two hours waiting for her court date. Her eyes scanned the faces behind the defense table as she sat in the bench area designated for defendants. There was not a soul there to support her. She fumed at the thought of her lawyer not calling her family to let them know she had court this day.

Judge Grand was only spending three minutes tops on each defendant that day. He was either issuing a personal bond or remanding people to the custody of the U.S. Marshals. What he was really doing was following the recommendation of the prosecutor. If the government wanted a defendant detained, then Grand was ordering their detainment.

Taquana's lawyer was late getting there. Mr. Mulkoff rushed to the bench and tried to carry on a brief conversation with Taquana before their case was called. He had Taquana signing an acknowledgment of her indictment when the court reporter called their case.

"That's us. Come on," whispered Mr. Mulkoff. He was an older white man with silver hair who stuttered when he talked. He ushered Taquana up to the lectern.

Judge Grand looked down his nose at Taquana as the attorney for the government, Paul Kuebler, explained why she was a danger to the community as well as a flight risk.

Mr. Mulkoff stuttered as he tried arguing that Taquana had no prior criminal record and how the government's case was unfounded, but Judge Grand, a former prosecutor himself, waved Mr. Mulkoff off with his hand.

"I'm ordering that she be remanded to the custody of the U.S. Marshals. This matter is adjourned," said Judge Grand.

Taquana was pointed back to the bench by one of the marshals. Mr. Mulkoff had slipped away, leaving Taquana pissed. She had hired him because he'd beaten some cases for Slim in the state. But what Taquana was learning was that the Feds and the State were two different entities with their own separate rules to play by. She'd expected a bond of some sort or at least a tether GPS monitor. But no, this pink cracker had remanded her to the musty-ass Wayne County Jail.

Taquana folded her arms over her chest and stared out the large window across the courtroom. She shook her head from side to side. She told herself that she wasn't going out like that.

Chapter Thirty-three

As soon as Saw got back to Detroit, he called a meeting with Hood and Lano. They all had something different on their minds at the time, and the meeting would be the perfect time for everybody to put everything on the table.

They met at Hood's crib out in Troy, Michigan. Lano and Saw arrived within minutes of each other, and when they got there, Hood had steak and lobsters set out for each of them. They sat down at the dining room table, and Hood poured red wine around the table. There was silent tension in the air among them. Hood raised his glass and gave a nod before taking a sip from his glass. Lano and Saw both followed by drinking from their glasses.

"I want us to meet because I've been thinking about the future of the family," said Saw.

Hood and Lano nodded.

"And I think that now is the best time for me to walk away from this thing of ours," said Saw.

Hood's brow raised into a question mark, as did Lano's. They shot each other with a look of confusion. Neither of them believed that Saw would ever just leave the game, not unless it was in a casket.

"What'chu mean, walk away?" asked Hood.

"I mean, before it's too late—" said Saw, but Hood cut him off.

"I know you ain't finna let some bitch hang up ya jersey?" asked Hood.

This brought a wicked smirk to Saw's yellow face. He wanted to kill Taquana as badly as Hood, but the game gods were on the bitch's side at the moment.

"You know ain't no nigga or bitch can ever run me from nothin'. I'm hanging up my own jersey like Mike, Kobe, and the rest of the greats who won playing the game that they love. I won. I say that we all won," Saw said, looking from Hood to Lano. "I'm not going to keep playin' past my prime until the Feds hang up my jersey for me, you feel me?"

Hood slightly nodded, because he was feeling everything Saw had just put down. But he didn't know what had prompted it all. Lano said nothing, nor showed any emotion. He was really jumping for joy on the inside, because now he wouldn't have to face Saw about branching off and doing his own thing.

"So when is all this 'posed to take effect?" asked Hood.

"As of right now I'm done. All the money we still got on the floor right now you and Lano split down the middle. I'm good, you feel me?" said Saw.

Saw looked at it like his contribution to the game, leaving something on the table as he made his exit. Plus, Saw had known about the last-run jinx of the game. Every time niggas said that they would just make one more run, they never made it.

As Hood was talking, a shadow against the kitchen floor caught Saw's attention. It was coming toward them. He looked up from the legs of the woman and into the face of Karmesha.

There was a thick silence. Saw's jaws clenched in anger. He didn't need an explanation to see what was going on. Karmesha stood there fidgeting with her hands. Her legs were bare as she was only dressed in one of Hood's button-down dress shirts. The swelling in her face had gone down, and her beauty had been restored, but her jaw was still wired shut.

Lano kept looking from Saw to Hood, who both sat across the table from one another, glaring into each other's eyes. By the unwritten rules of the game, technically Hood was in the wrong, because all wives and baby mommas were supposed to be off-limits. Karmesha wasn't just some random chick Saw kept on the side. If she had been, then there wouldn't have been any harm done, because they all had shared jump-offs in the past. But Karmesha was the mother of Saw's daughter, which made her sacred.

Saw pushed back his chair and rose to his feet, setting his napkin on his plate. As angry as he was at Hood, Saw just turned to leave. What Hood had done required a death sentence, but Saw wasn't about to make any emotional decisions he'd look back on where he'd realize that he threw his life away over having a sucka stroke.

Hood watched as Saw went out the front door. He was having mixed emotions because, the way he saw it, Saw was dogging Karmesha out, and it wasn't like he was going to wife her anyway. They had a child together, but that was the extent of it. There wasn't any love between them. Hood was relieved that it was all out there in the open now, because Karmesha was his woman now, and Hood wasn't about to hide that from anyone.

Saw punched the steering wheel repeatedly as he got onto the interstate. His blood was boiling because of the betrayal from Hood. Sure, Karmesha was a sack-chaser, but she was his baby momma, which meant hands-off. Saw expected Karmesha to do her thing in the streets, because it was in her nature, but not ever to cross the line of fucking with one of his best friends. There was a hole in Saw's heart and a knife in his back.

He was thankful that he didn't have his gun on him inside the house, because he wasn't sure that everything he had planned would've kept him from killing Hood and Karmesha right there in the house. The main reason Saw couldn't afford to blow up inside the house was because he had been recording their meeting with a digital audio recorder. The recording would be his proof of him stepping away from his role in their conspiracy should the Feds ever bring an indictment against them. No one otherwise would ever hear the recording. It would be kept for safekeeping by Saw's attorney, Mr. Beres.

Saw was closing the door to the game because he realized that the door was closing anyway. He was just picking what side he'd be standing on when it did shut.

He dropped the recorder off at Mr. Beres's office, and gave him another $100,000 of good-faith money. He was hoping Mr. Beres wouldn't have to represent him in court anytime soon, but just in case, he was covered in full. He had already done something similar with Ms. Raben.

When Saw sat down to do an official count of how much real money he was holding—not what was owed to him, but physical cash—what he'd come up with was $35 million to the good. It wasn't the hundreds of millions that he wanted to be sitting on, but still at only 20 years old, he was full.

His plan was to lie low for about five years before he made any significant investments, because he didn't want the Feds sweating his money. Besides that, within those five years of downtime, Saw told himself that he should be able to learn the in's and out's of the legit game before he put his money up to play. Because if he was going to play, he wanted to be the best.

Chapter Thirty-four

Taquana stared back at her reflection as she stood in front of the scratched wall mirror that hung above the sink and toilet of her tiny cell. Life at the Wayne County Jail was harsh, and it was showing in Taquana's face as she tried fixing her hair. She had sweated her perm out days ago, and she was starting to look like the rest of the detoxing bitches she found herself surrounded by. She had a visit coming and wanted to look presentable at least.

The female deputy working her floor was clicking Taquana's door from the control booth, signaling for her to come out of her cell. Taquana stole one final glance at herself then at her dope-fiend white cellmate asleep on the bottom bunk. To God, she prayed her attorney had the good news she hoped for.

Taquana was pat searched at the door by the female deputy then pointed down a short hall that led to the visitor's booth. When Taquana reached the visitation booth, a male deputy told her that her visitors were in the contact room for attorneys.

Taquana opened the door, and her attorney, Mr. Mulkoff, was in the middle of a sentence when he turned with a phony smile. He stood and pulled out a chair for Taquana.

"Have a seat here next to me," said Mulkoff.

Taquana took a seat as she looked into the faces of the two white men across the table. She recognized the prosecutor as being the one who asked the judge to deny her bond at her initial appearance. Right off the bat, Taquana wasn't feeling him because of the look he held, which clearly said, "I hold all the cards to your freedom." And judging by the way things had played out in court with her bond, Taquana had no reason to doubt his hand.

Mr. Mulkoff made all the introductions. The prosecutor's name was Mr. Kuebler, and the FBI agent beside him was Special Agent Hopskins.

Mr. Mulkoff presented an agreement from his briefcase, which was a letter for everyone present saying that anything Taquana provided at the meeting couldn't be used against her unless she lied during their sit-down. It was called a proffer letter.

The prosecutor signed it behind Agent Hopskins, who pushed the letter back to Mr. Mulkoff to sign. The only signature left needed was Taquana's.

"Why can't I get a bond?" Taquana wanted to know if she were to sign the agreement.

"Right now, you're putting the cart before the horse. You be truthful here today and, trust me, you'll be back in court for a bond in the morning," said Mr. Kuebler.

Taquana looked at Mr. Mulkoff, who gave her a solemn nod. She sighed as she reached for the gold pen and signed her name to the document. Immediately she felt as though she'd just sold her soul to the devil himself. Mr. Mulkoff smiled a shit grin and tucked the agreement into his files.

"Now shall we begin?" he said.

Agent Hopskins opened his manila envelope and placed a lone photo on the table and pushed it toward Taquana. "Who is this?" he asked.

Taquana swallowed. "It's Saw," she heard herself say. The snitching had begun, and if she wanted to get out, it wasn't going to stop for hours as they sat taking notes of all the incriminating details that Taquana gave them.

The more she snitched, the easier it became. Taquana was just happy that the Feds' focus seemed to be more on Saw than what she was guilty of doing in the game. Agent Hopskins had one agenda, and that was bringing down Saw.

They treated Taquana like the star snitch she was by having Popeyes chicken and grape Faygo pop brought in to fuel her ratting. They wanted every single detail, and Taquana gave it to them.

When Taquana got back to her cell, it was with a full belly and a mischievous grin on her face. Her cellmate was still asleep as Taquana took to the window overlooking downtown Detroit. In her mind, snitching to the Feds was justified, because her brother had lost his life way too early. She told herself that other niggas were snitching, and she wasn't about to play herself by trying to keep it real to a bunch of niggas who very well might flip on her in the end. Taquana had done what the two agents told her when they first arrested her. She got down first.

As promised by the prosecutor, that next morning Taquana was taken over to the federal courthouse, where she stood before Magistrate Grand for a second bond hearing. The prosecutor said something to the effect of Taquana's release would serve the ends of justice. Magistrate Grand caught the drift. She was now playing ball by cooperating, and the government wanted her released. He saw it every day in his courtroom.

"Granted," was all Magistrate Grand said.

Taquana couldn't stop cheesing like the rat she'd become, because she wouldn't have to go back over to the county jail. They would release her right from the federal courthouse.

Mr. Mulkoff had an exchange with the prosecutor, and then he stepped back over to the bench and kneeled to whisper to Taquana. "They're going to have you testify before the grand jury tomorrow, so you need to be back here at nine o'clock," said Mr. Mulkoff.

"Okay," agreed Taquana. She would have agreed to anything to be free.

Chapter Thirty-five

"You're doing right by yourself," said Ms. Raben as she stood over Saw's shoulder, watching him sign the needed legal documents.

They were at her law office in downtown Detroit. Saw was seated at the conference room table beside the Realtor Ms. Raben had suggested Saw work with. Saw was liquidating all of his estates and selling his investment properties. This all came at the advice of Ms. Raben, because she thought it would be best to start over from scratch. She didn't want the Feds trying to seize anything in court, should they bring charges against Saw. Fighting a conspiracy was one thing. But the forfeiture process was an entirely different legal battle that Ms. Raben wanted none of. So when and if the Feds came a-knocking, there wouldn't be anything for them to squabble over, because all of Saw's money from his real estate sales would be safe and secure in a bank over in Canada.

Ms. Raben had laced Saw's boots about the Feds not being able to freeze any accounts he held in

Canada, because the Canadian government didn't allow the U.S. or any other government to seize accounts being held in their country.

Saw was soaking up all the game his two attorneys were blessing him with. He left Ms. Raben's office knowing in his gut that he'd done the right thing. He had to keep reminding himself that he had already won the game, and now it was time to move on to something better.

Ms. Raben's assistant, Kathleen, came rushing out to the parking lot just as Saw was backing out his black Hellcat. She waved a white envelope in her hand. Saw stopped and let his window down.

"I'm so sorry, but this came in the mail for you today," said Kathleen as she handed Saw the envelope.

It was a letter from Wink. "Thanks," said Saw.

Kathleen smiled brightly. "Oh, you're welcome. Be careful now," she told Saw as she waved goodbye and headed back inside.

Saw put the car into park and tore at the seal of the envelope. Wink hadn't wasted any time getting back to him.

> Dear Saw,
> From one real one to another, it was a blessing having received your letter. I'm glad to know that you've got a good head on your shoulders. Keep studying the law,

*because that's a black man's only defense in
this crooked system. Most of us wait until
we're in here before we ever crack open
a law book, and a lot of times it's too late
because we done played ourselves. But you
got one up learning this shit now, you feel
me? One thing that did interest me was the
investigative notes from my case that you
mentioned. The ones you speak of are news
to me, and it would help a lot if you could
send me a copy. I would really appreciate it
and then some. On another note, they got us
on lockdown right now about some prison
bullshit that goes on in a place like this. Ain't
no telling how long they're going to keep us
down, but I'ma get the ball rolling on the
DNA test as soon as they let us up, a'ight?
How's your mom doing? Tell her that I send
my best. And, man, you be easy out there.
I'ma fall back and vibe with my young cellie.
In a minute.*
    Wink

Saw folded the letter and put it back into its envelope. He hadn't seen his moms since she'd been
shot at his club. Saw had stayed away because of
guilt. But now he couldn't stop from thinking how
she was doing. He put that on his list of things to
do, to go check on Denise. But first he had some

important stops to make. He was first going to meet his jeweler Bazzi at the Greenfield Plaza in Southfield, Michigan. Saw had over $3 million worth of watches and fine jewelry, but it all had to go. He didn't want the Feds having the satisfaction of taking a single token from him.

Chapter Thirty-six

Sherise had just finished seeing about her assigned patients at the hospital when her coworker stopped her coming out of a room to inform her that someone was there to see her.

"Did they say who it was?" asked Sherise.

"No, but he had some flowers in his hand and was looking good, too." Her coworker smiled, then headed down the hall.

Sherise headed toward the front lobby, all the while wondering who was there to see her, and with flowers. Saw was the last person she expected to see standing there with a beautiful arrangement of flowers. He was dressed nicely, and he smelled good and not like the streets he loved to run so much.

"Thank you," said Sherise, accepting the flowers. She put them to her nose as she looked up at Saw. There was something different going on about him, but Sherise told herself to keep up her guard.

"Can we go somewhere and talk?" asked Saw.

"Yeah, but I have to get back to work in a minute," said Sherise.

Saw followed her to an empty section of the waiting lobby. She was looking good, as she always did in her hospital scrubs. She wore the powder blue set that Saw liked so much. She looked up at him again with those beautiful brown eyes. He missed the feeling of her full lips kissing him all over.

"Remember how you always wanted to move to Atlanta?" asked Saw.

"Yeah, I remember."

"Well, I just bought a house down there. It's not a mansion or anything, but it's a nice-enough house for us to move into."

Sherise drew her brow into a skeptical question mark. "Saw, why would I be moving into a house with you in Atlanta when my life is here?"

"Look, I done left the game alone."

"Oh, yeah, and for how long? Saw, you ain't gonna do nothin' but go right back to the streets and all ya other skank bitches as soon as you get bored with me. Now I don't know what's gotten into you, but you can't just pick me up and then set me down whenever you feel like it because—"

"Sherise, I'm not just asking you to come with me to Atlanta. I'm asking you to come with me as my wife," said Saw.

He reached into his pants pocket for the black ring box and broke down to one knee. He opened the box, revealing the five-carat flawless diamond ring set in platinum. Sherise gasped and put her free hand to her mouth. People started gathering in the lobby.

"Sherise, will you marry me?" asked Saw.

Sherise smiled as a tear cascaded down her pretty face. "Yes, yes, I'll marry you."

People clapped as Saw stood and slipped the ring on. They embraced for a passionate kiss, and as Saw held Sherise within his arms, he had not a single doubt that he was making the right choice. Sherise was like a dream in his arms. The whole time she'd been right there. Except he'd been too foolish to know Sherise was the one woman God had created to be his wife.

Saw allowed Sherise to finish up her workday, but he promised that he would fill her in on everything when she got off work. Sherise's coworkers crowded around her as Saw left the hospital. They all were congratulating her and admiring the beautiful rock that adorned her finger. Saw had sold off all his Rolexes and fine jewelry for a lump sum of cash along with a trade-in for Sherise's engagement ring.

Sherise was on cloud nine as she worked the rest of the day. She was already making her own plans for when they made the move to Atlanta.

She would enroll in nursing school full-time and become a registered nurse. She wanted to open her own assisted-living centers. That was her endgame. She used to always try to talk about the future with Saw, but he was only focused on the present. But maybe now he would listen and invest in Sherise's vision. And if not, she told herself, she would just grind it out. As long as they were a family and together, she didn't mind waking up every day and busting out her grind. She just prayed that Saw's heart was sincere about not returning to the streets.

Saw had driven up to his mom's hair salon. He parked across the street in front of the coin laundromat and just watched the women move about inside the shop. His heart relaxed at the sight of his mom as she crossed the floor smiling and running her mouth as she loved to do. She was okay, and that was enough for Saw to be thankful.

He still couldn't bring himself to get out of the car and go see her face-to-face, although he knew that she deserved that much and that she would've loved to see him. Saw just couldn't find the will to go inside the salon. He made a promise to himself, though, that before he left for Atlanta, he'd stop and see his OG.

He pulled away from the curb and headed to his newly leased condo to get things set up for the night with Sherise. He was going to take her out to a nice, fancy restaurant, then take her back home and make love to her all night.

Chapter Thirty-seven

I belong to you and you belong to me.
Girl, you are the love of my life, baby.

The smooth voice of Rome filled the bedroom as Saw and Sherise made passionate love beneath the black satin sheet. Sherise was on top, riding Saw slowly to the music. With her eyes closed and her nails dug into his shoulders, Sherise enjoyed every thrust as it brought her closer to her zenith.

Saw knew Sherise's body like a road map, and he loved having her on top because it was the sure way to undo her every time. He sped up his stroke and palmed her ass with a firm grip, and he kept it there as he watched her sexy pout gape, and a soft moan escaped her.

"Ahh, I'm cumming," announced Sherise.

"Wait for me, baby," Saw said in a hoarse voice. He sped up his strokes and came just as Sherise climaxed.

Sherise collapsed onto Saw's chest, their hearts racing against each other. Saw ran his hands up and down Sherise's sweaty back, resting on the cuffs of her ass cheeks.

"When are we leaving for Atlanta?" Sherise asked in a small voice.

"I say in about two weeks. I just gotta square some things up with my lawyer on all my properties."

The two weeks sounded good to Sherise, because it would give her the needed time to let her employer know she'd be leaving, and she could settle her other affairs. She stole a glance at her ring, and a smile creased her chocolate face.

"What'chu smiling so hard about?" asked Saw, pulling back his own smile.

"At you." Sherise gave him a love tap. "Why'd you make me wait so long?"

Saw searched the ceiling for the right answer, then looked at Sherise and said, "You're the type of girl a man marries. And me, in the life I was living, I was the type of man a woman doesn't marry."

"But you're done with that life, right?" Sherise searched his eyes.

"I promise you that I'm done."

Sherise reached up and kissed Saw gently. She believed him, and she knew that their new life in Atlanta would surpass her biggest dreams. She was overwhelmed with happiness because the man she loved so much would soon be her husband. Sherise gushed inside at the thought of planning their wedding. No date had been set, but Sherise was already envisioning a summer wedding set somewhere on an island, surrounded by their true loved ones.

Sherise wanted a big family, also. So she had plans to get pregnant soon after she finished nursing school and got her assisted-living facility up and running. She couldn't wait to see the house in person that Saw had bought down in ATL. He'd shown her pictures and a virtual walk-through on his phone, but she wanted to physically see it so she could start designing it the way she wanted to.

Saw hadn't told anyone about their engagement, but Tammy seemed to know already, because she was blowing up his phone, leaving all sorts of messages about how he needed to be a better father to their son. Tammy had seen Sherise's post on social media announcing their new engagement. It probably didn't help any that Sherise had tagged a picture of her sparkling rock that said, Flawless, bitches.

Saw could just imagine what drama would follow once it was learned that he and Sherise were moving to Atlanta. Tammy and Karmesha were likely to flip their wigs, especially Tammy, seeing that she didn't have a man. She always blamed not having a man on Saw leaving her to be a single mother to their son. She claimed that no real man wanted a woman with kids.

So to avoid the headache, Saw asked Sherise not to post anything about the move to ATL until they were gone. He had more than enough on his plate already to deal with.

Sherise rolled out of her bed naked and padded to the bathroom. Saw clutched his growing erection as he watched her sexy backside slip into the bathroom. He stroked the length of his manhood in anticipation of what he would do to her when she returned.

Chapter Thirty-eight

Lano had called a meeting at the club on 7 Mile and Syracuse. He wanted to inform the members of their street family of Saw's departure from the game and that from then on he would be the head of the family. Everyone was in attendance except Hood. Lano had purposely not called to inform Hood of the meeting, because after witnessing Hood with Karmesha, Lano had seen another side of Hood that couldn't be trusted. Lano feared that Hood would stand in his way, and so he had another plan altogether for Hood.

As the members stood inside the club listening to Lano declare himself their leader, it was evident from the side conversations taking place that not everybody was feeling Lano. He was a good hustler and all, but he didn't have their respect. Lano had never put in any work in their eyes, and they were all official goons, so it just made it hard for them to follow his lead.

Thugga and Maine definitely weren't down with taking orders from a soft nigga like Lano. They were salty that Saw hadn't told them himself about his move and even more so to stick them with Lano's creep ass. Thugga and Maine walked out of the club as Lano tried detailing the way he wanted things handled now that he was in power.

"You hear that bitch-ass nigga in there?" asked Maine as he opened the passenger door of the Challenger.

"Nigga done lost his mind if he think I'm workin' for 'im," said Maine.

Thugga had slipped behind the wheel and sparked the half-smoked wrap from the ashtray. He said nothing as Maine vented about Lano being in charge and their position in the family. As far as Thugga was concerned, there was no family except the nigga at his right. The rest of them were out for self. That family shit sounded good, but talk was all that it was. The true definition behind family was to want for your family what you wanted for yourself. And Thugga knew better than to believe a creep-smiling nigga like Lano wanted them to prosper.

"What we gon' do?" asked Maine.

"What we should've done a long time ago," answered Thugga as he put the car into drive and skirted away from the curb.

Back inside the club, the meeting was over, and all the members were enjoying the free liquor flowing from the bar. Saw had never let everyone just hang out inside the club, because it was his sanctuary and throne, so to speak. But Lano was set on doing everything differently from what the family was used to. He had plans of expanding their operations into gambling and escort services, which was just a legal way of selling pussy. And Lano also wanted the family to tap into the fraud game surrounding them.

Lano had noticed Thugga and Maine's sudden departure, and he made a mental note to have a personal sit-down with them, because he recognized them as the top enforcers of the family and needed them to be happy.

The movement inside the club ceased at the sight of Taquana crossing the floor, flanked by two massive bodyguards. She was adorned in fine jewels and wore an all-black pantsuit with heels, looking like she belonged on the cover of *Don Diva*. She and Lano were the only two smiling as Lano stood from his perch at the dominoes table.

Whispers filled the club as Lano kissed Taquana's hand. He ushered her out of sight of everyone and into the back office, where he shut the door. Taquana held her phony smile in place as she took a seat across from Lano.

"Can I offer you anything?" asked Lano.

"I'm good but thank you." Taquana's head was on a swivel as she seemed to be expecting something. "Where's Saw?" she asked.

"He's no longer in the business," said Lano.

Taquana's smile evaporated. "What do you mean?" She frowned.

"From now on, I'm the head of the family. Saw sorta went into retirement, which is good for business. He personally would have never agreed to a meeting with you. Saw's stubborn like that. He'd rather a thousand bodies lay dead in the streets until one side wins the war, but I'm not like Saw. I called you here today to offer a truce so that our families can stop killing each other and get back to making money," said Lano.

Taquana squinted at him. She didn't like Lano because she could tell that he was spineless and weak. But she forced herself to pull back a phony grin. "A truce would be nice," she said. "I'm all about keeping the peace, but what happens when Saw decides he wants to come outta retirement?" asked Taquana.

Lano had thought about this as well. "I give you my word that if he were to return, I would personally retire him myself," said Lano.

Taquana had no reason to believe Lano because she could smell the fear seeping from his pussy across from her. She didn't know what type of game Saw was running from behind the scenes, claiming to be done with the game, but until she found out, she would play along with Lano's plan on calling a truce.

"So we are in agreement then?" asked Lano.

Taquana rose from her chair and held out her manicured paw to be kissed. "Yes, we are in agreement."

She led the way back into the club, where silence hung in the air as she and her men crossed the floor to the exit. As the door closed behind them, everyone turned to Lano. He explained that they had entered into a truce with Taquana because it was bad for business and the war was making them all hot with the police. Most of the members nodded in agreement, but there were still some rumblings about how Saw would've never agreed to a truce. He would've kept the war blazing until they ran the other side into the dirt.

For those loyal to Saw, things just weren't making much sense.

Chapter Thirty-nine

Special Agent Hopskins had been listening in on Taquana and Lano's sit-down via the wire Taquana wore on her chest. Hopskins and two other FBI agents were parked in a white van down the street from the club, and they had a team of agents in unmarked vehicles nearby just in case things went sour during the sit-down.

Lano had been the one to reach out to Taquana about the sit-down. Agent Hopskins told her to accept the meeting because it could lead to more incriminating evidence. But Hopskins, as well as everyone else, had expected Saw and Hood to be at the meeting.

The only voice the Feds caught on tape was Lano, and all he was talking about was calling a truce between the families. Agent Hopskins slammed down his headset after listening to the recording a second time. He was pissed because he didn't know what to make of this business about Saw no longer being in the business. That was not how it worked. Hopskins had never seen a guy of

Saw's stature just up and leave the game. It just didn't happen. No, they played the game enough for Hopskins to gather enough evidence that he would later use to either flip them into becoming rats or nail them to the cross.

Saw didn't come off to Hopskins as being any exception to the rules, but still it was irking the hell out of him not knowing just what angle Saw was playing.

"You get that bitch on the phone and tell her that I said to meet us downtown right now!" Hopskins ordered his field agent.

Taquana was summoned to the federal courthouse on Lafayette Boulevard. No court proceedings were taking place because it was after five o'clock, but the agents kept an office upstairs for briefing and snitching.

Agent Hopskins ordered the rest of the agents to leave the room as Taquana walked into the conference room. Taquana was in fear that she'd done something wrong and that her bail would be revoked. "You wanted to see me?" she asked.

"Sit down," ordered Hopskins. The look on his face said it all. He was pissed and wanted answers. "What's this shit I hear about Saw not being the head of his organization anymore, and why wasn't he at the meeting?"

"I swear, I don't know what's going on with that. I was expecting to see him at the meeting as well—"

Hopskins cut her off when he slammed his hand against the table and stood up. "You listen to me, you little slick bitch. If I find out that you're lying and you're trying to play me, I'll have your black ass back in front of a judge and thrown back in jail. Do I make myself clear?"

"I swear—"

"Damn it, do I make myself clear?"

"Yes," said Taquana in a defeated voice. She had no idea that when she started working for the Feds they owned her, and in owning her they'd talk to her like the snitch she'd become.

"You find out what the hell's going on with Saw," said Hopskins. He waved his hand for Taquana to leave his sight. He wanted her beak to the grindstone like the rest of his snitches working to get their time reduced, while some were even working on behalf of a loved one doing time in the Feds trying to get their sentence chopped down.

Meanwhile, Agent Hopskins had his agents looking into Saw's latest movements. He was sure it was some sort of play, maybe to get Taquana to lower her guard, and then he'd kill her. Hopskins played with the different theories in his head as he sat alone inside the conference room. It never crossed his mind that Saw just might very well be done with the game.

Taquana had already testified at the grand jury, and there was a sealed indictment returned against all of her people as well as for Saw, Hood, and Lano. The federal prosecutors had the indictment sealed because they feared many would flee, and because they were still working an ongoing investigation.

Taquana left the federal building, feeling cheap. She had the mind to say, "Fuck the Feds," and just take off in the middle of the night. Her thoughts of where she could hide out took over her mind as she rode in the back seat of her tinted black Escalade. She had millions tucked away from all the years Slim had run the west side of Detroit. The Feds were putting too much pressure on her to get to Saw. Giving up information was one thing, but now they had her wearing wires and seeking niggas out. That was supposed to be their job, and it made Taquana wonder just what she had signed up for. *They can kiss my ass.* She'd made up her mind to make a run for it. She knew just the place, and it was perfect because the Feds would never guess that she would be hiding there.

Taquana fixed herself a double shot of Patrón from the minibar to settle her nerves. She fired up a cone filled with her favorite, Cookie. She looked out the window at the city that she loved so much. It was a shame that she had to leave it all behind, for a good while anyway. She wasn't sure how long the statute of limitations was, but whatever it was, she planned to run it out.

Taquana ordered her driver to take her home. She wanted to unearth her millions from safe-keeping, so by nightfall she'd be all set to board a private jet on a one-way flight to St. Thomas. Her moms was from the islands, and she'd raised her kids to know about their heritage, so every summer when Taquana and Slim were coming up, their moms would take them to her native land of St. Thomas to visit relatives.

Slim still owned a mansion and a few businesses on the island, so that would be Taquana's getaway from the Feds. She loved it there almost as much as she loved Detroit, so it wouldn't be so bad leaving, she told herself.

Chapter Forty

Hood was sitting on the living-room floor between Karmesha's legs as she sat on the sofa oiling and twisting his dreads. Hood sat with his eyes closed because Karmesha's touch was intoxicating. The classic movie *A Thin Line Between Love and Hate* played on the massive TV mounted over the fireplace.

Karmesha hadn't left Hood's side since she came home from the hospital. She had the wiring removed from her jaw and was doing better with each day that passed. Hood had taken her shopping for a new wardrobe and even surprised her with a brand-new Range Rover Sport. Hood wanted her to know that she was wanted and that she was his woman.

Neither of them had heard from Saw since the awkward day at the house. But Karmesha had seen Sherise all on IG showing off her engagement ring. It made Karmesha cringe with jealousy, because in her eyes she was more of a bad bitch than Sherise and Tammy put together. Karmesha told herself that the only reason Saw even asked the bitch to marry him was because he was probably salty about her and Hood being together.

Karmesha held a satisfied smirk on her face at the thought as she twisted the last of Hood's dreads. She wiped the oil on her hands onto the white towel draped around Hood's neck, then patted his head. "All done," she said.

Hood had dozed off. A smile creased his face as he opened his eyes and sat up. "Thank you, baby," said Hood.

"You can thank me by cleaning all this up," said Karmesha as she swung her leg over Hood's head, then stood up. She wore black capris, a wife-beater, and furry house slippers.

Hood stood up and pulled Karmesha to him by her small waist. He gave her small kisses around her neck then on her lips. "How do I look?" he asked.

"Like my man. My man who's about to cook me dinner," said Karmesha with a smile as she threw her arms around Hood's neck. Hood had been spoiling her with his skills in the kitchen, and he had promised to cook up some lamb chops with all the trimmings.

"I got'chu," said Hood, allowing his hands to slide down to the cuffs of her plush ass cheeks.

"I'ma go up and take a shower while you do that." Karmesha stole a kiss and turned to leave, but not before Hood could slap her across the ass.

She turned and giggled like a schoolgirl and headed up the spiral staircase. Hood stretched and yawned until his muscles cracked, then he started to gather up the combs and rubber bands Karmesha had used to do his dreads. He was bare chested with a pair of black cargo shorts on and no shoes or socks. Hood was a big, natural swoll nigga who looked like he'd always just finished working out even when he hadn't.

He stood up and pulled his dreads back into a ponytail, using one of the rubber bands to secure it. As he was doing so, a shadowy figure against the wall in the kitchen caught his eye. The figure was accompanied by another figure, and both were hunched over with assault rifles in their grasp. Hood flipped the cushion up on the sofa and snatched the black AR-15 he kept for situations like this. Hood had the AR-15 aimed for the entrance of the kitchen as he stood in the cut. He opened fire on the first man as soon as he rounded the corner. Kaa! Kaa! Kaa!

The man stumbled back from the impact of the bullets, and his finger squeezed the trigger, causing his AK-47 to spray wildly. Hood ducked out of the way while still busting back. The second intruder let off a series of shots, tearing through the kitchen wall into the living room, but they were all cover shots as he made his getaway, leaving his crime partner for dead.

Hood gave chase of the second man, but by the time he reached the backyard, there was no sight of the man anywhere. When Hood walked back inside the house, Karmesha was coming downstairs with her hair wrapped in a towel and a Smith & Wesson .40-cal at her side. Hood had shown her how to use it so that she would always know how to defend herself.

Hood stood over the dying masked man with his AR-15 pointed down at his head. The man's chest slowly rose then fell, letting Hood know that he was on his way out. Hood reached down and yanked the mask from the man's head, then studied his face.

"Who is he?" asked Karmesha.

"I don't know," said Hood, which was the truth, because he had never seen ol' boy before a day in his life.

The man's eyes fluttered then rolled to the back of his head. Hood knew that at that very moment the man was fighting with the Angel of Death, who was there to claim his soul. But before he went, Hood wanted to know who sent them.

He slapped the man up until their eyes met. "Who sent you?" The man's mouth opened as if to speak, but his last breath was all that came out. Hood slapped him some more. "Who sent you?" he demanded of the dead man.

"Baby, he's gone," said Karmesha.

She stepped to Hood's side as he rose to his feet. She curled under his massive frame, afraid of the unknown to follow. She wondered who would want to kill Hood.

Hood had his gut telling him one name. *Saw.* He was the only one even crazy enough to try Hood like that. Hood had seen the look in Saw's eyes the day Karmesha walked in on their meeting. Hood knew then that it was going to be a problem. There were only two people who even knew about Hood's crib, and that was Lano and Saw. Hood just couldn't believe that it had really come to them playing the murder game with each other. But as Hood looked around at the damage done by the bullets through his home, he accepted the fact that one of them must die. And Saw had already taken the first shot, so now it was his turn.

But Hood was laughing because Saw would know better than to send two rookies to get at him. The two lames he'd sent were still wet behind the ears, so he really couldn't have expected them to come back with his blood on their hands.

Hood mule kicked the dead man in the face. "Stupid mothafucka." Police sirens were nearing the house. Undoubtedly, one of the neighbors had heard the gunfire and called the police. Hood instructed Karmesha not to say anything. He would do all the talking and allow the scene and evidence to spell out what really happened, which was that the two men had committed a home invasion, and Hood shot one of the men in self-defense.

Chapter Forty-one

Hood set out on a bloodthirsty mission to kill Saw the next day, because in his heart he knew that it was Saw who had tried killing him. Hood was up early in the morning, driving as the sun came up. He'd driven out to each of Saw's estates, only to find them all empty with huge SOLD signs staked into the front lawns. Hood had been out of the loop since he and Karmesha had been playing house. He had no idea about Saw's plans to move down to Atlanta with Sherise, nor did he know about the new condo Saw was holed up in until they moved down South.

Hood pushed the black BMW 750 onto the interstate, headed for the club. Lano of all people had to know where Saw was. When Hood pulled up to the club on Syracuse, niggas were just starting to post up, some rolling their first blunt of the day. They all still had sleep in their eyes and were moving slowly.

Lano stood among them, barking orders and talking with his hands. He hadn't seen Hood because Hood parked on 7 Mile and crossed the street. When Hood rounded the corner of Syracuse, Lano looked as if he'd seen a ghost. His thin frame froze with fear as Hood closed the space between them.

"I need to holla at you," said Hood.

"What . . . what up doe?" stammered Lano.

"Inside," said Hood, then walked around Lano to the entrance of the club. All of their men gave Hood nods, but no words were spoken.

When Lano came inside the club, he was a nervous wreck. His eyes were wide with fear and more so guilt. But Hood was so zoned out that he hadn't picked up on Lano acting shifty. Hood was behind the bar, pouring himself his second shot of 1738 Rémy Martin. As he tossed the shot back, his black T-shirt rose at the hip, giving Lano an eyeful of the Desert Eagle Hood was packing. Hood slammed the glass against the bar and looked across at Lano. "Somebody tried to kill me last night," said Hood.

"You bullshitting. Where at?" asked Lano.

"Two niggas came to my house of all places. But I got one of 'em, and the other got away," said Hood.

"Who was they?" asked Lano. He had a nervous knot in his stomach.

"The nigga died on my floor before I could get him to talk. But I know who sent 'em at me," said Hood.

Lano's eyes bucked with fear like he'd been caught in a woman's panty drawer. "Who?" his ashy lips quivered.

"Saw sent them rookies at me. He still mad because of Karmesha," said Hood. "He wanna kill me about some pussy, then so be it."

Hood and Lano both knew there was more to it than that. Hood had crossed the line of disrespect and loyalty. But Lano wasn't about to tell him that. He was just glad that Hood wasn't there to kill him. He secretly rejoiced at the idea of Saw and Hood wanting to kill each other. That was killing two birds with one stone.

"Where that nigga at? I went to all his spots, and they were empty with SALE signs out front," said Hood.

Lano frowned because it was news to him about Saw letting go of all his properties. "I don't know where Saw's at. The last time I seen him was at your crib," said Lano.

"Well, I want you to call him and tell him that you wanna meet with him later," said Hood.

"Hood, you know y'all my niggas, so I ain't tryin'a be in the middle of y'all shit. How would you feel if I lured you to a meeting—"

Hood put on his ice grill and leaned over the bar. "I'm not asking you. I'm telling you to call the nigga and have him meet you here."

Lano swallowed the dry lump in his throat. "Okay," he agreed as he pulled out his cell phone and scrolled down to Saw's name. "It's ringing," he informed Hood.

Saw didn't answer, but he sent a text: What up doe?

Lano showed Hood the message, then texted back: I need 2 holla at u so come 2 da club later.

A few moments passed, then Saw texted back: C U at 5.

Hood read the last text and was satisfied that at five o'clock he'd have Saw standing before him. He poured himself another shot and downed it. "I'll be back in a li'l while. Don't go anywhere," ordered Hood.

Lano watched as Hood left the club, and he thought, *see, this is exactly why I gotta kill both y'all asses*. Lano cursed himself for sending the two amateurs to try to kill Hood. All they did was piss him the fuck off and wake up the beast inside of him. Lano knew that he was up against the clock, because he didn't feel right having Saw and Hood in the same place. It was his guilt that had him paranoid. He needed to kill them in two separate locations. But first he needed the right shooters for the job. Someone who he knew wouldn't miss.

Lano called Thugga and pleaded with him to come to the bar. Thugga and Maine hadn't been back to the bar since they walked out during Lano's speech. They were in the cut plotting their own takeover.

"I promise that it'll be worth your time if you come and hear me out," said Lano.

Thugga and Maine reluctantly showed up to the club to see what Lano had up his sleeve. They viewed him as the coward that he was, because Lano always wanted the next nigga to do something that he himself was afraid to do.

Lano might've been a coward, but he was willing to pay like a boss. As soon as Thugga and Maine walked into the club, there was $1 million piled high on the bar top.

"This is a million dollars. Let's call it a good-faith payment. For this money I want you to kill Saw. And I got another mill for y'all to kill Hood," said Lano.

Thugga was tempted to pull out and just kill Lano for the million on the bar, but the second million he promised was what saved his life without him knowing it. "So let's get this straight. You gon' give us this mill right now to kill Saw, and then another mill after we kill Hood?" asked Maine.

"That's what I'm saying." Lano nodded as he rocked back on the heels of his blue Gators with his hands shoved into his slacks.

Thugga felt they could press for more, so he did. "Plug us in with ya coke connect and we got a deal."

Lano pulled back a wide shit grin and held it as he seemed to be thinking it over. There was no way he would ever enrich the two killers before him with that type of money and power. They would surely kill him next. "Okay," lied Lano. He'd agree to anything right then if it meant killing Saw and Hood. He'd deal with Thugga and Maine when he came to that bridge.

Lano pulled out his phone and sent Saw another text: Change of plans. Pretty Woman at 3.

Saw texted back: It's on.

Lano nodded as he rounded the bar for a fifth of Hennessy. He took down three shot glasses and filled them. He took a shot with Thugga and Maine, then poured another round. He laced them up about the three o'clock meeting he'd set up with Saw. That was where they were to kill him. And then at five o'clock, they were to be back at the club to kill Hood.

"Your other million dollars will be waiting for you then," promised Lano.

Chapter Forty-two

Pretty Woman was an old strip club on the east side of Detroit off Van Dyke and 7 Mile. Saw hadn't been inside the hole in the wall in a minute, but he liked their steaks, so he didn't mind meeting up with Lano there. As he cruised through the afternoon traffic, the purplish clouds ahead promised a coming storm, so Saw raised the top on the platinum BMW he was manning.

When Saw made it to Pretty Woman, the parking lot was almost vacant with about four cars in it. From the tattered teal-green booth, the valet popped out bearing a yellow smile at Saw's driver window.

"What's happening, playa?" asked the old timer as he opened the door for Saw and moved his hand about. "You must've come for the steaks, because the booty ain't in yet."

Saw laughed and passed the ol' head a crisp twenty. He headed inside the bar while eyeing his phone for the time. He was ten minutes earlier than three o'clock. A faint smell of cheap leather and humped pussy met Saw at the door as he stepped into the dimly lit remnants of the club. The music was low, and the stage was bare. Only one barmaid stood behind the bar, washing glasses.

"Can I get'chu something, baby?" she called out without looking up at Saw.

"Yeah, I'll have one of ya steak dinners," said Saw as he bellied up to the bar. The Channel 4 news played behind the bar.

"And can I get'chu anything to drink?"

"I'm feeling like a double shot of Crown Royal."

The barmaid smiled up at Saw. "Coming right up."

Saw watched as she poured his drink. She was a pretty redbone with short, wavy hair, heavy chested, but with no hips or ass to complete her resume. She placed the drink in front of Saw, then tried throwing her makeshift ass as she headed down the bar.

As Saw sipped, the door of the club opened, and he turned to see Thugga and Maine walking in. An eerie feeling came over Saw as the two goons crossed the bar in his direction.

"My nigga, you lucky we fucks with you," said Thugga, flashing a genuine smile.

"Yeah." Maine nodded. They both bellied up to the bar beside Saw.

"Let me guess, Lano sent y'all at me?" asked Saw.

"Yeah. Nigga gave us a ticket up front to down you right here," Maine informed him. "He wants us to kill ya manz Hood next," said Maine.

"Facts," added Thugga.

Saw could only shake his head because he hadn't seen it coming. First Hood wanted to go behind his back with Karmesha, and now Lano was putting money on his head.

"But you know we could never bring you no fucked-up move, ya feel me? You always been a hun'd with us," said Thugga.

"But let me ask you this," said Maine. "What's up with your leaving the game and leaving us to work for Lano's creep ass anyway?"

Saw wiped a hand over his face. "The Feds are building a case as we speak, so I gotta fall back and stay out of the way, ya feel me?"

Thugga and Maine nodded. They respected Saw's decision, but at the same time they wanted his blessing to do their own thing.

"My nigga, you know me and Maine have always been loyal to you through the whole flick, and while we respect yo' mind on getting out of the game, we was hoping you'd turn us on to a connect," said Thugga.

"Say less. I'ma plug y'all in with my peoples out in Houston, but on y'all's word, you gotta always deal palms up," said Saw.

"On everythang, we got'chu," said Thugga.

Saw's mind returned to Lano trying to have him killed. "This is what I want y'all to do. I want y'all to go back and tell Lano that y'all put me in the trunk and drove me somewhere and killed me. I want him to think that I'm dead, ya feel me? And then when are y'all 'posed to kill Hood?"

"We 'posed to hit him at the club about five o'clock," said Maine.

"A'ight. I'ma meet y'all there," said Saw.

Thugga and Maine left Saw to his steak dinner as they went to put their plan in motion. Saw cut into his tender steak and fed himself a bite. *You want me dead, huh? We finna see.*

Chapter Forty-three

Lano was pacing the floor of the club as he awaited word from Thugga and Maine about killing Saw. He checked his gold-face Rolex for the hundredth time. It was almost four o'clock, and he was starting to worry. They hadn't shown back up at the club, nor had they called. But then again, neither had Saw. He had to be dead, because he would've called by now to see why Lano hadn't shown up. *Yeah, it's done,* Lano assured himself as he fired up a Newport to try to calm his nerves.

The front door of the club cracked open, and Lano nearly shit himself. It was only his doorman, Ricky, letting him know that Thugga and Maine were pulling up. "A'ight, but knock next time," said Lano. He was on edge about everything. He took a hard pull from his cigarette, then stubbed it out in an ashtray atop the bar.

He tried to appear calm as Thugga and Maine crossed the threshold into the club. He searched their faces for any tells, but they showed no emotion. "Well?" asked Lano with desperation.

"It's done," said Thugga.

"Yeah, we put him in the trunk, then drove him to the north end and put two in him," added Maine.

There was a ton of relief in Lano's smirk. "Did he beg for his life?" he wanted to know.

"Nah, but he did offer to double whatever you were paying us," said Maine.

This made Lano laugh. "Y'all know the most Saw's cheap ass ever paid y'all was fifty thousand. I wish I'd seen the look on his face right before y'all put his lights out," laughed Lano.

He rounded the bar as Thugga and Maine each took a stool. He set a fifth each of Hennessy in front of them. Suddenly, Lano was in a festive mood. Half of his plan was taken care of, and the other half would be settled in less than an hour.

"You got that other ticket ready for us?" asked Thugga.

"It's in the back all counted out on my desk." Lano smiled.

Thugga kicked Maine's foot under the bar, and they both stood up, drawing twin Glock .40s from their waists. Lano threw up his hands and proceeded to plead his case.

"Wait a minute. If it's about the money, I can give you guys more. That's not an issue."

"Shut the fuck up," growled Thugga. He motioned for Maine to go get their money out of the back.

"Bring yo' bitch ass around here and sit down," ordered Thugga, directing Lano to a seat at the dominoes table.

Lano complied with the man of the hour and took a seat. He was rifling through the pages of bullshit in his mind, looking for the right words that would hopefully save his life, but he found none worthy. So he sat in fear and silence as Thugga stood over him with the Glock flirting with his face.

"I never liked yo' snake ass for nothing in the world. I knew you was the type to cross out ya manz in the end," said Thugga.

Lano started to speak, but Thugga grimaced. "Say something and I'ma blow yo' shit back," promised Thugga. He despised Lano with a passion. In his eyes, the only real reason he was ever in the position he was in was because he came up with Saw and Hood. Lano was a weak nigga, and Thugga had peeped it, but he was Saw and Hood's man, so he always had a pass.

But today, Thugga was going to expose Lano for the creep he truly was. And then he was going to take pleasure in being the one to blow his brains out all over the club's floor.

Maine came back to the front with a black pregnant duffle bag over his shoulder. He set it down on the table in front of Lano.

"Before we kill him, we should make him up some mo' bread. You heard him say he got mo', ya feel me?" said Maine, speaking as if Lano weren't sitting there listening.

"Nah, we good with two million," said Thugga as he met eyes with Lano. He didn't want to give the weasel before him any extra time to breathe. The $2 million they had already should be enough to get things going with the connect Saw was to plug them with, reasoned Thugga. He figured if a soft nigga like Lano could get niggas to follow him, then he and Maine would run the city.

The front door of the club burst open, and Ricky yelled, "The Feds coming up the block." Ricky had disappeared from the doorway just as fast as he had appeared. The sound of car doors slamming and engines starting could be heard coming from outside.

Damn! thought Thugga as he looked into Lano's eyes, realizing that he'd have to let him live for now. Maine snatched the bag of money, and he and Thugga raced out the front door, which no one ever used to access the club. They made it out just in time, because the Feds were only houses away from closing in on the club. They had come the long way, down by Nevada Avenue.

Lano was happy to be spared his life, but at the same time, he wasn't trying to taste jail either. He bolted out the side exit of the club, straight into the hands of a dozen or so federal agents. The Feds had nabbed a few of Lano's men who were too slow getting away, and they formed a perimeter around the club for anyone who may have been hiding nearby in the alley or one of the neighbor's yards.

Special Agent Hopskins made the scene and stepped dead into Lano's face as two agents placed him in handcuffs and frisked him.

"So what's it gonna be? Are you going to help yourself or are you gonna go down with your friends?" asked Hopskins.

"That depends on what you talking about," said Lano.

Agent Hopskins knew a snitch when he saw one, and Lano fit the description to a T. "Take him to my office," ordered Hopskins.

Agent Hopskins scanned the area but saw nothing deserving of his time. What he needed was a new star snitch in Lano, so he got into his SUV and headed downtown. Hopskins had learned from his field agents that Taquana had fled the city of Detroit, and without her testimony their case against Saw didn't stand a chance of holding up in front of a judge, let alone any would-be jury.

Lano had to be the key, and Hopskins was willing to have the government offer him full immunity for his cooperation against Saw and Hood. Hopskins viewed Lano as the lesser of the two evils. It was simple. He wanted Saw.

The Feds had put bugs in the club the last time they had raided it, so agents had caught Lano's murder plot all on audio. That was how they knew to move in, because they couldn't risk allowing a shoot-out to ensue once everyone showed up at the club.

Agent Hopskins had ordered that his agents make Saw's and Hood's arrests simultaneously along with those named in the sealed indictment.

Hood was coming up off the Davidson Expressway when he saw a herd of red and blue lights flashing in his rearview mirror. As he reached the corner of Conant Avenue he pulled over to the curb, thinking that it was an emergency convoy needing to pass, but he found himself being boxed in by the tinted vehicles. A blue Tahoe rammed him in the rear, and before he could blink, there were agents closing in on him with their guns drawn.

"Let me see your hands! Show me your hands!" ordered the red-bearded agent inches away from the driver's window.

Hood grimaced. *Ain't this about a bitch,* he fumed. He had a mind to make them crackers use them shits, but he thought about Karmesha and the life he planned on spending with her. Hood found himself raising his hands, and as he did, the car door opened and he was snatched out to the street with knees planted into his back. The agents ripped the Desert Eagle .44 from his waist, then stood him up and knocked against the bullet-proof vest adorning his wide chest.

"What's this?" asked one of the agents.

But Hood stood silent.

"I'd say that's five more years, Jim-Tom," another agent said sarcastically. "That is, on top of your other sentences," he added.

They ushered Hood to the back of the Tahoe that had rammed him. "Watch your head there, Timmie," cracked the agent as he put Hood inside the truck.

The only thing Hood could do was put his face against the front seat and close his eyes. He knew that whatever the Feds wanted with him wasn't going to be as simple as a call to his attorney this time. He had seen it in those crackers' smirks that the shit was real this time.

Chapter Forty-four

Saw was on his way to the club to surprise Lano that he was still alive when he got the text from Thugga letting him know not to go to the club because the Feds were raiding it. *My hitta,* thought Saw as he made a U-turn on Gratiot Avenue and headed for I-94. His heart was telling him not to turn around because the Feds must've unsealed their indictment. Saw would've bet his life on it that his name was number one on whatever indictment the Feds had cooked up on them.

Saw thought about Sherise as he merged onto the interstate. She was still at work, and he didn't want to alarm her that he was leaving without her. He decided that he would call her once he landed in Atlanta and tell her to catch the next flight out.

Saw knew the day was coming when the Feds would come a-knocking, and he had done every-thing in his power to plan for it. But he still wasn't ready to go sit in anybody's jail while his lawyers fought to clear his name. If the Feds wanted him, then they'd have to arrest him. Saw couldn't see himself turning himself in no matter what his lawyers said.

He gunned the BMW until he reached the Metropolitan Airport out in Romulus, Michigan. His phone was blowing up as he walked through the double automated doors of the terminal. It was Denise calling. Of all times she picked then to be calling.

Saw let his voicemail pick up, but as he approached the counter, his mom was calling again. Saw ignored the vibrating of his phone as he offered a cheap smile to the woman working the ticket counter.

"And how may I help you today?" asked the pudgy blonde with freckles.

"I need a one-way ticket to Atlanta. Do you have anything leaving soon?" asked Saw.

The woman stabbed at her keyboard. "We have a flight leaving in about forty minutes. That's with American," she said.

"That's fine," said Saw.

"First class or coach?" she asked.

"Um, first-class, please," said Saw.

"And how will you be paying today, sir?" she asked.

"Cash," answered Saw as he unearthed an enormous bankroll and paid for his ticket.

The woman snatched the receipt from the register and passed it to Saw along with his ticket. "Have a nice flight," she said.

When Saw turned around, a band of FBI agents stood behind him, stone-faced. "Going somewhere, are we?" asked one of the agents as he reached for the ticket and receipt in Saw's hand. "Atlanta, Georgia," read the agent, looking at the designation. "One-way," he said with emphasis. "That's too bad, because the only one-way you're going is to federal prison. Cuff him and get him outta here," said the agent.

Chapter Forty-five

The back seat of the Crown Victoria felt like a prison on wheels as Saw sat slouched in the cheap leather while he tried blocking out the tightness of his handcuffs. The agents had purposely put them on too tight because they were all pissed about the many long nights they'd spent chasing Saw. It was their way of saying, "We've got your ass now!"

Saw didn't complain or show any emotion, for that matter. He wouldn't dare give them the satisfaction. Besides, Saw was a rare breed. He'd known that the job was hard when he took it, so having to sit down was just part of the game he played.

The tinted black Crown Victoria drove with urgent purpose as the lead vehicle of a three-car caravan. As they came up off the Lodge Expressway, Saw could see the Wayne County Jail on the skyline. It was a dreadful feeling knowing that was where he was headed. Saw enjoyed the last sights of freedom as the car pulled off Gratiot. People were out enjoying the last of the summer, many walking the short distance to Greek Town Casino.

Saw sighed as the car pulled up to the gated garage of the jail and honked its horn a few times. Moments later, the gate went up and the car escaped into the dimly lit, filthy garage.

"Here we are. Home sweet home," said the driver as he killed the engine.

The passenger held a wide shit grin on his clean-shaven face as he stood with the door open for Saw. "You've been here before, right?" he asked, trying to be funny.

But Saw had no rap for their asses. He shuffled past the agents and into the sliding door of booking. A strong welcoming whiff of crotch met Saw at the door, causing his nose to frown. He had entered the bowels of the Wayne County Jail where only a smell like that could exist.

The agents stopped Saw at the registry booth and handed him over to the deputy along with their needed paperwork.

"He's got a federal hold. Probably have court in the morning," one of the agents informed her.

"Okay. You guys are all set," said the wide-frame black chick from behind the glass. She pointed toward holding cell three.

"Someone will be with you shortly," she lied.

The agents left, still smiling at Saw as he headed to holding cell three. The fat bitch knew that it would be hours upon hours before anyone would see Saw. Saw had known she was just talking from the fifty-something bodies that stood dick to booty, crammed inside the tight cell. He said, "Excuse me," as he inched his way toward the phones lined against the wall. But just like his last visit to the county, none of the phones were working. Two of them had wires coming out of the receivers, while the other one simply didn't work.

Saw looked around at the assorted faces, mostly petty dopefiends and drunk drivers, but no one to be cautious of. Being in the county a nigga always had to be aware of his surroundings because it was a sure meeting ground for new and old beefs. The only thing was that they checked the guns in at the door, so niggas were playing by a much different set of rules. It was called "get your man by all means necessary," which translated to "sneak attack." A nigga would sneak you in a minute if you let them.

A glimmer of hope came over Saw at the sight of a young nigga huddled low in the back using a cell phone. Saw wasn't the type to be cutting into anybody for a favor, so he came bearing a crisp blueface. The young nigga looked up at Saw and the money in his hand as if neither meant anything. And in reality, inside a place like Wayne County Jail, $100 wouldn't get you far, maybe some cigarettes from the trustees or some zoom-zooms and wam-wams, but a phone was considered a hot commodity.

Saw respected the game, so he tore off another $400 and presented it to the youngster, who accepted it this time. He promptly ended his call and handed Saw the phone.

"How long you need?" asked the youngster.

"I just need to make a couple of calls and I'll be out ya way," said Saw as he crouched down as the youngster stood as the lookout.

The first person Saw called was Mr. Beres, who promptly confirmed Saw's fears of the Feds unsealing their indictment. Mr. Beres told Saw that he'd have court in the morning and that he and Ms. Raben would both be there. Saw thanked Mr. Beres, and then called Sherise.

She answered crying her eyes and soul out into the phone. She blamed Saw for being where he was because she believed that he was still somehow involved in the streets.

"I can't do this with you, Saw. You lied to me," cried Sherise.

"No. Baby, listen to me. I didn't lie to you," pleaded Saw.

But he couldn't get through to Sherise. Her heart was broken into a million pieces, because they were supposed to be moving on to better things and here Saw was taking them backward. Sherise had watched her own mother try to carry on a marriage with her father from the penitentiary, and her mother was never happy. She was only trying to hold on to a love who didn't love her back. Sherise told herself that she couldn't do the same thing.

"I can't. I gotta go," cried Sherise.

"Sherise. Sherise?" Saw lowered the phone at the sound of the dial tone. *Damn.*

Saw went into a haze for a moment. It was crazy what a new day had the power to bring about. He thought back to the morning, how he and Sherise were in bed, him running his fingers through her hair, when Lano called then texted him.

Saw could only shake his head, because he would've given anything to be back in bed with Sherise instead of where he was at. The youngster pulled back up, breaking Saw's train of thought.

"You straight? You don't need to call anybody else?"

"Nah, maybe later. Good looking, tho'," said Saw, handing him his phone.

The youngster crouched down and started texting, leaving Saw to his racing thoughts. Saw dusted a spot on the floor, then slid his back down to the cool tile. He sighed and tried to envision himself walking out of the federal building like George Jefferson with his arms swinging behind him. He had confidence in Mr. Beres's plan, but it still meant some time until things got sorted out. Time away from Sherise and the new life they'd been planning together.

The deputy didn't start processing people out of the holding cells until after midnight. Saw was one of the last ones to be fingerprinted, photographed, and then strip-searched. Saw hated the strip search area because they made everybody line up ass naked and bend over to show the cracks of their asses. And that was what it smelled like—fifty years of ass crack.

Saw had been to the county enough to know to sneak some cash upstairs with him to quarantine. He cuffed $1,000 and had the deputy put the rest on his commissary account. He was shuffled up to medical for screening and then taken to the quarantine pod. The youngster with the phone and a few others all went into the same pod as Saw.

The pod was designed to house ten men, but there was a total of sixteen people, some having to sleep on plastic beds they call "boats." By the time Saw lay down in his boat, the deputy was calling names over the intercom for court. "Listen up for your name!"

Saw heard his name and went to splash some water on his face. The mirror above the sink was so battered that Saw couldn't see his reflection. He fell to the back of the line, hoping that he wouldn't be returning after court. The line moved around to a bullpen, where the group waited for over an hour until the deputy ran them downstairs on the elevators. Saw looked at the aged clock down in booking. It was four thirty in the morning, and yet the wheels of justice were already turning. Because Saw was going to federal court, he was put in bullpen two, where he was fed a cereal breakfast and orange juice. Saw made himself aware of his surroundings. A huddle of migos sat off to the side, while two old-timers, both of foreign descent, talked in hushed tongues of their native language.

As Saw finished the last of his orange juice, the bars of the bullpen slid open, and Hood rounded the corner. Saw looked up and met the cold stare of Hood, who had his murder mask on.

"You missed," said Hood.

"What?" Saw frowned. He didn't know what the hell Hood was talking about.

"Them li'l rookies you sent at me, they missed," said Hood.

Saw shook his head no. He realized that Lano must've put some niggas on Hood too. Saw patted the empty spot on the bench beside him. "That wasn't me," he said.

Hood pulled up and listened, because he had never known Saw to be a liar. If it had been Saw, then Saw would've straight out told him that yeah, he'd been the one.

"I'm listening," said Hood.

"It was ya manz Lano. He tried to pay Thugga and Maine to hit me yesterday. And then he wanted them to see you next," said Saw.

Hood thought back to the day before the club. "That's why his ass was acting all funny."

"Yeah. Had it not been for Thugga and Maine, I wouldn't be sitting here talking to you." said Saw.

"Where they get you at?" asked Hood.

"At the airport," said Saw, wiping his hands over his face.

"Shit, at least you made it that far. They snatched me out in the middle of traffic," said Hood. "But what about Lano? Did they pick him up too?"

"I don't know. I ain't even know that they grabbed you," said Saw.

"Something's telling me that we finna sit for a minute on this one."

Saw had that same feeling in his gut, only because it was the Feds and they didn't play by the rules. But still he wanted to remain optimistic. He had an ace in the hole when it was all said and done.

They had settled the issue of Hood thinking Saw had tried to kill him, but there was still an elephant in the room about Hood being with Karmesha. Neither spoke on it, although they both were thinking about it. Really, there was nothing Hood could say to clean up the betrayal Saw felt. The damage to their life-long friendship had been done. The only thing that they could do at that point was stand solid, and hopefully they'd both see the streets again.

Chapter Forty-six

Over at the federal courthouse, Saw and Hood were placed in the same freezing cold holding cell. They both bundled up into the sleeves of their hunter green county jail shirts. Hood lay across one of the benches, using a roll of tissue for a pillow, while Saw paced the small cell. They knew not to talk while in the federal building because they were sure the Feds had each cell tapped and could hear anything they may have said.

A couple of hours passed without any movement until the door leading into the hallway buzzed and clicked open. It was one of the Marshals escorting Lano to a holding cell beside Hood and Saw. Lano had met eyes with Saw but shifted his eyes to the floor as he passed by.

Saw had seen something within Lano's eyes that he didn't trust, and it wasn't because he'd tried having him killed the day before. It was something that Saw didn't want to believe. He nudged Hood's leg to wake him.

"They just brought Lano in. He's next door," said Saw.

Hood got up and went to the iron gate and waited for the Marshal to leave. "Lano," called Hood.

"Yeah," responded Lano. It sounded like he was at the back of the cell with his head in his shirt for warmth.

"Nigga, come to the gate," snapped Hood.

Lano could be heard approaching the gate. "What up?"

"Shit, you tell me," said Hood. "I got ya message, so I'm just wondering what other surprises you got for me."

"You'll see," said Lano.

"Nigga, what?" Hood grabbed the gate. "Tell me what I'ma see."

But Lano could be heard lying back on the bench. Hood slapped the gate hard, then turned and looked at Saw. Both of their fears had been confirmed. Lano was working.

The reality had taken the fight out of Hood. He had to go sit down and digest that his best friend had turned State. Lano knew a whole lot, which made Hood wonder just how much he'd told the Feds. Lano knew enough to park Hood and Saw for life without any possibility of ever coming home. It was a sickening feeling that Hood didn't wish on his worst enemy.

The Marshal reappeared and called for Saw to step out of the bullpen. "Your lawyers are here to see you."

When Saw got to the attorney-client room, behind the mesh wire sat Ms. Raben and Mr. Beres. They both offered faint smiles, and then Ms. Raben got down to business.

"Did you see Delano back there? He's now working with the Feds," said Ms. Raben.

"Yeah, I seen him. Who else has agreed to cooperate?" asked Saw.

"Well, they had a girl, Taquana. She testified at the grand jury, but she's since gone on the run," said Ms. Raben.

"You think they'll give me a bond?" asked Saw.

"That's what we're gonna ask for today," said Mr. Beres.

"But with Delano now snitchin' on you guys, there isn't any telling what all he's told the Feds, and the government's going to use that in court today," advised Ms. Raben. She didn't want Saw to get his hopes up high for a let-down. She believed in always telling her clients the truth.

While that wasn't news Saw hoped to hear, he trusted that the two wise minds across from him wouldn't let the fight end there. "Well, see what y'all can do," said Saw.

"Okay. We're going to head on up. They should be calling you shortly," said Ms. Raben as she and Mr. Beres stood.

They left Saw to his thoughts. *Damn,* he thought at the possibility of being denied bond. He wondered how long it would take for Mr. Beres to make his power moves with the recording of him stepping away from the conspiracy. It was all a wait-and-see game with the Feds, because even if you beat them in the end, they still got some time out of you along the way.

About ten minutes later, the door opened, and the Marshal pointed to a spot against the wall for Saw to stand next to Hood. They were both still shackled at their feet, but now the Marshals were cuffing their hands so they could go into the courtroom.

The Marshals walked them around to the elevator, and they rode up to the sixth floor. The marble halls were buzzing with lawyers and court clerks. Saw scanned the faces moving about, in search of Sherise. He didn't see her among the people, and it dampened his spirits because he needed her love and support. Everyone else's at the time had proven to be fake love.

Who Saw saw upon entering the courtroom were Denise and Karmesha. They were seated together behind the defense table. Saw nodded to his mom but didn't acknowledge Karmesha's presence. He didn't know if she was there for him or Hood.

Hood smiled and waved at Karmesha, making things even more awkward between him and Saw. Saw was hurt that Sherise wasn't there to hold him down. He understood that she was upset and disappointed, but he needed her to believe that he hadn't lied to her about quitting the game and that he was going to come up from under whatever the Feds were trying to stick on him.

Ms. Raben and Mr. Beres emerged from behind the swinging bench and took to the lectern. The court had just called their case, so Ms. Raben waved Saw over to stand with them. Hood's lawyer had made it, and she was kneeled down, going over everything with him.

"All rise! Judge Grand presiding. Calling case number . . ." read the court clerk.

Magistrate Grand took his seat behind the bench, and he glared down his eagle beak at Saw with contempt in his eyes.

"You may be seated," ordered Judge Grand. He had everyone state their names for the record, and then he allowed the government to state their case.

Assistant United States Attorney Paul Kuebler was the lead attorney for the government. He started by informing the court that Saw was named as the number one defendant in a conspiracy indictment. He highlighted that Lano had agreed to fully cooperate in the investigation, so a superseding indictment was likely to soon follow.

"The defendant is a danger to the community as well as a flight risk, Your Honor. When the agents made his arrest, it was at the airport, where he was buying a one-way ticket to Atlanta," said Mr. Kuebler.

"I see," said Judge Grand. He looked at the defense. "Would the defense like to share anything?"

Ms. Raben was to speak. "Your Honor, my client had every right to purchase a ticket to Atlanta. He had no knowledge of the unsealed indictment against him. He's not on probation or parole, which would otherwise restrict his travel. So unless the government has any clear evidence that proves he's an actual flight risk, it is my position that the government's rhetoric is unfounded, just as this purported indictment is unfounded," said Ms. Raben.

"My client is not a convicted felon, nor does he have a violent criminal history. Based on the Bail Reform Act, the court should explore granting the defendant some sort of bail, which is what we're asking for today," said Ms. Raben.

"Denied. I am remanding the defendant to the custody of the U.S. Marshals until further proceeding," said Judge Grand. And it was so ordered.

Hood and his mouthpiece, Camilla Barkovic, took to the defense lectern. Ms. Barkovic and her father were known to be good lawyers, but mostly in the state. Judge Grand promptly denied Hood's bail as well, remanding him to the custody of the Marshals.

Ms. Raben promised she'd be over to the jail later to see Saw as the Marshals ushered him and Hood out of the courtroom. They both felt a bit of defeat, because sitting in the county jail was not the least bit desirable. The first couple of weeks were always the hardest because they were still fresh off the streets. But after they got into the routine, things wouldn't be that bad.

Hood and Saw separated once they made it back to the county. Hood went one way, while Saw was taken back to the musty pod he'd prayed earlier not to return to. Saw was glad in a way that he and Hood weren't around each other all day in the county, because he didn't know if he could look at him. Saw just couldn't understand how he, Hood, and Lano had ended up the way they did. They were made men. And most importantly, they were family, or so Saw had thought.

Lano had been the only defendant in front of Judge Grand to be released on bond that day, primarily because he had signed on to be a government informant. He'd been screened by pretrial services, and he'd given the probation department the address to his ranch in Adrian, Michigan. He was then released straight from the federal building, but not before Agent Hopskins reminded

him that he was due to testify before the grand jury
next week Monday.

Ricky picked Lano up from the courthouse and
drove him to his ranch. The streets were already
talking about Lano snitching on Hood and Saw,
which was what Ricky filled him in on during their
drive. "But you know I'm on yo' side," said Ricky.
"Them niggas was greedy and grimy, and to keep
to a hun'd, shit, I would've bagged they asses too."

Lano listened to Ricky go on and on about why
he was justified in snitching on Hood and Saw.
Ricky was a bad-body, big-face nigga with no neck
and a sketchy smirk. He didn't give a fuck about
Hood, Saw, or Lano. Ricky was only loyal to the
bag. Whoever had the bag, that was whose dick he
was going to ride.

Lano knew that was the case with most of the
niggas left in his crew. As long as he kept the bag
moving, no one would care how many years he put
Hood and Saw away for. Lano had seen the same
thing with other major niggas who had told, and
when they came home, niggas were still fucking
with them. Why? Because they had the bag and
were feeding niggas.

Lano peered out the passenger window of the
Audi A7 SUV at the passing traffic. He was cooking
up his master plan. If a nigga wasn't with him,
then they were against him, and he was going to
bust their wig, meaning he'd feed them to the

Feds. Lano didn't want to be one of the ones who snitched and still had to do time. He told himself that after he finished telling, he'd never see the inside of anybody's prison, because he'd get time served at sentencing.

Lano thought about Hood and Saw lying in the cells at the county jail. *Fuck you niggas. Die slow.*

Chapter Forty-seven

Taquana was laid out on the massage table overlooking the view of the crystal blue water that surrounded her white mansion in St. Thomas. She purred at the touch of the masculine hands working the stress out of her shoulders and lower back. Two bare-chested dreads served as her personal masseurs. She had a full staff of sexy islanders who serviced her every desire. *This is the good life*. Taquana smiled to herself.

Her troubles back in Detroit were a million miles away, or so she'd thought. Taquana opened her eyes at the tight grip around her wrists. Her eyes were wide with fear as she thought the worst: that her island workers were kidnapping her for a king's ransom.

"Don't move! You're under arrest!" said one of the men who'd been massaging her just a minute ago.

He and his partner were local DEA agents. They worked as undercovers and only focused on suspected drug traffickers, and Taquana fit the profile.

They didn't know who she was exactly at first. They thought that maybe she was on the island looking for a drug source or route. But after they'd done some digging, it was discovered that she was a fugitive wanted by the Feds in Detroit.

"Wait, I'll pay you a million dollars if you let me go," said Taquana as the cold steel clasped around her wrists. Her bribes fell on deaf ears as the two agents took her by the arms and ushered her through the courtyard. Her entire staff had been undercover federal agents. They were combing the estate for evidence and tagging everything to be seized.

Taquana was taken inside so she could dress. The agents had already arranged her travel plans back to Detroit, and a jet was waiting for them at the airport. Special Agent Hopskins had said he wanted her brought back forthwith. Her little vacation was over.

Taquana felt like she was trapped inside a bad dream as the jet skirted to its landing at the Detroit City Airport on Gratiot Avenue and Connors. The jet taxied around the strip and stopped beside a motorcade of tinted vehicles. Agent Hopskins stood with his hands on his hips, his sharp eyes concealed behind mirrored gold aviators.

"Enjoy the flight?" Hopskins asked Taquana as she stepped down off the plane.

"Not with these on," said Taquana, raising the cuffs and belly chain.

"Well, you might as well get used to traveling with those for a good while," said Hopskins, taking a hold of Taquana's arm.

He steered her to the back seat of his Crown Victoria and placed her in the car. Hopskins waved goodbye to the agents who'd flown Taquana in, and then he got behind the wheel and pulled out. Hopskins drove alone. He preferred having no partner riding with him watching his every move, because he didn't always play by the rules. In his eyes that didn't make him a dirty agent. It was his way of equalizing the scales. Hopskins felt as though he wasn't wrong if he had to falsify some evidence or lie on a guy to make the conviction stick. He told himself that he wasn't wrong because he was only locking up criminals who the system would never be able to otherwise convict without his equalizing tactics. So in a strong sense Hopskins felt justified.

He peered through the rearview at Taquana, who held his gaze. "Give me one good reason why I should give you a second chance."

"Because I'll do whatever you tell me," said Taquana in a small voice.

"That's right, bitch. And if you don't, let's just say you don't want to find out."

Taquana had caught Hopskins's drift, and she wasn't ready to test his patience. There was something in his eyes that told her jail would be the least of her worries if she didn't stick to the script.

Meanwhile, the Feds moved Hood to St. Clair County Jail out in Port Huron, Michigan. Hood was pissed because he had clout in Wayne County Jail from all the younger blacks who worked there and knew his name in the streets. At the St. Clair County Jail, Hood was just another black inmate. The deputies were all white and chewed tobacco. Hood didn't have anything in common with the deputies or the other inmates. The inmates were either petty drug addicts, or they were federal inmates who'd been there for years waiting to testify against someone. Hood's lawyer had told him not to talk about his case with anyone and that she'd see about getting him moved somewhere else.

The Feds had moved Hood for two reasons. They wanted to make him uncomfortable, and also it was their way of separating him and Saw.

Hood was feeling down since being moved because he hadn't been able to get Karmesha on the phone. He didn't want to believe that she'd given up on him so soon.

Chapter Forty-eight

The youngster who'd let Saw use his cell phone had been to court on a possession charge, and he needed $1,200 more to make bond. Saw made him a deal that he would have him bonded out if he left the phone with him.

"Bet," agreed the youngster.

Saw called Mr. Beres, and within a couple of hours, they were calling the youngster's name for release. The first person Saw called was Sherise. He hadn't spoken to her since the day he got arrested.

"Hello," she answered in a small voice.

Saw closed his eyes at the sound of her voice. "Baby, don't hang up, okay? I know you don't believe me, but that's why I had my lawyer send you the proof," said Saw.

"I got it in the mail this morning," said Sherise.

"Then you know that I wasn't lying to you," said Saw.

There was a pause.

"Sherise?" said Saw.

"Yeah, but that doesn't change where you're at right now."

"You think I wouldn't rather be at home next to you?"

"But you're not, Saw. What do you want me to do?"

"I need you to hold us down. I need to know that you're not like all the rest of 'em," said Saw.

"I can't believe you could even say that to me."

"Who do you expect me to believe, Sherise, you or my lying eyes? 'Cause right now all I see is a train that says LEAVING SAW'S CORNER. Everybody else is already on that bitch, and it's waiting for you," said Saw.

Sherise had never heard Saw speak with so much passion before. She heard it in his voice that he loved and missed her. It brought a smile to her heart and face.

"I'm not going anywhere, Saw. I'm scared, that's all."

"Baby, it's okay to be scared. I'm not asking you not to be. But I need for you to believe that I'ma walk outta here and marry you when it's all over."

Sherise hadn't taken her ring off. She looked down at the rock and envisioned walking down the aisle, being handed off to Saw.

"It's us against the world right now, you hear me?"

"Yeah," answered Sherise in a small voice.

After Saw finished tightening his game up on Sherise, he called Thugga and Maine because they had yet to be caught by the Feds, and Saw wanted to put them up on game.

"What up doe, my baby?" answered Maine.

"Shit, where y'all at?" asked Saw. He could hear the excitement in Maine's voice.

"We down here messin' with ya manz," said Maine.

"Okay," said Saw. They were down in Houston with Saw's coke connect, Chelo.

"What up, my nigga! It's live down this bitch, you hear me?" said Thugga over Maine's shoulder.

Neither Thugga or Maine knew that the Feds had snatched Saw, so he laced them up about the whole play and how they were named numbers four and five on their indictment. He told them that Lano was working and was free on bond.

"Say less," promised Thugga. He still had unfinished business with Lano anyway. "We be back that way in a couple days."

"Y'all niggas be careful. I can't afford to see y'all in here with me, you hear me?" said Saw.

Thugga's wicked laugh came over the phone. "Shit, I'ma make them crackas kill me," he said.

Saw didn't doubt that he would. But Thugga and Maine were his other ace in the hole. He needed them now more than ever before. He prayed that they'd be safe and take care of the business. Saw could just imagine all the secrets Lano was telling to the Feds. There was no way he could let those stories make it into the courtroom.

Saw kicked back on the bottom bunk of his cell and thought about when times were much simpler. Back when they first started in the game, and all they wanted was new clothes and a chain. Saw still remembered the day he, Lano, and Hood all bought their first cars from BT Auto Sales. They had dropped three box Chevys on blades. A smile crept across Saw's face at the memory, because couldn't nobody tell them nothing as they pulled off the lot back-to-back and flew down 7 Mile. The first place they went was up to Pershing High, so that they could post up and be seen by all the haters and sack-chasers.

Of all the cars Saw had bought, he had never gotten rid of his candy blue Caprice. It still sat in his mom's garage like his first pair of baby shoes.

Saw's relishing of the past was short-lived as reality struck him like a ton of bricks. His dopefiend cellmate had roared off a fart that vibrated the bunk, and the smell bounced off the wall down to Saw's nose and mouth.

His cellmate, an older black man, grunted, then drifted back into his light snore. Saw was pissed. Not at the old-timer, but at himself for being there in the first place. He thought about Wink for the first time since he'd been arrested, and he wondered how he'd done twenty years.

Chapter Forty-nine

Over a hundred bottles of champagne and liquor filled the tables Lano and his underlings took up at the King of Diamonds on West 8 Mile Road. Lano had weeded through those who he felt were loyal to him and the money he provided, versus those who were keeping up his name for snitching. He had surrounded himself with his closest men, and they were living it up, popping bottles and throwing money all night long at the beautiful strippers.

It was clear who was in power from the way niggas and bitches kept whispering into Lano's ear as he sat draped in gold chains, a pair of diamond-studded Buffs, and a busted-down Roly. Lano smiled continuously as people took turns kissing his ass. He was undoubtedly the man of the hour. Every stripper in the club wanted to be the one he picked to go home with, only because they knew Lano was a big trick and he was going to pay top dollar.

But not everybody in the club was feeling Lano that night. J-Rock was an east-side nigga from East Warren. He had a bag and had clout in the streets just as much as the next nigga. He was at the club with his niggas really just out to have a good time, but J-Rock wasn't enjoying himself because he couldn't take his eyes off Lano across the club.

J-Rock had known Saw and Hood from coming up in the game, and he'd heard about Lano snitching on them.

"Rock, what's up?" asked Heff, seeing the look on his friend's face.

"Look at that rat-ass nigga over there," said J-Rock as he took a swallow of his liquor.

Heff's eyes followed J-Rock's stare. Lano was laughing it up and throwing money at the two strippers dancing for him.

J-Rock despised snitches. In his mind, they had only one place in the game, and that was the cemetery. J-Rock slammed back the rest of his drink, then stood up heading for Lano's section.

Heff was like, *here we go with the bullshit*. But he was a solid nigga, so he fell behind J-Rock as they crossed the club. When they got to Lano's table, a couple of his men blocked J-Rock and Heff while looking back at Lano.

"It's cool," said Lano. He sat back against his seat in a dignified manner. "What's up?" he asked.

"It's fucked up you got them boys down there in the county like that. You know I fucks with Saw and Hood," said J-Rock.

"So what'chu saying?" asked Lano with his mouth twisted.

"I'm saying . . ." J-Rock went to pull the pistol from his pants, but one of Lano's men wrestled his hand down. Boom! The .40-cal erupted in J-Rock's pants, and the club went crazy.

Heff snatched a bottle from the table and cracked the nigga over the head who was still tussling with J-Rock. Boom! Boom! Two more shots licked off, followed by another succession from across the club. Boom! Boom! Boom!

The glass behind Lano's booth shattered as two of his men rushed him to the exit. People stormed out of the club and into the parking lot where more gunshots lit the night's sky.

Lano was thrown across the back seat of an Escalade, and Ricky stomped down on the gas. Bullets hit the hood of the truck as Ricky made a sharp turn onto 8 Mile Road. Ricky looked in the back seat at Lano, and he was laughing his ass off. "What the fuck you laughing at?" asked Ricky.

Lano sat up, smiling. "These bitch-niggas don't want it with me. Any nigga running they mouth, they gon' get the same thing."

J-Rock and Heff both had been slain in the shoot-out. For Lano it was a victory and a message that he still had shooters who wouldn't hesitate to get niggas together if they acted up.

Meanwhile, the Feds had been close by the club watching the shoot-out unfold in the parking lot. Two agents were assigned to keep tabs on Lano at all times because he was their star witness. Once the agents had seen that Lano was safely driven away from the club, they relaxed and stood down from intervening in the gun battle. For all they cared, the rest of them could kill each other.

Agent Hopskins was pulling out all the stops on successfully getting a conviction against Saw and Hood. Hopskins had paid Saw's baby momma Tammy a visit at her home in Eastpointe. He was good at deciphering when a woman was ready to jump ship on their recently locked partner. Hopskins had been secretly listening to Tammy's calls, and he'd pulled up all her texts between her and her friends. It was clear that Tammy was pissed with Saw for asking Sherise to marry him and also for not leaving her with any money when he went to jail.

Agent Hopskins saw an opportunity to turn Tammy against Saw, and he seized it. He gave her $20,000 to testify in front of the grand jury and promised another $20,000 when she testified at trial. Tammy, being the larceny-hearted bitch she was, accepted the money and terms without any hesitation.

Agent Hopskins smiled like the devil himself. He fed Tammy a script of lies she was to say. With her on the stand as Saw's child's mother, Hopskins was sure any jury would believe her story.

Chapter Fifty

Houston turned out to be a beautiful city for Thugga and Maine. The city had its own vibe that was Southern but not country-bama. Maine liked the women down in H-Town because they were fine and knew how to take care of a man. He had met a thick redbone with green eyes by the name of Jaquita. She was about her money, too. Jaquita owned a growing commercial cleaning service and moved pounds of weed on the side. Thugga had hooked up with her sister, Laquita, who had brown skin and was thick as hell with a sexy gapped-tooth smile.

Laquita owned a Southern eatery, which was where Thugga and Maine had met the sisters. The women of H-Town loved out-of-town niggas, especially if they were from big cities and chasing a bag. Thugga and Maine had been kicking it with the sisters every day since they'd met them. It was good having someone to show them around and put them up on game.

What Thugga liked the most about Houston was that the niggas down there stuck together and supported each other's grind, unlike in Detroit. Niggas were steadily trying to pull each other back down to the bottom in Detroit. Thugga told himself as he got his money up he would buy a crib down in H-Town and treat it like his second home.

The connect Saw had plugged them in with, Chelo, had enough bricks to pave all of downtown Houston. Chelo was a short, fat, but fly Mexican born in the United States. His family were originally from Mexico, but they had settled in Houston, where the men of the family set up a hub for the coke and heroin coming in from across the border.

Chelo was only 24 years old, but he'd had a hard-knock life, so he could pass for 40 easily. He had a mouthful of diamonds set in yellow gold, which he flashed at every opportunity. That was how the niggas showed their wealth in H-Town—by their grills and by their slabs (cars).

Chelo had a fleet of slabs, everything from old schools on eighty-fours and Vogues to Bentleys and Ferraris. He lived to get money and to shine. He'd promised Thugga and Maine that if they stayed with him, they'd be as big as Saw was.

Thugga and Maine had driven down to Houston with $200,000 in cop money. Chelo was letting them get each brick or $16,000 since they were coming to get them and driving them back. He told them that, from then on out, whatever they bought he'd front them the same number. It was a way to help them run up a bag a lot faster. Chelo even provided them with a cargo van equipped with vacuum-sealed compartments. There was a special combination of pumping the brakes and the AC controls to access the compartments. The secret stashes were foolproof and could hold up to fifty kilos each trip.

Thugga and Maine left H-Town with enough work to start a temp service. They were on in a major way, because they could easily let each brick go for $30,000. Ever since Big Meech and his brother Big T got knocked, the prices had gone up and had never come back down. The ticket for a brick was $36,000 firm, so Thugga and Maine would have niggas flocking to them with the low ticket they planned to put out there.

They had it all mapped out how they would take over the city, but there was one thing standing in their way, and that was Lano. As soon as they made it back to Detroit, Thugga and Maine set out on a mission to find Lano. They had given Saw their word. Plus, their own lives depended on it as well. Lano was capable of sinking everybody, and for that he had to go.

Thugga and Maine donned their all-black monkey suits and loaded up the choppers for a manhunt. The first place they went looking was the club on 7 Mile and Syracuse. When they pulled up behind the tinted windows of an Impala, niggas outside the club were nudging each other to check out the car driving slowly by. The black Impala looked like something the police would be in.

There was no sign of any of Lano's cars, but that didn't mean he wasn't inside the club. Maine did a U-turn down at the end of the block and came back up the one-way at full speed. He got the reaction he wanted out of the niggas posted outside when they all took off running in opposite directions.

Thugga and Maine bailed out of the car at the curb with AKs in hand. There was no one to stop them from going inside the club, so Maine snatched the door open wide and led the way in.

Ricky was behind the bar watching UFC when Thugga raised his AK to his chest. "Where that nigga Lano?"

"He ain't here," said Ricky with fear in his eyes.

Maine checked the rest of the club, but Ricky was the only one inside. "Ain't nobody back there," Maine informed him.

Thugga looked back at Ricky and opened fire, tearing flesh from his chest and neck. Lakaa! Lakaa! Lakaa!

Lano would get their message. He was next.

Chapter Fifty-one

Every year around the end of the summer there was a big party at Atkinson Park across from the projects. This year was no different as the sack-chasers were out like they'd been deployed by the National Guard. Their mission: to catch a balling-ass nigga.

Luxury cars and tricked-out old schools wrapped around the square mile of the park, while bumper-to-bumper traffic inched by the party. People had been out at the park since the afternoon, some grilling while most drank and talked shit. There was a pick-up basketball game and a dice game going down as well.

As the sun went down, the older folks started packing up their things and heading home. They had been living in the hood long enough to know that the yearly picnic never ended on a peaceful note. Every year some fools started shooting.

Thugga and Maine were out on the prowl in search of Lano. The nigga had been missing in action since they got back from Houston. Thugga wanted to kill him so bad it made his dick hard just thinking about it.

"Where you at, bitch?" Thugga mumbled over the music. His eyes scanned the faces standing on the sidewalk as Maine crept along the side street, Hillsdale.

Atkinson Park was still jumping, so Thugga hoped to spot Lano somewhere in the mix because he knew how much he liked to show off and stunt.

"Right here, right here," said Thugga as he bailed out of the car with his AK-47 on full display.

Screams from a group of chicks walking by alerted everyone that something was about to go down. Thugga had broken into a sprint. He'd locked eyes on JC and Twan posted up by the basketball court. They were kicking it with two chicks when the panic happened. Twan saw the masked gunmen coming straight for them, so he grabbed one of the females and spun her around to catch the first bullets meant for him. Kaa! Kaaaa! Kaaaa!

Twan pushed the chick toward the gunfire and tried to make a run for it, but Thugga cut him down in his tracks with a hail of gunfire. Kaaaa! Kaaaa!

Twan grimaced on his way down as he crumbled to the center of the basketball court. The park had cleared out. Thugga walked over to Twan and let the rest of the fifty-round clip go into his back and head. He was pissed that JC's little bitch ass had slipped away, so Twan would pay for the both of them.

Thugga and Maine made their getaway in the blue Malibu they had stolen earlier. They switched cars and stayed on the hunt for Lano. It was on sight with him or any nigga who was a part of his circle. Twan was one of Lano's runners who moved a lot of work out of town. He and JC were best friends.

The way Thugga saw it was that he and Maine were crippling Lano's operation with every member of his crew they killed, and eventually they were going to smoke him out of whatever hole he was hiding in.

But Lano hadn't been hiding from anyone. He didn't even know that Thugga and Maine were back in the city and were gunning for his head. Special Agent Hopskins had two agents pick Lano up at his ranch the morning after the shoot-out happened at the King of Diamonds. Agent Hopskins had told Lano that he didn't care what he did in the streets, so long as it didn't jeopardize his investigation.

"I'm keeping you under watch at least until after the grand jury," said Agent Hopskins.

Lano was pissed because he had an operation to run in the streets. "Ain't nothing gon' happen to me."

Agent Hopskins cut Lano off. "It's nonnegotiable. You can either stay here, or you can go sit in lock-up with the rest of 'em."

Lano weighed his options, which were either stay put inside the hotel room the agents had him stashed in, or go sit inside of the Wayne County Jail. Needless to say, he picked the first option. The suite at the Hilton wasn't all that bad. Lano was sure he could stick it out.

Lano settled into his rat hole and called his man Chip. Chip was an up-and-coming boss in the game, and Lano had taken a liking to him because Chip knew how to stack his paper. He wasn't like the rest of the niggas who worked for Lano who spent their profits no sooner than they came in. Chip reminded Lano of himself, because he was into having a bankroll versus anything else.

Lano had called Chip and given him the rundown on how he wanted him to run the show in his absence. Chip stepped up and said that he'd hold down the fort, but he also laced Lano up about Ricky and Twan being killed in the past two days.

Lano could only hold one group of niggas responsible. He told himself that it had to be them East Warren niggas coming back about J-Rock and Heff. "Just keep everybody together," Lano told Chip.

"I got'chu, boss," said Chip.

Chapter Fifty-two

"Mail call! Coming down!" yelled the CO from the mouth of D block. His keys could be heard at his side as he stopped at the cell doors issuing mail to the men who'd been lucky enough to get something from the outside world.

CO Edinger stopped in front of Wink's cell and looked at the face tag on the door, then at Sharky, who was at the door waiting.

"You's an ugly son of a bitch," laughed CO Edinger. He was the third generation of Edingers at USP, Lewisburg.

Sharky just glared at the cracker like, *if this door weren't between us, I'd beat shit down ya leg.*

A white manila envelope fought to come underneath the door until the CO had enough sense to open the food slot and pass it through. "It's for you," said Sharky, handing over the parcel to Wink. Sharky climbed up on his rack and put his MP3 on random. For him the day was over with.

Wink tore into the envelope and removed the treasures he'd been patiently waiting for. Saw hadn't forgotten to send him all the investigative notes from his case. It was all there in black and white how the Feds withheld Willie's history of lying from his defense. It was a clear Brady violation, and no court in America could deny not vacating his convictions.

"Thank you," whispered Wink as he closed his eyes with the papers still in his grasp. He had waited over twenty years for that one moment, and it had arrived. For he was about to be vindicated.

Wink felt the need to write Saw and thank him for holding true to his word. He had no idea that Saw was lying in a cell the same size as the one that confined him and that he was also now fighting for his own life.

The prison was still on lockdown since the murders, but word had been circulating on inmate.com that the warden was talking about letting them come up next week. Wink sure hoped so, because he needed to rush to the law library and whip up his new emergency appeal.

As Wink began penning Saw's kite, the sounds of shower shoes scratching against the floor let Wink know that a fight was taking place somewhere close by. The thud of bodies bumping against the metal walls told Wink that it was his two next door neighbors going at it.

"You know you want this dick!" It was D.C. Mike trying to wrestle the asshole of the young light-skinned nigga the guards had put in with him the night before.

It was crazy that such occurrences had become normal to Wink over the past twenty-plus years.

Chapter Fifty-three

The women inside Top-Notch hair salon had all ceased their midday gossip and were standing under the plasma TV mounted in the waiting area. One of the stylists, Karen, stood with her arm wrapped around Denise for support as they watched the live news conference on Channel 4. Federal Prosecutor Matthew Schneider stood at the lectern, flanked by Detroit's mayor, Mike Duggan.

There was a photo of Saw, Hood, and others posted on the screen as the prosecutor explained to the public that a federal grand jury had just returned an eleven-count indictment against the men shown on their screens.

The news conference was being held on the steps outside the federal courthouse. The cameras caught a picture of everyone who was said to have testified before the grand jury. Lano came walking out the glass doors dressed in a blue Armani suite. He was ushered to an awaiting Lincoln by a host of agents.

"Snitchin' bitch," said Denise.

Moments later, Tammy pushed through the glass doors of the federal building. She flipped her hair back and put her shades over her eyes.

"Isn't that one of Saw's baby mommas?" asked Karen.

"Yeah, that's Tammy's trifling ass," confirmed Denise as she watched Tammy cross the street out of view of the cameras. Denise and the crowd of women dispersed from the front of the TV. Everybody was saying something to Denise to try to lift her spirits because many of the women had lost loved ones to either the penitentiary or the graveyard.

Seeing her son plastered all over TV had pissed Denise off, because she knew that not everything they were claiming Saw had done was the truth. She had known Saw was not an angel, but he was neither the monster that they portrayed him to be.

Denise grabbed her purse and left the shop for the rest of the day. There was no way she was about to sit around and watch her son be thrown to the wolves by the very people he'd helped.

Denise took out her earrings as she pulled up to Tammy's house in Eastpointe. *This bitch done lost her mind if she think I'm finna watch her help put my son away.*

Tammy's Lexus truck was parked in the drive-way, indicating that she was home. Denise pulled her hair back into a ponytail, then got out and rang the doorbell. Tammy came to the door but left the screen between them. She and Denise never did really like one another, so she wondered why Denise had pulled up to her domain unannounced.

"Yes?" said Tammy, rolling her eyes all over Denise.

"Girl, you betta open this damn door up," snapped Denise.

Tammy sucked her teeth and went against her better judgment by unlocking the screen door. Denise pushed inside the house and rushed Tammy into the wall by her throat.

"Get the fuck off me!" yelled Tammy as she struggled for her next breath. She was trying her best to free herself.

Denise choked her with one hand while she beat her face in with the other hand. "Bitch. Bitch," said Denise with each landed blow. "Bitch. Bitch."

Tammy's cousin, Rachel, came running from the back of the house. She grabbed at Denise's shoulder, but Denise spun around and unearthed a neon orange box cutter from her bosom. "Bitch, I'll kill you," warned Denise.

Rachel backed away, realizing that whatever reason she was beating Tammy's ass was none of her business.

Denise turned back to Tammy as she lay against the wall struggling to breathe. "You listen to me," said Denise. She reached down and grabbed Tammy's hair into a fist. "Before I let your stinking ass help bury my son, I'll kill you myself. If I find out that you so much as talk to the Feds again, they gonna find yo' ass facedown floating in the river. Do I make myself clear?" growled Denise.

"Yes," whimpered Tammy.

"Good," said Denise. She cut a chunk of weave from Tammy's head, then tossed it at her face on her way out of the house. Denise had meant what she told Tammy. She was still very much connected to the streets and wouldn't hesitate to have Tammy touched if it meant Saw's freedom.

Denise got in her car and drove straight to see her old, crazy uncle, Du'shan. Her uncle was a hit man from back in the day. He'd done twenty-five years in Jackson State Penitentiary on a murder that he later beat at the appeal level. He'd come home still crazy as he was before he'd gone to prison. When he came home, Denise had thrown him a party and helped him get on his feet. When she asked her uncle what he needed, he told her two .45s and a box of shells. That was his only request because that was all he needed to play his role in the game.

Denise still had blessed him with some money and a car, but Du'shan was going to always be a hit man. He came home, and the first people he focused on killing were the snitches who'd sent him to prison. He hated snitches because he was from the old school, where snitching was the worst thing a man could ever do. He hated the new generation because all they knew how to do was try to snitch their way out of trouble.

When Denise pulled up on Du'shan, he was sitting behind the screened-in porch of his corner house on Eureka Street. He had an old towel spread across his lap and a can of WD-40 next to him as he cleaned his arsenal of assault rifles.

"Hey, baby girl," said Du'shan as Denise opened the screen to the porch. "How's my favorite niece?"

Denise was still fuming about Tammy and Lano. Du'shan set aside the SKS he'd been oiling, stood up, and walked over to the seat Denise had taken.

"Now you know I don't get involved in no domestic violence, because all my sisters and they kids call me to go 'round there because they nigga done went upside they head. Then a day later they back with the same nigga. Nah."

"It's not that, Unc. It's Saw," said Denise.

"What's wrong with my nephew?"

Denise filled him in on what was going on and how she feared that Saw would get a lot of time. But Du'shan told her not to worry about it and that he would take care of it. Saw was family, and Du'shan wasn't about to let anybody send him off to prison on account of snitching, not if he had anything to do with it.

***

Lano had been freed from his lockdown status of the hotel room because he had testified before the grand jury. He didn't spare any details either while testifying. He wanted Hood and Saw to be put away forever so that he'd never have to come face-to-face with them again. He feared them, but he feared the Feds a lot more.

The club on 7 Mile and Syracuse had yellow crime tape still wrapped around the entrances from Ricky's murder. The police had shut the club down because of all the shooting that kept happening. So Chip opened up another club on Moenart and 7 Mile right beside BB's Diner. Chip had done a good job of keeping the profits rolling in Lano's absence. And he'd kept everyone alive since Twan had been killed.

Lano couldn't have been any happier with the way Chip had handled the business. Chip was showing Lano around the new club, which had a second floor that was an apartment. The downstairs had a bar and two large pool tables. It was a step up from the old club.

"You did well," said Lano.

But he was ready to resume his seat on the throne. His first order of business was to settle the beef between him and the East Warren niggas. Lano was only about making money, and if he could avoid a war in the streets, he would. He sent

Chip over to East Warren with a peace offering of $100,000, but the niggas of J-Rock and Heff rejected it at the door. They wanted Lano's head. Fuck him and all the money he had, because he was two things they weren't: a coward and a rat.

Their rejection of the money was unnerving for Lano because he'd know East Warren to have some real shooters, and he doubted that they'd stop at nothing until he was dead. So Lano did the only thing that he figured would save his life. He called Special Agent Hopskins and put the Feds on the East Warren crew. He told Hopskins that they were threatening to kill him because of his cooperation against Saw and Hood.

Lano knew that this would make Agent Hopskins jump to it, because the Feds needed him to stay alive until the trial. That was how Lano was playing the game. If he feared a nigga, and he couldn't buy him off with money, then he was putting the Feds on his trail.

Chapter Fifty-four

Ms. Raben had been to see about Saw at the Wayne County Jail. She hated that she had to be the bearer of bad news, but that was all she had for him as she told him everything that Lano had testified to before the grand jury. The conspiracy charges were the least of Saw's worries. Lano had told the Feds about all the murders Saw and Hood committed and ordered. They were looking at multiple life sentences.

Before Ms. Raben left, she gave Saw a letter she'd received at her office from Wink. Saw opened the letter as he got back to his cell. He lay across his bunk and kicked off his slippers.

> *Saw,*
> *What's the word with you? I got your package with all the notes we talked about. You just don't know how much of a game changer this is going to be. I can't say thank you enough! We're still behind these doors, but as soon as we come up, I'm on you with the testing forms from the DNA.*

I was just getting at you, my guy, to let you know that that was a touchdown. Get at me when you can. And good looking out again. Real niggas do real things.
Wink

Saw was happy at least one of them had gotten some good news. He hadn't enclosed a letter to Wink with the package he'd sent him because he didn't want Wink to know that he was locked up. He didn't know why it mattered, but he just didn't want Wink to know. Saw figured he would've been out by then, but from the looks of it, he was in it for the long haul. He hadn't heard from Maine and Thugga, but he told himself that they were loyal and that they would handle up.

Saw's racing thoughts were disturbed by the clicking of his door lock. He stuck his head out of the cell, and the female deputy told him that he had a visitor waiting.

Sherise stood behind the steel barrier separating Saw from the visitor's side. He looked her over through the slender plexiglass. Her eyes were swollen and red from crying, and her hair was unkempt.

"Saw," she cried and put her hand up to the glass.

"I'm here, baby. Talk to me," said Saw, placing his hand on the glass to match Sherise's.

She'd seen the news conference, and the streets were saying that Saw and Hood would never walk the streets again.

"Why is this happening to us?" cried Sherise.

Saw wished he had the answer. He had been wondering the same thing. How had his life taken a drastic turn? He felt bad, but he knew that he had to be strong for Sherise.

"They're saying that you're never coming home," said Sherise.

"Who's saying that?" asked Saw.

"The news. And everybody in the hood," said Sherise, wiping her tears.

"They're saying that because that's what they want to see happen to me. But ain't one of 'em the judge of me. Sherise, I need you to believe in your heart that I'ma walk outta here. Do you believe that?"

Sherise looked down. "I want to, but . . ."

"Ain't no but's. I need you to believe that I'm coming home to you."

Sherise wiped her face and looked up at Saw. The only thing that she could think about was her mother going through hell trying to carry on a prison marriage.

"You better come home to me," was all Sherise said.

And that was all Saw needed to give him the strength to keep believing himself that he would rise above whatever charges the Feds and Lano cooked up.

Chapter Fifty-five

Hood was going through the same thing as Saw. His lawyer had been to see him with the news about Lano. The only thing Hood could see were all the bodies that he'd dropped coming up in the game. Those were his skeletons in the closet, and they'd come back to haunt him. Hood was starting to be extra paranoid about everything and everyone around him. His lawyer had told him not to talk about his case to anyone, but Hood had taken it a step further.

He drew up an affidavit and made several copies of it for the other inmates living in the pod with him to sign, which said that at no time did he discuss his case or personal life with them. It was to be his insurance later down the road, should any of them try to jump on his case and come to court on him.

Everyone had signed their affidavits except his cellmate, which was a mistake on his part. Hood already didn't care for the nigga, because he sounded like those crackers from out there in Port

Huron, and he was always on some secret squir-
rel shit, walking around with a yellow pad and a
pencil, writing down the conversations around the
pod.

Hood waited until it was lockdown time so
the nigga couldn't run. He snatched the nigga
off the top bunk by his ankles, then ripped his shirt
clean off his back. The man had a thin black wire
taped at the center of his chest. He started yelling
and screaming some code words, for his cover had
been blown.

Hood was enraged that the nigga would even
have the balls to try him like that. He heard the
sound of keys responding and knew that they'd
put him in the hole anyway, so he figured he might
as well go for a good enough reason. He started
beating the sleeves off the nigga until the deputies
had to pull him off the nigga.

As Hood lay in the hole with nothing but the
beige brick walls, lots of time, and his thoughts, he
wondered how he'd gone from sugar to shit seem-
ingly overnight. They had the world in the palm
of their hands, young millionaires. Now though it
was a trial to see who would stand tall in the paint.

Hood hoped Saw was holding up. He knew that
Saw was as solid as the bricks inside his cell, but

then he had snaked Saw by getting with Karmesha behind his back. In the game, Hood had known that niggas nowadays looked for any excuse to snitch, so if Saw were looking for one, he sure didn't have to look far.

Hood was beginning to regret ever crossing those boundaries with Karmesha. She'd proven not to be worth the cost of his friendship with Saw. She'd come to court that one time and had been missing in action ever since.

What Hood didn't know about Karmesha was that she could never be wife material and hold him down in his times of need. Her love was one-sided and only benefited her. Saw had known this about her, which was why he never entertained the thought of them ever seriously being together. Hood had to live with the fact that he'd traded his life-long friendship with Saw for a chick who didn't love either one of them.

Hood didn't have a family to call his own. His moms had died in a car crash, and his father was a heroin addict. Hood had been raised by the streets. He lived with his aunt growing up, but she'd married and moved to Florida when he was 12, leaving Hood to fend for himself. Saw and Lano were the closest thing he'd had to a family. When Hood was hungry, either Saw or Lano would sneak food out of the house so Hood would have something to eat.

And in the winter months, Saw would sneak Hood into the house to save him from a freezing night of sleeping in the abandoned houses he'd been living in that had no heat.

Denise had seen Hood sleeping at her house plenty of times, but she never said anything to Saw about it. She knew Hood's story, and she liked him as much as her son did, so Hood was always welcome inside her home.

Hood lay on the cold green mattress on the floor of his cell in the hole. He thought back to his days of coming up poor without a family. Karmesha, he'd thought, would fill that void. Hood had let her into his world, opened himself up to her like he'd never done before with another woman, and all he felt was an empty hole in his heart.

Meanwhile, Karmesha was living her best life and not bothering herself with the woes of Hood or Saw. *Such is life,* was her attitude toward their current situation. Karmesha was older than Hood and Saw, and she'd been in the game much longer, so they weren't the first two ballers she'd sunken her claws into. She'd watched many niggas rise only to fall. That was the game. Her position was to enjoy the ride, then move on to something new when that ride was over and done with.

In her eyes, Hood and Saw's run in the game was over, and she didn't do jail for nobody. Right after she heard the judge deny Hood's bond, it was over with. She drove out to his crib and cleared out the safe where he kept his jewelry and spending money. Karmesha hawked the jewelry for a nice sum, and she was having the time of her life trying to spend the money. She and Kim shopped for new designer bags in Manhattan, New York. They were living it up, and Karmesha hadn't thought about Hood's ass.

Chapter Fifty-six

Du'shan was a sneaky nigga by nature. His beady black eyes always stayed moving, which was why he kept dark shades on to conceal his eyes. He was a loner and a real killer by fate. Du'shan had been killing people since he was a kid growing up in the sixties on Detroit's east side. He used to work for this old hustler by the name of Maurice, running numbers. But numbers wasn't the only thing that Maurice was into running. He had a strong hand in the heroin trade at that time. His dope was some of the best in the city, and he was a very rich man. But he kept getting robbed.

There was a crew of deadly robberies during that time, and none of Maurice's men could get close to them. Du'shan had been in the back room sorting his numbers when he heard old Maurice complaining about the robbers to one of his men.

"I'll do it," said Du'shan.

Maurice and his counterpart looked at Du'shan, then laughed. But Du'shan wasn't dismayed. He stood there with a straight face until they had stopped laughing.

"I can handle it for you," said Du'shan.

Maurice regarded Du'shan for a moment. He'd met a lot of killers in his time, and he'd seen that look in Du'shan's young eyes. "You take care of this, son, and I'ma pay you ten thousand," said Maurice.

Du'shan had climbed underneath the target's car at night, and he lay there until the sun came up the next morning. The guy's name was Bam, a certified jack boy. If he and his crew learned that a nigga was touching major money, best believe they were coming.

But Bam had made the mistake of shitting where he ate. He was a robber by trade, but he was also a family man whenever he wasn't in the streets jacking people. Every morning he liked to drive his two daughters to school.

When he came out of the house that morning and rounded the hood of the gold Caddy he drove, Du'shan rolled from underneath the driver side and filled him with all six shots from the black .38 Special Maurice had given him for the hit.

Du'shan stood and met eyes with Bam's two daughters, who were seated in the car. They broke into crying fits at the sight of their daddy getting shot. Du'shan just turned and ran down the side of the house and slipped away from the scene.

That was his first hit. He'd lost count of how many he'd done in between. Du'shan had a thirst to kill. The money he was paid to kill was just an added bonus. He had this thing where he liked to do a drive-by so he could meet eyes with his victim days before he would kill them. It was like soul gazing, only his victims had no idea that they were being stalked.

Such was the case with Lano. He had no idea that the old bum walking past the club was really one of Detroit's most notorious hit men. Du'shan stumbled past the club sipping from a pint of Bumpy Face. He was dressed in a thick, worn winter coat and a skully rolled up high like a wino. From behind the dark shades he wore, Du'shan looked dead into Lano's eyes as he stood in the center of about twenty niggas in front of their club on Moenart and 7 Mile.

Du'shan flashed a sucka's grin, but no one paid him any mind. He stumbled on, satisfied that he'd sealed his date with death soon. Du'shan fantasized about killing Lano. He wanted him to have that same smile on his face when he got the drop on him. *Yeah, you just keep that same energy when I run down on ya ass.*

Chapter Fifty-seven

Saw and Hood were taken back to court so they could be arraigned on the new superseding indictment. The courtroom was packed to standing room only as news reporters occupied the majority of the benches. The story had gained national attention, so the case was expected to be covered by the news throughout the trial.

Denise smiled and waved at Saw, then at Hood. She blew them a kiss and mouthed the words, "Y'all stay strong."

Sherise was seated beside Denise. She looked good, but Saw could see the stress in her face. She pulled back a weak smile and mouthed the words, "I love you."

"I love you too," Saw found himself saying in a low voice. It was the first time he'd ever told Sherise that he loved her, but it was true. He did love her, and he had loved her for a long time. It was just crazy that he had to be in the middle of fighting for his life before he could tell her how he really felt.

The court date was just a formality. The prosecutor read the indictment into the record, and Judge Grand denied Saw's and Hood's requests for bail.

"I guess I'll see you at trial," said Hood to Saw.

"Yeah, that's what it's looking like," said Saw.

Hood wanted to try to talk to Saw as they were put back into the holding cell awaiting transport back to the county jails that held them. But Hood just couldn't find the right words to say. "I'm sorry" didn't seem sufficient enough, so they sat in silence.

Saw's mind was turning a million miles per second. He needed Thugga and Maine to handle up, and fast, because their trial had been scheduled to start in less than seventy days. Saw wasn't thinking about the situation with Hood and Karmesha anymore. They had both betrayed him, and as far as he was concerned, that was spilled milk. He was focused on coming up from under the murders Lano had put on them.

Hood was the first to be called by the Marshals to leave. St. Clair County was there to get him. He dreaded going back to that jail in particular because he was still in the hole for having whooped the snitch in his cell.

"I'ma holla at you, my nigga," said Hood on his way out.

Saw gave him a simple nod as the gate slammed shut. It pained Hood's heart that Saw really wasn't fucking with him, but he told himself that he'd been the cause of it.

Chapter Fifty-eight

Taquana winced at the ankle monitor around her left leg because it was ugly and it was cramping her style. She was back in the Feds' good graces after testifying again before the grand jury. Judge Grand had reinstated her bond, but with the condition of her wearing a GPS tether. She was restricted from leaving her home in Sherwood Forest for any reason without the approval of the probation department. Being at home sure beat the hell out of being stuck in a jail cell, but Taquana still found herself going stir crazy.

She had remembered there was a time when Slim was on tether for violating his probation. Slim was never at home though, because he would wrap his tether with aluminum foil several times, which blocked the GPS signal. And he had the house phone forwarded to his cell phone in case they called to check on him.

Taquana wrapped her tether just as she'd watched Slim do a hundred times, and she was in traffic. The club was calling her name, so she hit up a new club called Clout downtown. She wanted the streets to know that she was back like she never left, so she flossed in Slim's platinum Phantom Drophead. She had her girl April riding shotgun. When they pulled up to the club, everyone standing outside in line turned and watched as Taquana stopped at valet parking and as she and April walked straight into the club. They were greeted with bottle service and shown to the best section in VIP.

The club was modern and sleek. The waitresses wore next to nothing, but remained sexy and classy at the same time. There were three bars on the lower level with another two bars on the upper level.

Taquana and April settled into their seats and sipped the peach Cîroc they'd ordered. "This is nice," April said as she looked around the club.

"Yes," agreed Taquana. And it was just the night out she needed.

Across the club, lurking in the shadows, were Thugga and Maine. They'd been stalking all the clubs in hopes of Lano showing up, because they knew how much he liked to club. But they had spotted Taquana instead. Maine tapped Thugga and jerked his head over at Taquana. She'd been missing in action, but she was still on their to-do list.

"Look at the fleas on Fluffy," said Thugga as he downed the rest of his Hennessy. There she was, sitting on their plate. Taquana was so busy enjoying herself that she hadn't even noticed Thugga and Maine slip out of the club.

Thugga and Maine parked across the street from the club and watched the front door. A couple of hours passed, and finally people started coming out of the club. Taquana and April emerged hand in hand. They were tipsy and laughing at each other. They stumbled for the valet, totally oblivious to the two masked gunmen crossing the street in full pursuit of them.

Thugga took aim at Taquana as he neared the curb. Kaaa! Kaaa! Kaaa! Taquana's body shook violently, and she staggered away from April to the velvet rope around the door of the club. Thugga took pleasure in the fear of death wide in Taquana's eyes as she fought to stay on her feet.

Thugga raised the AK-47 to her stomach and unleashed a series of rounds, twisting and turning Taquana's body with every bullet. She spun to the ground, and Thugga stood over her, emptying the remainder of his clip into her skull.

Maine had chased April out to the middle of the street, where she suffered a death similar to Taquana's. Neither of them would have the luxury of an open casket. Their heads had been shredded beyond recognition. The way Thugga and Maine saw it, all rats deserved to die in that fashion.

Chapter Fifty-nine

When the homicide detectives made it to the murder scene at club Clout, the first thing that the lead detective noticed was the GPS tether around the victim's ankle. Before he got there, someone had removed the foil from the monitor, so the signal had pinged to the federal authorities, signaling that Taquana had violated her tether.

Within minutes the FBI was on the scene. One of the agents phoned Agent Hopskins at home to inform him of Taquana's death. They were able to ID her from her driver's license found inside her clutch.

Agent Hopskins was pissed because he had gone against his better judgment in having Taquana's bail reinstated. He knew she was trouble from her fleeing, and now she was dead because she'd tampered with her tether.

This prompted Agent Hopskins to have Lano brought into custody. He was to remain under the watch of two agents twenty-four hours a day until after he testified at trial. Hopskins could tell from the way Taquana had been slain that someone wanted her dead, and he didn't doubt that those same people wanted Lano dead as well.

Agent Hopskins had a hunch who was behind Taquana's murder, and he'd thought he would send them a message loud and clear.

The sound of the cell door slamming against the wall jerked Saw from his sleep. Before he could get his bearings, a storm of deputies adorned in SORT gear snatched him out of bed, rag dolling him to his feet.

Saw was stripped naked right there, and the deputies found the cell phone stuffed down in his briefs. That was exactly what they'd come for—the cell phone. Agent Hopskins ordered that Saw's cell be torn apart, and that he be put in the hole to have zero contact.

Saw was thrown in an empty, dark cell with nothing but his briefs on. The toilet was clogged with days' old shit and piss, and the steel frame where his mattress was to go was rusted and filled with crumbs.

Saw felt like he was trapped inside a bad nightmare. He hadn't any idea why he'd been thrown in the hole or how long he'd be in there. None of the deputies would stop and talk to him during their rounds. He could only hope that Ms. Raben or Mr. Beres would check on him soon.

Chapter Sixty

Thugga and Maine weren't letting up on the pressure. They hadn't seen any signs of Lano, but they didn't let that stop them from trying to smoke him out of his rat hole.

Chip had become Thugga and Maine's focal point since he was handling all of Lano's money and managing their street team. Chip was much like Lano in the sense that he didn't want any problems. He was a soft nigga by nature who always tried to disarm people with his smile. They called him Chip because one of his front teeth was chipped. He was a fail nigga with a pea-sized head and bugged eyes.

Killing Chip would mean that Lano's crew would be without a leader to feed them. Thugga and Maine were still wanting to build their own team, so getting Chip out of the way would have niggas wanting to be down with them.

Maine had walked inside of Broadway's men's clothing store right off Gratiot Avenue. Clutched at his side was a .40-cal that had gone unnoticed until he raised the barrel to Chip's head as he stood at the register paying for a new suit.

The woman standing next to Chip screamed, but the roar of the Glock drowned out her frantic screams. Boom! Boom!

Maine had fed Chip two dome shots through his temple, knocking his brains all over the screaming woman. Maine walked out as if nothing had happened, while Chip lay dead in a growing pool of blood and brain matter.

Thugga and Maine were playing for keeps. They knew that if anybody could run the city, it was them, because they were about their issue before anything else. They put in their own work and never had any smut on their names as far as them messing with the police. Niggas were going to either get in line or be outlined in chalk. It didn't make any difference to Thugga and Maine who they had to kill. They were set on taking over the city.

They just had to find Lano's snitchin' ass. They knew Saw and Hood were counting on them to handle up, and neither of them wanted to let them down. Besides that, Lano had their names tied up in over a dozen hits, and the Feds had them on the indictment as enforcers. So finding Lano was Thugga and Maine's number one priority.

Chapter Sixty-one

Special Agent Hopskins examined the cell re-
cords and texts sent and received on the phone
found in Saw's cell. It was clear that Saw had been
communicating with Thugga and Maine. But what
Hopskins didn't understand was why none of his
agents had filed for a warrant that would allow
the Feds to track Thugga's and Maine's locations
through the GPS embedded in their phones. They
were wanted men, and for murder.

Agent Hopskins was frustrated that he had to
do everything himself if he wanted it done right.
He got the warrants drawn up, then signed by a
duty judge. Hopskins called an emergency meeting
on the ninth floor of the federal building. The
only ones allowed in the room were highly skilled
marksmen who had the necessary skills to take
down extremely dangerous people like Maine and
Thugga.

Agent Hopskins kept the meeting short as a
mugshot of Maine and Thugga shone against
the white projector screen. "These men are to be

considered armed and dangerous, so deadly force has been authorized. We're all going home to our families tonight. Do I make myself clear?" asked Agent Hopskins.

No one said anything in response. They had their orders.

"All right, let's move out," said Hopskins.

It was close to midnight when the team of agents piled into their caravan of vehicles set for the designation pinging on the GPS locator that Agent Hopskins held in his hand.

Thugga and Maine had taken over the Alderwood Apartments on the corner of 7 Mile and Outer Drive. It was a massive high-rise that sat off a set of railroad tracks. Back in the day the apartments were held in high regard, but then the crack era happened, and the building had changed into The Carter, which was named after the crack apartments in the movie *New Jack City*.

Thugga and Maine were the latest drug dealers to stake claim to the million-dollar-a-day operation. They were holed up in an apartment on the sixth floor, where camera monitors decorated the living room. They had an angel at every entrance and hallway of the apartments. They had seen their faces flash across *Crime Stoppers* enough to know that they were hot with the Feds, so they'd decided to stay put until Lano surfaced again.

Thugga was seated in the front room, smoking a blunt while playing *Madden*. Maine had dozed off with his AK-47 and phone in his lap. They'd been taking turns napping, because they were on high alert, plus they had to stand on their money, which was coming in nonstop.

Thugga sat up to thumb the ash from his blunt, and he saw a sea of black helmets rushing up the staircase. At first he didn't want to believe his eyes, but they were coming.

"Nigga, get up!" yelled Thugga, hitting Maine's leg.

Maine jumped up with his AK-47, looking half crazy because he was still sleepy. Thugga was slapping a clip into the ass of his fully automatic AR-15.

"The Feds is coming!" yelled Thugga, sliding into his black vest.

Maine witnessed the sea of black helmets climbing the fourth-floor staircase. Not another word was exchanged between him and Thugga. They hit the door and went in opposite directions. It was all part of the plan: never get caught together. They hoped at least one of them would get away while the other one shot it out to the death. Thugga and Maine were both willing to die for each other, and they'd vowed never to be taken alive. They'd done too much dirt, so a life sentence was the only thing that they could expect if captured.

As Maine was running down the hall, he heard the drumming cadence of the agents' gear and boots. They had made it onto the sixth floor and were headed in his direction. *Damn*, thought Maine as he skidded to a halt. He turned to the apartment door he was in front of and kicked in the door. A woman's scream echoed from inside the apartment.

"Freeze!" ordered an agent. Then he opened fire as Maine rushed inside the apartment. Boom! Boom!

Wood from the frame of the door splintered from the impact of the two missed bullets intended for Maine. The team of agents lowered their stance as they crept toward the open door of the apartment. It was silent, and then a crackle came over the radio.

"Officer down! I repeat, officer down!"

The sound of gunshots rang out somewhere downstairs.

I'll kill this bitch!" warned Maine. He had taken the woman and her small daughter hostage. He held them both in front of him as human shields.

"No one has to die! Just put down your weapon, and show us your hands!" said the front agent.

Maine responded by letting off a blast of gunfire. The bullets tore through the cheap walls, nearly hitting two of the six agents.

"Stay back!" ordered Maine. He had pushed the woman and her daughter into the bedroom. Maine snatched the sheets from the bed and began tying them together. He eyed the window overlooking the railroad tracks. He wasn't about to let them take him in.

Maine let go another series of shots. "Stay back!" he warned. He quickly tied the sheet around the base of the bed frame and moved over to the window.

"Again, sir, no one has to die here tonight," said one of the agents. His voice was much closer, and Maine could tell that he was inside the apartment.

He panicked and tore through the walls with his AK-47. Laaka! Laaka! Laaka!

A thick cloud of gun smoke hung in the air of the bedroom, and the walls looked like Swiss cheese. The woman held her daughter close to her chest as she prayed with her eyes closed. The agents had cowered into corners of the apartment, signaling to each other to get ready. They were lying when they'd said no one had to die. They had orders to use deadly force, and that was what they intended to do.

The front agent gave the signal to move in, and the team of agents all rushed into the bedroom guns at the ready, but the only thing they found was the woman and her daughter and the sheet hanging out the window. The front agent peered down into the darkness, but Maine had vanished into the night. *Motherfucker!* The team of agents was supposed to be the best in the department, but now they had to tell Agent Hopskins and the powers that be how they'd allowed two wanted killers to escape.

Thugga had made it away from the apartments after a brief shoot-out he had with three agents standing guard on the first floor near the entrance. Thugga had killed one agent and wounded the other two agents as they cowered for cover.

He and Maine knew to meet at the crib on Barlow. It was their safe house that no one except them knew about. It was a simple ranch-style brick house with a two-car garage. Whenever they went to the house, they would be behind tinted windows and would pull straight into the garage.

Thugga was waiting in the living room, smoking a Newport. He'd heard Maine pull into the garage and was thankful that his crime partner had made it out safely. They had been in some shoot-outs before, but none like that.

Maine walked into the living room smiling. He reached for the pack of Newports sitting on the coffee table and fished one out. "Fuck wrong with you?" he asked, putting the cigarette in his mouth and lighting it.

"You got ya phone on you?" asked Thugga.

Maine patted himself and thought back to the apartments. "Nah, it must've fallen or something," said Maine.

"That's how they knew where we was at. They tracked ya phone."

"You think so?" Maine took a pull off the cigarette. He had a quizzical look on his face.

"How else did they know where to find us? I kept telling you to get another phone," said Thugga.

"That's the only number Saw got though," said Maine.

Thugga drew a deep breath and sighed heavily. The Feds were hot on their trail, and he didn't know if it would be wise for him and Maine to keep on the hunt for Lano. They wouldn't be any good to Saw or to themselves if they were to be killed in a blaze of glory with the Feds.

But even knowing all that, and that the odds were stacked against them, Thugga just couldn't see turning his back on Saw. It just wasn't in him to do so.

Chapter Sixty-two

Special Agent Hopskins walked inside Saw's cell and stood over him with his hands shoved into the pockets of his cheap slacks. Saw was asleep. He was exhausted from days of hunger and restless nights since he'd been placed in the hole. He stank bad from not being allowed to shower. His outer appearance was a mess, but his spirits remained intact.

Agent Hopskins saw the fighter in Saw's eyes when he kicked his leg to wake him. Saw looked up at Hopskins with the same contempt he had when they'd first met.

"I take it you're ready to get outta here," said Hopskins.

"I just got here," said Saw.

Agent Hopskins pulled back a smirk and regarded Saw for a moment. He hated Saw because he couldn't break the man. He stood for something, and he wouldn't roll over the way Hopskins had grown accustomed to everyone else doing.

"You really are your father's son, aren't you?" asked Hopskins.

Saw glared at Hopskins, not following him.

"Wink. He's your daddy, right? What, you didn't think I would find out about the letters you've been exchanging with him through your attorney? I've read all y'all letters."

"Then you know he's on his way home," said Saw.

Hopskins threw his head back and laughed. "You believe that jail-talk bullshit he's feeding you? Every soul in that place has this dream that keeps 'em going, that one day they're going to walk outta that place. But let me be the one to tell you that that's all it is, a dream. Wink's gonna die in prison."

"Cracka, fuck you. If he does die in prison, he'll at least die a man and not one of your rats," said Saw.

Hopskins's jaws tightened from Saw's blatant disrespect. "I'm going to see to it that you get a cell right next to his so that y'all can dream of getting out together," promised Hopskins.

Saw rolled over, facing the wall. "Pardon my back," he told Hopskins, then closed his eyes. He heard the steel door slam shut with finality.

Saw could live with never seeing the streets again if it meant keeping his good name and honor intact. He knew the job was hard when he took it and that prison was just like the grave. They both came with the game.

He couldn't help but think about the promise he'd made to Sherise that he would come home to her. He knew deep down that she deserved better. And he started to think about the best way to tell Sherise to move on with her life, because things were looking bleak. He hadn't heard anything from Thugga or Maine, and as far as he knew, Lano would be at trial singing about the dirt he and Hood had done.

Saw closed out all his worries and pretended he was at home in bed with Sherise. For there wasn't any other place he would've rather been than close to her.

Hood's cell had been raided by the deputies at St. Clair County Jail. They'd stripped him down to his boxers and left him with a bare mattress and the four walls that contained him. The AC pumped ice-cold air from the vent above the sink. It was a tactic the deputies used whenever they wanted to implement punishment. But Hood was a warrior. He was built for whatever tricks them crackers had up their sleeves.

He paced the cold tile floor barefoot, and the only voice he could hear was Larry Hoover's from a skit he'd dropped from prison on Scarface's album. The King of the GDs had said, "All they want is a nigga to roll over and tell something."

Larry Hoover had been in prison over forty years, locked down at the ADX supermax in Florence, Colorado. Hood told himself that if Hoover could sit underground for all those years and not break, then so could he. Hood couldn't see his legacy as being a nigga who rose to the top of the game but then folded in the end. He thought about lyrics from one of his favorite rappers, Jadakiss:

And I'm tired of hearing about old niggas that had it,
And be the same old niggas that ratted.

Hood told himself that was not how his story would end.

He thought about Saw and wondered how he was doing under the circumstances. He hoped that Saw was doing much better than he was at the time. *Damn, my nigga, I fucked up.* He was blaming himself for them being in the position they were in. Hood reasoned that if he had not been caught with Karmesha, then he and Saw would've seen the Feds coming. He blamed himself that they hadn't been talking leading up to their arrest.

Hood had never done any sucka shit in his life. But he admitted to himself that fucking with Karmesha was just that—some sucka shit. He told himself that he had to redeem himself and that he couldn't let Saw go down with him.

Chapter Sixty-three

Ms. Raben and Mr. Beres stood in Judge Goldsmith's chambers at the federal courthouse. They had filed an emergency motion because the Feds had ceased Saw's visitation at the jail, including visits with his attorneys. They were arguing that this violated their attorney-client privileges as well as Saw's constitutional right to have access to a legal defense.

"Not if he's putting murder-for-hire contracts on witnesses' lives from his jail cell," argued the prosecutor, Paul Kuebler.

"Are you insinuating that I am somehow involved with a murder plot?" asked Ms. Raben.

"I am not ruling anything out," said Mr. Kuebler.

"The fact that you're an idiot hasn't been ruled out either," shot Ms. Raben. She'd had about enough of Mr. Kuebler.

"Let's settle down," said Judge Goldsmith.

The room fell silent as Judge Goldsmith seemed to be considering the arguments of both sides. He set aside the papers before him and laced his fingers together. He was ready to issue his ruling. He addressed the prosecutor. "While you present an argument, it comes with no facts. The defendant has only been considered responsible for these murders, but they have not been charged. Nor have you convinced me that either of the counselors would ever involve themselves in a murder plot. I am therefore granting the defense's emergency motion forthwith. And your office is to refrain from preventing their visitation with their client. This is my ruling."

Needless to say, Mr. Kuebler was hot around the collar. He had gone in hoping that the judge would side with the government based on the circumstances. But Judge Goldsmith had always been a champion of constitutional rights. He was fair and impartial.

Ms. Raben and Mr. Beres drove straight over to the Wayne County Jail with their court order in hand. The deputies tried stalling because they didn't want Ms. Raben and Mr. Beres to see the shape Saw was in. But Ms. Raben pitched a fit and threatened to file a civil suit if they didn't let them in to see their client.

Ms. Raben took one look at Saw, and she knew from experience that they'd been mistreating him. Cruel and unusual punishment was an understatement. Saw was already a skinny guy, but he was on the verge of looking sick.

"I'm getting you out of here," said Ms. Raben.

Saw didn't argue because he hadn't the energy, plus he knew that Ms. Raben would have her way regardless.

The following morning, Saw was moved to Genesee County Jail in Flint, Michigan. Saw wasn't really feeling the move because Flint was a forty-five-minute drive from Detroit. The niggas were different, and they really didn't like out-of-towners. Saw peeped that the first day in his pod. But he was a solid nigga, so he wasn't worried about no geographical shit them niggas were tripping off of.

The other thing he wasn't feeling was that there weren't any cell phones floating around the jail. Saw couldn't understand how all those Flint niggas were right there in their own backyard and nobody was making any moves.

Saw stayed to himself, and when he wasn't doing that, he was burning up the blue phone talking to Sherise. He still hadn't found the courage to let her go. He told himself that he was being selfish, but he just couldn't let her go.

The threat of the trial loomed in the back of Saw's mind. Every day that passed with no news

about Lano being killed was a day closer to the
reality Saw didn't want to face. He just couldn't
imagine Lano up on the stand pointing him and
Hood out for the prosecution. In the beginning,
Saw would've bet the house that neither Hood or
Lano would speak a thing.

Chapter Sixty-four

The warden at USP, Lewisburg had finally let convicts out from the lockdown. The yard was filled with thick tension because no one could ever say for certain what was on the next man's mind. As far as both sides of the conflict between St. Louis and Florida were concerned, somebody could decide to pop off at any given time.

The convicts who'd been down a minute knew to handle their most important business as soon as the doors unlocked, starting with a shower, a phone call, and a warm bowl for the night with a bucket of ice for a cold soda later.

Wink had done all of the above and shot to the law library, where he knew his old homie, Sag, would surely be. He found Sag typing a brief at his reserved table. Sag was a real-life jailhouse lawyer who'd freed many good men with his legal genius. He just had yet to free himself from the life sentence he was serving.

Sag was an ink black cat who stood at six feet five inches, and he was well-built for his age. He had his ways, which often got him into run-ins, particularly with the youngsters. They'd want to try to put hands on old Sag, but he'd always go get Wink to smooth things over.

Wink respectfully interrupted Sag from typing, then took a seat beside him. Wink handed Sag the thick manila envelope from Saw's attorney.

"That's it right there, Sag," said Wink.

"You hand me this like this is the key to something," said Sag. He had a sense of humor that only Wink appreciated.

"Just check it out, would you?" said Wink.

Sag pulled the papers out of the envelope and began reading. Besides Wink, Sag had known Wink's case better than anyone else, including his attorneys. Sag had been helping Wink since they'd met years back.

Sag solemnly nodded after he'd finished reading the investigation notes. "I assume you want this done ASAP?"

"What'chu think?"

"I think you're about to be a free man within the next thirty days," said Sag.

They shared a victorious smile. It had been a long time coming, and Sag would finally get to see his comrade walk out of the hellhole that he, himself, was trying to escape.

Wink hadn't shared his good fortune with anyone else, not even his family. He didn't want any big fuss about him coming home, no parties, nothing that would cause a stir. He wanted his appeal to kiss the panel's desk without any conversations beforehand to conspire to deny him relief. Wink just wanted what was due to him: his freedom.

Chapter Sixty-five

A nervous fart threatened to escape Saw as he sat beside Hood at the defense table. They were both dressed to the nines in black Armani suits and loafers, but Saw wasn't convinced that their attire made them look any less guilty in the eyes of the twelve jurors staring a hole through them. It was the first day of their trial, and they'd just concluded jury selection.

Saw and Hood were pissed behind the blank expressions their lawyers had coached them to wear at all times while in front of the jury. They were pissed because all of the jurors were from some rural area where the citizens viewed law enforcement as their friends. They didn't buy into the realities of police corruption and brutality. The twelve jurors sure weren't peers of the defendants, as the law states.

Mr. Beres leaned over to calm Saw's nerves. He'd told him to let him and Ms. Raben worry about the jurors. He was a successful trial lawyer. That much he knew about Mr. Beres. So Saw tried to relax and trust that, in the end, he and Hood would be acquitted.

Hood was struggling to find that same confidence in his lawyer, Ms. Barkovic. She'd never been to see him at the jail except for one visit, and she was late getting to court. But she wanted Hood to trust her. It was all she kept saying. What she didn't know was that Hood hadn't any qualms about breaking her jaw.

Saw turned around in his black swivel chair and stole a glance at the people in the back rows. Many were reporters. But his mom was seated three rows back. She smiled and waved. Beside her was some light-skinned nigga with wavy hair. He pulled back a closed smile and gave Saw a nod of assurance. Saw wondered who he was, but his eyes continued searching the courtroom for Sherise. She wasn't there. *Maybe she's running late,* Saw told himself. He didn't even want to begin to believe that Sherise wouldn't be there to support him.

Hood didn't bother turning around because he was sure there wasn't a soul there to support him. The only loved one he had in the world was sitting beside him, and they were about to start the biggest fight of their young lives.

Judge Mark A. Goldsmith sat on the bench. He ordered the government to start with their opening arguments. AUSA Mr. Kuebler gave the women and men of the jury a detailed summary of what he intended to prove throughout the trial and why it was their duty to convict Saw and Hood. Ms. Raben followed with a strong and assertive counter, calling the government's case a ham sandwich.

"You can indict a ham sandwich, and you can dress it up however you like," she told the jury. "But what the government's trying to feed you is bologna. It doesn't chew the same, doesn't taste the same, and it sure doesn't cost the same. As the evidence unfolds here, you all will see that the government doesn't have a case, but a theory, based upon the lies of informants who have cut side deals to save themselves." Ms. Raben left it there for the jury to consider.

Saw watched the expressions on a few of the jurors' faces. He could see that at least two older white women had regarded Ms. Raben.

Judge Goldsmith fixed his spectacles and laced his fingers. He was a small man in stature, but the bow ties he always wore gave a glimpse into his personality beyond the bench. He was a settled man who loved the law. He was as interested as any to see the final outcome of the trial, so he got things moving. He ordered the government to call their first witness.

Hood and Saw exchanged a nervous look. They just knew that Lano would be the first witness to grace the stand, but to their surprise, Mr. Kuebler called Tammy as the government's first witness.

As she stood and raised her right hand, Saw
couldn't help wanting to jump over the table and
beat her ass all around that courtroom. *Really,
bitch! After all I've done for you, you gon' come in
here and do me dirty?*

Ms. Raben squeezed Saw's hand, reminding
him to relax. He couldn't let the jury witness him
being angry, because if they saw him in that light,
it would be hard to convince them that he wasn't
capable of all the ill things he was accused of doing.

Tammy took a seat in the witness box, and Mr.
Kuebler regarded her with a warm smile. "Ms.
James, could you tell the court what your relation-
ship is to the defendant?" said Mr. Kuebler.

"I'm not sure," answered Tammy.

Mr. Kuebler held in his hand a copy of the testimony she'd given before the grand jury. He
presented it to Tammy. "You said here that you've
known the defendant for years. Do you remember
testifying to that at the grand jury?"

"No."

Mr. Kuebler was getting frustrated because
Tammy wasn't following the script that they'd
rehearsed in the days leading up to the trial. "So
it is your testimony here today that you don't
remember making this statement?" Mr. Kuebler
set the three-page statement down in front of
Tammy, but she wouldn't look down at it. "Ms.
James, would you like to read over your previous
statements?"

Tammy locked eyes with Denise, and she flashed back to the promise Denise had made her. "I don't need to read that because it's not true what it says." Tammy pointed to Agent Hopskins, causing everyone's head to turn. "That agent paid me twenty thousand dollars to say those things. And he promised to pay me another twenty thousand after I testified here today," said Tammy.

There was a bustle of side conversations around the courtroom. Saw smiled on the inside because the truth was coming out, and there was no way that the jury could disregard what Tammy had just thrown in their laps.

Judge Goldsmith banged his gavel for order to be restored. He wasn't into saving either side, so he pressed the government to proceed. "Are you done with your witness?" he asked.

"Yes, Your Honor," answered Mr. Kuebler. He was visibly pissed as he rounded the oak table for his seat.

Ms. Raben stood up and walked over to the witness box, but instead of looking at Tammy, she regarded the jury. She drove home her point that the government's case was unfounded and even conjured up by people who had zero credibility and who were trying to save themselves. Tammy was clear evidence, she said, of the government's willingness to practice deceit.

Mr. Keubler didn't call any more witnesses for the day. He couldn't afford any other surprises like the bombshell Tammy had dropped in the courtroom.

Ms. Raben gave Saw an assuring smile as the Marshals ushered him out of the courtroom so that he could be taken down to the bullpen. Judge Goldsmith had ordered everyone to return to the next session at 10:00 a.m. to resume the trial.

Hood and Saw were put into the same bullpen, and they couldn't help but be excited. Hood gave Saw a play.

"My nigga, did you see that cracker's face when Tammy flipped the script up in that bitch?" asked Hood.

"He looked like he shit a brick," said Saw.

They shared a laugh, which was good for both their souls.

"I ain't gon' lie. I ain't know what that bitch was gonna do. She been on some bullshit ever since I asked Sherise to marry me," said Saw.

"I never did get the chance to tell you this, but congratulations on the engagement," said Hood.

Saw nodded, and there was a brief silence that followed.

"I hope dawg come in there and have a memory lapse too," said Hood about Lano with his good-snitching ass.

"No bullshit," agreed Saw.

They had a good start at trial with Tammy's blunder, but Lano held the trump card. He would be the determining factor whether the jury believed that Saw and Hood were really the cold-blooded murderers the Feds painted them as.

The van from Genesee County Jail had arrived to pick up Saw. "In the a.m.," said Saw as he closed the gate of the bullpen.

"It's on," said Hood.

Hood lay across the cold bench with a smile plastered across his face. He was optimistic that they were going to beat every charge against them. *But then what? What you gonna do with your life after that?* a voice asked in his head. Call it divine intervention or whatever, but Hood didn't ignore the message being conveyed to him. The game was over. There weren't but a few loyal men left. And the Feds were building more penitentiaries every day. Hood didn't want to beat the Feds only to have to suit up and fight them again on another charge later. He had to make a change.

Chapter Sixty-six

AUSA Paul Kuebler vented to his counterpart, AUSA Frances Carlson, about Tammy's testimony. He was livid that she had gone off script the way she had. If he could've choked her, he would've.

"I should charge her ass with perjury," said Kuebler.

"And what, risk her going to trial and revealing that she was in fact paid to testify? I don't think so," said Ms. Carlson. She was the chief prosecutor over the violent crimes division, and she had the final say as to the direction her office went regarding prosecution. She'd been a federal prosecutor for nearly twenty years.

She and Mr. Kuebler were seated in her office awaiting the arrival of Special Agent Hopskins. He had some explaining to do, because by paying Tammy for her testimony, he had violated several ethics codes. But neither Mr. Kuebler or Ms. Carlson was concerned about the ethics violations. They wanted to be clear on one thing, which was that Hopskins had acted alone. It was time to do damage control. Hopskins would take the fall because he'd been the one to illegally pay Tammy for her testimony. Ms. Carlson was an experienced prosecutor, so she was sure the defense would latch on to Tammy's testimony for all that it was worth should they lose at trial.

Agent Hopskins arrived at the meeting late. He had known why the two prosecutors wanted to see him, and he wasn't particularly happy about the ass chewing he knew to expect. He sat like a child being scolded by his parents for being expelled from school.

"I'm warning you, Hopskins, if this thing blows up in my face, you're on your own. And that means an investigation, and the possibility of your career," said Ms. Carlson.

"Save me the speech, okay?" Hopskins knew the drill. He was expendable to them just like the snitches he put on the streets were to him.

It was all good so long as he kept the convictions rolling in. Everybody at the prosecutor's office would be cheesing and calling him their favorite agent, because more convictions meant more promotions and money. But as soon as there was a little mishap in the way he went about getting them the evidence they needed to obtain their convictions, everybody wanted to panic and part ways.

Agent Hopskins wasn't going to let a little tramp like Tammy be the one to destroy his career in the Bureau. He had something already in the works for her that would ensure no courtroom would ever hear her testimony again. If she couldn't take the stand, then the defense couldn't use her.

Hood and Saw weren't the only ones who could make a witness disappear. Two could play that game.

Tammy had just finished picking up her clothes from the cleaner's when she was driving home and was pulled over by an unmarked black SUV. She squinted in her side mirror as she pulled over to the curb. "Shit," she said to herself. She knew she hadn't been speeding, and she used her turn signal. She didn't understand why they had pulled her over.

She watched as a white man with dark shades got out of the driver's side and approached her door. Something told Tammy that the situation didn't seem right, but before she knew it, the man was at her window.

She had already let the window down due to the heat of the summer. "Did I do something wrong, Officer?" she asked.

The last thing Tammy saw was the silencer attached to the handgun being pointed into the car at her. The man jammed the silencer into her chest and fired several rounds. Tammy's body jerked with every bullet, and her eyes bucked into a stare of death. She slowly released her grasp from the man's arm as she succumbed to her death.

The man calmly walked back to his car and turned the flashing lights off before driving away.

Chapter Sixty-seven

The next morning, Hood and Saw were transported downtown to the federal courthouse to resume trial. Ms. Raben had learned about Tammy's death, but she didn't convey that knowledge to Saw because she didn't want to upset him during the trial. She and Mr. Beres had been to see Saw in the attorney-client cell, and they went over what they should expect the government to present in court. They all suspected that the government wouldn't waste any time calling Lano to the stand. He would surely start the day to make up for the blemish of Tammy's testimony.

Saw wanted to take the stand in his own defense, but Mr. Beres and Ms. Raben were both against the idea, calling it too risky. They'd explained to Saw that all it would take was for the jury to hear him speak and there would be a good chance that they would consider him guilty.

"Why is that?" asked Saw.

"Because for one, you're arrogant," said Ms. Raben, giving it to him raw. Saw didn't know how to back down or bow out gracefully when needed.

Mr. Beres nodded in agreement.

"Besides that, you'll be open to questioning about your expensive lifestyle, which you would have a hard time explaining," said Mr. Beres.

Saw didn't like it, but then again, that was what he had paid them to do—protect him, even if that meant protecting him from himself.

"I guess we'll see you upstairs," said Ms. Raben as she stood and gathered her duffle bag.

"A'ight," said Saw with a sigh. He needed a minute by himself anyway. He closed his eyes as the door closed behind his attorneys. The moment of truth wasn't but an hour or so away. Saw prayed to the game gods for a miracle.

Du'shan dipped his head down into his lap and snorted a greedy line of coke from the CD case. He looked up into the rearview mirror of the minivan he sat parked in. His eyes were glossy, like he'd just finished swimming. He grunted from the drain he felt from the coke as he thumbed his nose.

He hadn't snorted coke that good since the nineties. He was high as a kite as he sat across the street from the steps of the federal courthouse. Du'shan had always said that whenever he died, he wanted to go out high as "E-mothafucka," as only he could say.

He was getting there. He dipped down for another line of coke. He sat up and shook his head with sheer satisfaction. He was on cloud nine and ready to meet his Maker.

Du'shan reached for the white bucket on the floor of the passenger seat. A white towel sat at the top of the bucket. He donned his gas-station shades and reached for the door handle.

He crossed the street to the steps of the courthouse and went into his pitch about being homeless. "Come on and help a brotha out with some spare change," he begged as people passed by the courthouse.

Du'shan collected a few dollars and some loose change, but he readied himself as the black convoy approached the steps of the courthouse. He watched as Lano emerged from the back of a Suburban with his head on a swivel. Lano shrugged into the fit of his suit jacket and buttoned it closed as he was led by a group of agents across the sidewalk.

"Y'all think y'all can spare some change? Help a brotha out," said Du'shan as he tried approaching the circle around Lano.

One of the agents held out his hands to stop Du'shan. "Sir, you need to step back," said the agent.

"All I'm asking for is some loose change," said Du'shan.

Before the agent could blink, Du'shan had come out the bucket with a mini AR-15. Lano turned and looked at the gun as the first blast exploded through the agent's head.

Lano instinctively tried to make a run for the glass door of the courthouse, but Du'shan took aim at his back and fed him a series of shots. Lano stumbled up the steps, then crashed to his side from the hail of gunfire.

The agents had opened fire on Du'shan in return. He had known that he wouldn't be able to kill them all, so he took his shot at Lano. As long as he got to Lano before he could perch himself on the stand against his nephew, Du'shan could live with the chance of dying.

He lay on his back with a cheap smile across his face. The coke he'd snorted made his passing an easy one. He closed his eyes, still smiling, and accepted the grip of death taking hold of him.

Inside the courtroom, there seemed to be a lot of whispering going on at the prosecution table. Marshals and agents rushed in and out of the courtroom.

"What's going on?" Saw leaned over to ask Mr. Beres.

"I'm not sure." Mr. Beres was wondering the same thing.

Ms. Raben was over at the prosecution table arguing with Mr. Kuebler. She threw up her hand as she walked away. Judge Goldsmith had run out of patience and demanded to know what the holdup was all about.

Ms. Raben took delight in informing the court of the recent developments. "The government's star witness has passed away, Your Honor," said Ms. Raben.

"He was killed, Your Honor! He was killed outside the courthouse moments ago!" said Mr. Kuebler.

"Which has no bearing on my client's right to a speedy trial," asserted Ms. Raben. "The defense is ready to proceed," she said.

Judge Goldsmith gave Ms. Raben a look. She was correct, but at the moment, she was coming off too strong for his taste.

"Counselors, approach the bench," ordered Judge Goldsmith.

Saw and Hood kicked each other underneath the defense table. The game gods had delivered them the miracle they needed. Saw smiled inside at the thought of Thugga and Maine. They hadn't left him for dead. *My hittas.*

After the judge finished talking to Ms. Raben and the prosecution, he ordered a forty-five-minute recess. The purpose of the recess was for the government to offer a last-minute plea deal to Saw and Hood.

"They're offering you guys ten years," Ms. Raben informed them.

"I'm not taking a single day," said Saw.

"Me neither. Tell 'em to run it," said Hood, meaning to get on with the rest of the trial.

Mr. Beres presented the prosecution and the judge with the evidence proving that Saw had stepped away from the conspiracy prior to the indictment. And without Lano's testimony, the government had nothing tying Saw to any of the unsolved homicides.

Judge Goldsmith agreed that there was insufficient evidence to proceed against Saw, and he entered a judgment of acquittal. Hood wasn't so lucky though. He had been convicted for having the bulletproof vest and firearm upon his arrest. He'd beaten all the other charges. Hood was expected to get five years at sentencing, but that was a long way off from the life sentence the Feds wanted to give him.

Chapter Sixty-eight

Saw stood up from the cold bench of the holding cell and stretched his muscles. He'd been waiting hours for the Marshals to tell him that he could go home. They were all pissed around the federal courthouse that Saw had beaten his charges. In their sick and twisted minds, everyone charged by the Feds were supposed to lose at trial.

But that was a day for the books. The Feds loved to boast about having a 97 percent conviction rate, but they never publicized their losses because they hated losing. Saw had a wide shit grin across his face knowing that he could honestly say, "I beat you bitches," and he didn't ever once waver.

Finally, the door clicked open, and the Marshal called for Saw to come out. Hood had already been transported back to the county jail. "You ready to get out of here?" asked Murphy. He was the head Marshal at the courthouse and really the only straight one.

"Yeah, I'm ready to blow this spot," said Saw, walking past Murphy.

"Well, the good news is that the only way you'll ever come back is if you decide to," said Murphy.

That was a true bill. Saw was a free man with the absolute power to remain free or make the choice to be captured again. Saw liked the first option of remaining a free man.

The sun kissed his yellow face as he descended the steps of the courthouse. Saw took a moment to close his eyes and smell the fresh air that was free of another man's ass. *Freedom*. He exhaled.

When he opened his eyes, news cameras swamped the sidewalk, and reporters with microphones all asked the same question. "How does it feel to be freed from all charges?"

Saw dignified them with his answer. "I never doubted my lawyers from the start. They're the best in the business and the reason I'm not still in there," said Saw. He spotted Ms. Raben and Mr. Beres pushing through the crowd, so he met them halfway.

The reporters tried getting a comment from the lawyers, but neither were into posing for the cameras. They let their work do the talking for them. Saw kissed the crown of Ms. Raben's head as they crossed the street with their arms locked together.

"You guys are the best," said Saw, turning to Mr. Beres.

But neither smiled. "I want you to lie low because not a lot of people are happy to see you standing where you are," said Ms. Raben. They had stopped in front of the black iron gate of the paid parking lot.

"They're going to come after you again," admitted Mr. Beres.

"Why?" asked Saw. His mood was dampened.

"Because that's what they do when you beat 'em. They just keep coming until something sticks. But you can't give 'em what they need. You have got to lie low," said Mr. Beres.

Saw nodded as he looked across at the massive courthouse that he was sure had given out millions of years in sentences. He was just one of the few who'd slipped through the cracks. He made a vow never to be back in the clutches of the Feds again, not of his own accord.

"Looks like you've got some people here to see you," said Ms. Raben.

Saw looked over her shoulder. His mom was making her way toward him with the guy from the courtroom. Denise rushed to her son and gave him the biggest hug she could muster. "Thank you, God," she said, giving thanks as she rocked with Saw in her arms. Her son was a free man and in good health. That was all she had asked God for.

Denise turned to Ms. Raben and Mr. Beres, and she thanked them from the bottom of her heart for fighting for her son.

"Ah, he's not a bad guy." Mr. Beres smiled.

"Just remember what we've said," Ms. Raben reminded him. She and Mr. Beres said their good-byes and left Saw to his mom.

Saw looked from his mom to ol' boy she seemed to be keeping company with. "Baby, I want you to meet your father," said Denise.

Wink pulled back a smile and opened his arms to embrace Saw. Saw was having mixed emotions, but he went with it and hugged Wink back. There they stood, two living legends across from the same building of devils who wanted to take their lives from them.

"When did you get out?" asked Saw.

"A couple weeks ago. Those notes you sent me busted my case wide open. Soon as I put my appeal in, the prosecution ordered my release because they didn't want the truth getting out there," said Wink.

"These some dirty mothafuckas," said Saw.

"You don't have to tell me. I'm still going to put the truth out there. My manz Kevin Chiles gon' give me the next cover of *Don Diva*," said Wink.

"Can we talk about this someplace else?" Denise smiled. She was just happy that her son was a free man, and she wanted to get him away from that god-awful building.

They went to Flood's and had their famous steak dinner with red wine. Saw and Wink did much of the talking. They seemed to be bonding. The only thing Denise had ever wanted for Saw was to have a father in his life. She'd picked Wink up from the Greyhound bus station when he got out, and she made him promise to stay out of her son's life if Wink was about to try to reclaim his glory days in the streets. Wink understood Denise's concerns. He'd told her that he had no desire to run the streets, and he only wanted to live out the rest of his days surrounded by family. He'd been surrounded by the walls of the penitentiary for so many years that he knew there wasn't any love inside those bricks. There were only regret and pain, both of which Wink wanted to save Saw from experiencing.

As Wink looked across the table at Saw, he didn't need any DNA test to tell him that Saw was his son, because he saw himself in Saw. The topic about the DNA test never came up at the table, and Wink had no plans of mentioning it either. His only plans were to restore his own life and be in Saw's life as much as he would let him.

Denise noticed that something was bothering Saw, so she asked him what was wrong. He admitted that he had hoped Sherise would be outside the courthouse waiting for him, but she hadn't been. He hadn't talked with her much since the start of the trial.

Denise put her hand over Saw's as his eyes fell into his lap. "Baby, go get her. She'll be happy to see you," said Denise. Denise had always liked Sherise, and she just hoped that her son would one day realize that Sherise was the right woman for him.

Wink gave Saw a nod like, *what are you waiting for?* "Go 'head. Me and ya momma gon' hang out a li'l bit," said Wink.

Denise gave Saw the keys to her Infiniti truck along with a few hundred dollars. "Be careful," she said as Saw made his way to the door.

Saw found his mom's silver truck and climbed behind the wheel. The plush leather seat felt good against his back. It felt good to be home. He cranked up the radio as he pulled away from the curb, and Tee Grizzley's "First Day Out" poured from the speakers: "You ever went to trial and fought for your life?"

Saw sang along with the lyrics, because that was exactly how he was feeling on his first day out. As he drove to his apartment to wash up and change clothes, he spotted a black Crown Victoria in his rearview. It had been following him for over a mile, and it wasn't trying to hide the fact that they were tailing him either.

Saw thought back to what Mr. Beres had told him outside the courthouse. *"They're going to keep coming."*

Chapter Sixty-nine

Lay your head on my pillow.
Here, you can be yourself

Alicia Keys poured from the Bose speaker beside Sherise's bed as she lay with her eyes wide open. She had taken off from work since the start of Saw's trial, and she had locked herself up in her house. She cut off her phone and had totally cut herself off from the rest of the world. She didn't watch TV because she didn't want to see the news covering the trial. Sherise just wanted Saw to walk through the door and get into bed with her, where he belonged. She closed her eyes and enjoyed the soft notes of Alicia Keys. Her music had always brought Sherise the comforting words she needed to hear when things weren't going well.

She hadn't seen Saw walk into the bedroom. He smiled as he kicked out of his shoes and quickly undressed down to his boxers. He crawled up the length of the bed and planted a soft kiss on Sherise's full lips.

Her eyes flew open in surprise, and she threw her arms around his neck, pulling him ever so close to her. She kissed him back and kissed him some more until she had tears in her eyes. She couldn't believe that he was there with her.

"Are you really here?" she asked with a smile.

"Yes. And I'm not going anywhere," promised Saw as he wiped the lone tear streaming down her face.

"Promise?" asked Sherise in a small voice.

"I promise," said Saw, and then he kissed her again.

Their kisses were long and passionate. Saw ran his fingers through her hair, grabbing a fistful of it, letting Sherise know how much he'd missed her. His erection against her leg confirmed this as well.

Sherise reached down and found his manhood through the hole of his boxers. She stroked the length of him while watching his reactions. "I want you inside of me," she confessed.

She helped Saw out of his boxers, and then he peeled her out of the lavender panties she wore. Saw positioned himself between her thick thighs and pierced the split of her love nest with the throbbing head of his dick.

"Ahh!" cried Sherise as Saw quickly filled her up. He pulled out and drove balls deep again, resting for a second, before delivering his stroke.

Sherise clung to Saw by digging her nails deep into his back. She arched her back, greedy to have all of him inside her. He felt so good, almost like a dream. "Yes. Fuck me! Ahh!"

Sherise sank her teeth into Saw's shoulder because of the pleasure he was bringing her. "I love you," she confessed.

"I love you too," said Saw in a hoarse voice. He was on the verge of unloading. He'd been anticipating the feel of Sherise beneath him for months, and now that he had her, the feeling was surreal.

They came together, and Saw continued his stroke until he went soft inside Sherise. He lay on top of her, still inside of her. He kissed around her neck as she lay with her eyes closed and with a smile of satisfaction across her face.

She pinched his ass cheek, making him jump a little. Sherise giggled like a schoolgirl. "I just wanted to make sure you were really here with me," she said.

Saw pinched her nipple, then nestled against her neck. "Yes, I'm really here, so believe it."

Sherise rolled them over to where she was on top of him. She could feel him hardening inside her, so she slowly ground her hips in encouragement. She raked at his stomach with her nails while biting her bottom lip and looking deep into his eyes.

Saw palmed her small waist and began guiding her to their satisfaction. They made love all afternoon and into the night.

Chapter Seventy

Saw had put the rush on making the move down to ATL. He wanted to give Detroit a good long break because, as Mr. Beres told him, the Feds were going to keep coming at him until something stuck. At least in Atlanta no one really knew Saw, so he could just focus on building a life with Sherise.

Karmesha had up and moved to California with Saw's daughter, Lovey, and Marco, Saw's son with Tammy, went to live with his father. Sherise accepted Marco with open arms and included him in their plans to move to ATL. Saw wished his daughter could come, but Denise had told him just to go down there and be happy, because he'd only drive himself crazy trying to please everybody. It was the best motherly advice she had ever given him. She told him that Detroit wasn't going anywhere, and that it would be there when he came back.

Wink helped Saw load up the U-Haul truck with the items Sherise deemed necessary to take down to Atlanta. It was mainly shoes and her extensive wardrobe, but Saw didn't mind. She was to be his queen, and she could have anything that she wanted.

As they loaded the boxes into the bed of the truck, Wink stopped, and he looked at Saw for a moment.

"What's up?" asked Saw. "You tired, old man?" he joked.

"Nah," laughed Wink. "It's just I'm sending you off to Atlanta, and we're just starting to bond."

Saw had stopped and wiped at the sweat over his brow. He took a seat on one of the boxes, and Wink joined him. They looked out at the traffic moving along the residential street. There was a small group of boys shooting ball on a rollout rim just a few houses down. It made Wink and Saw both think.

"I'm sorry that you had to grow up without a father in your life, Saw," said Wink. He sighed, then continued. "I can't say that had I known you were in your mother's stomach, I would've picked another route, because I was deep in the game. I'm proud of you though, because you made the right choice at the right time, and because of it, you're going to have the blessing of watching your kids come up."

"We can watch 'em come up together. You are their grandfather," said Saw.

A wide smile creased Wink's face. "I'd like that," he said.

Saw gave Wink some dap, and they leaned over for a half-hug. They both accepted the past for what it was, but they'd made a concerted decision to live their best lives from then on.

Saw would get to raise his kids while building his own relationship with his father. He was all for it and even invited Wink to visit them in ATL whenever he wanted to just hang out and chill.

"It's on," said Wink.

They finished loading the truck at Sherise's strong request. She brought them each a glass of iced tea, then told them to finish up because she was ready to see her new house. There was much to do, and ATL was calling her name.

Sherise had already started planning their wedding and dreaming up how she wanted everything to be. She wasn't a diva, but on her special day she wanted to be perfect.

Wink really liked Sherise and was happy his son had found her. "You hold on to her," he told Saw.

Chapter Seventy-one

Meanwhile, Hood had been sentenced to forty-eight months to be served in the custody of the Federal Bureau of Prisons. He had never been in any serious trouble before, and he only had a four-year sentence, so Hood was supposed to serve his time out at a minimum-security prison. But Agent Hopskins and the dick-face prosecutor flexed their muscles and had Hood designated to the United States Penitentiary, Pollock, in Louisiana. The prison had earned the nickname "Bloody Pollock" because of all the murders and riots that occurred on a near-daily basis.

Hood had heard the war stories about the penitentiary. It was one of the sixteen that the Feds had spread across the United States. The day Hood got to USP, Pollock, the captain gave him and the new arrivals a speech before they hit the compound.

"I'm telling you right now, if ya ass is hot, this is your last chance to step to the wall," said Captain Ramos. The term "hot" was another word for a snitch.

Two men stepped against the wall, indicating that they were indeed snitches and feared for their lives.

"You two bitches wait here," Captain Ramos told the two men. "The rest of you, come with me," he said as he led the group from R&D to the main corridor. "I suggest y'all get with y'all homies, have ya paperwork ready to be checked, and get a good knife, because there's a hands-off policy here, which means ain't no fist fighting going on. Only knife play."

Captain Ramos escorted the men to the double doors by the kitchen that led out to the yard. He pushed open the doors and released the men to the wolves awaiting them. At the last minute, a white boy clung to the door, but Captain Ramos pushed him outside.

"Ya ass had the chance to check in. Now I'ma let ya homies bite that ass," said Ramos as he shut the door and locked it.

There was a mob of convicts lined against the gates beneath the gun tower. They were all awaiting the new arrivals for any signs of enemies or good-standing homies on the new.

Hood held his bedroll under his arm and walked in the direction of his assigned unit, B-2. "Any Gs out here?" called a voice at the gate.

"Any Damus?' asked another voice.

"Vice Lords?" asked another man.

There was a roll call of the gangs and organizations seeking out their own. Some of the new arrivals stopped to recognize their affiliations, but Hood kept one foot in front of the other until he reached the mouth of B-2.

A man drenched in blood shot out of the unit with two shirtless black men on his heels. They both had blood dripping from the blades of the knives held at their sides as they chased the man out onto the handball court, where he tripped and collapsed. The two men straddled their victim and took turns stabbing holes deep into his face and chest. The gun tower sounded its alarm, and the sliding window dropped out a flash grenade.

The two convicts ignored the warning shot fired from the AR-15 that the CO up in the tower had let off.

"All inmates get down on the ground!" So went the automated recording from the speaker mounted above the tower.

Hood crouched down as he'd seen the others around him doing. The two men were still slamming their bone crushers into the man, causing his body to jerk with every thrust. COs came rushing with pepper mace and beanbag guns. The two men had been subdued, but their victim had been slaughtered. There was no doubt that he was dead, but the two responding nurses still tried to work on him.

Hood and the others were rushed to the assigned housing units and immediately locked inside their cells. Hood had picked the wrong time to get locked down, because his new cellmate had just finished shitting. Hood balled his face up upon entering the cell. His cellmate was waving a sock filled with baby powder above his head.

"Smell like a perm, don't it?" asked the guy with a smirk.

Hood took up the window and put his shirt over his nose. He could only shake his head about the situation. The Feds had gotten him good. But he tried to find solace in knowing that his stay would only be temporary. In the meantime, he would adapt to his environment just as he had in the streets.

Hood watched a helicopter descend to the parking lot of the prison. Apparently the guy who'd been stabbed was still clinging to life, and he was being flown to the hospital.

"You gon' see a whole lot of that there," said the man behind Hood. He had just finished washing his hands.

Hood turned around to face the guy. He wasn't much older than Hood, but he was a lot thinner and wore wire-frame glasses. He hadn't stopped smiling since Hood walked into the cell.

"They call me Boo-Shay."

"Hood."

"Where you from?" asked Boo-Shay.

"Detroit."

"Okay. I'm from Inkster. We got a couple homies in the block. I'ma show you 'em when we come up from lockdown."

Boo-Shay was doing twenty-seven years and had been down for seventeen, so he laced Hood up on all the prison politics and the bullshit that came with doing time in the pen.

Chapter Seventy-two

Six months later, Saw and Sherise were getting married in the Bahamas in front of a small group of family and Sherise's girlfriends. The wedding was everything that Sherise dreamed it to be. The weather was beautiful, with not a cloud in the sky, and the ocean surrounding the gathering provided a tropical breeze.

Saw stood at the altar dressed in a black tux. Wink was his best man because Saw really didn't have anyone else close enough to ask to do the honor. In the months leading up to the wedding, Wink had been to visit Saw and his grandsons in Atlanta, and during that time he'd formed a bond with all three of them.

Denise sat in the front row with her family members. She was dressed to the nines because no one would outdress her on her son's wedding day. She couldn't stop smiling as she looked at Saw and Wink because they were so handsome in their tuxedos.

Sherise emerged down the aisle, escorted by her older brother. Saw smiled at how beautiful she looked in the custom-made dress that fit her like a glove. She was the most beautiful woman he'd ever laid eyes on, and he was happy that she was going to be his wife.

Sherise smiled into Saw's eyes as her brother handed her off. "I love you," mouthed Saw. The ordained minister from the island went through the rights and responsibilities of their proposed marriage, and then Saw and Sherise exchanged vows. Saw's vows were heartfelt when he assured Sherise that she was the one woman God created solely for him and that he was grateful to have found her in his lifetime.

A lone tear escaped Sherise because she had never heard Saw open up with his feelings, especially in front of a gathering of people. It was the affirmation that her heart needed, and he'd given it to her.

The minister announced them husband and wife, and Saw kissed his beautiful bride. It was official. They were now husband and wife and could forever live the good life.

Saw had gone all out for the reception. He rented a three-level 120-foot yacht that came with a captain and full crew. They crossed the ocean while dining on the best seafood the islands had to offer.

The biggest surprise though was when Musiq Soulchild came out and sang a string of his early hits. Sherise loved his voice and every song he made, so she was beside herself as she and Saw had the first dance.

See, I'll love you when your hair turns gray, girl.
I'll still want you if you gain a little weight, yeah.
The way I feel for you will always be the same,
Just as long as your love don't change, no.

Saw sang along to the lyrics as he held Sherise in his arms. She really felt like a dream in his arms.

Sherise rested her head against Saw's chest and closed her eyes. Her special day was everything that she had dreamed it would be since she was a little girl.

Chapter Seventy-three

Meanwhile, back in Detroit the game had moved on without Saw and Hood. Up-and-coming hustlers were fighting to fill the void that the drug supply had suffered at the loss of Saw and Hood. In the midst of the bloody war that was underway were Thugga and Maine. They were still on the lam from the shoot-out with the Feds, but it hadn't stopped them from trying to eat on a major level.

They had shot back to Houston for a while until they'd heard about Lano finally being killed. That meant they were in the clear about the murders he planned to snitch about. The only thing they had hanging over their heads was the shoot-out with the Feds, and they agreed to cross that bridge when they got there.

Thugga and Maine came back from Houston with 200 kilos, and they set their sights on the east side of Detroit to restart their operation. The only thing standing in their way was Turk, an old-school nigga who had just come home from the Feds after giving back a life sentence. They had heard that Turk was an official nigga and was about whatever any nigga wanted to get into about his money.

That rundown of Turk only made Thugga's dick hard, because he loved whenever he got to kill a tough nigga. He just hoped that Turk would keep that same energy when he ran down on his old ass. Thugga didn't give a fuck about the prison rep Turk had or about his glory days back in the eighties. None of that boo-game shit was going to cut it in 2020. Old niggas were getting it too if they were in the way.

Turk was an east-side nigga, so he had come home and set up shop all up and down 7 Mile to Gratiot. This nigga had crack spots like he was bringing back the Chambler Brothers era.

Thugga and Maine couldn't help but laugh the first time they saw Turk. He was standing out on the corner of Gable Street with a doo-rag wrapped tight around his prison waves. He had on some old-school jewelry with baggy clothes. Turk was still stuck in the era from which he'd been arrested. He had a gathering of youngsters around him listening to that old shit he was trying to run.

Maine stopped the tinted black Durango as he reached the corner, and he and Thugga bailed out with AR-15s dripping at their sides. The youngsters scattered in different directions, leaving Turk caught like a deer in headlights.

"Welcome home," said Thugga as he raised the barrel of his AR-15 to Turk's chest.

Thugga and Maine opened fire on Turk, but just enough to spin him to the ground. They didn't do him dirty by giving him any face shots on the strength that he was a real nigga. So they left him there to bleed out on the same corner he'd come up hustling on as a youngster himself.

Thugga and Maine climbed back in the Durango and peeled off. Turk was just the start of their takeover. Many more would die just as he had if they stood in the way of Thugga and Maine's rise.

Chapter Seventy-four

Within a couple of weeks, Thugga and Maine were running most of the east side of Detroit. They had a simple program going. You either bought from them or you didn't hustle anymore. They had laid down enough demonstrations around the city that niggas were starting to catch on. It was really a generous offer, Thugga thought. If niggas bought from him and Maine, they'd get the best work in the city and at a low ticket. And if that weren't enough, they also got to keep their lives.

Thugga was the brains of the operation. He was the one in the shadows plotting his and Maine's next move in the game. He had arrived to the position of power that he'd watched all those before him hold. Thugga told himself that the difference between him and those before him was that he was going to die at the top of his game. He wasn't going to be named a snitch at the end of his run, nor was he going to try to retire from the game. He was going to go out the same way he'd come in: hard as a mothafucka.

That was why Thugga wasn't cutting the streets any breaks when it came to his and Maine's money.

Dorian Sykes

He accepted the fact that he wouldn't rule forever, but while he did, it would be dick hard with no grease.

Thugga circled the steel chair that Ed Bone was tied to. He held an electric saw at his side and revved the blade as he came to a stop in front of Ed Bone.

"That's not what I wanted to hear," said Thugga as he lowered the spinning blade against the left wrist of Ed Bone.

"Ahhh!" Ed Bone let out a bloodcurdling scream as the saw cut through his bone, severing his hand from his arm.

Thugga held up Ed Bone's detached hand so that he could see it. "You still got one good hand. Should we go for that one next?"

"Fuck you!" screamed Ed Bone. Then he spat at Thugga but had missed his face.

Thugga pulled back a sinister smile and dropped the severed hand to the floor. He walked over to the tool shed of the musty two-car garage where he'd kept Ed Bone unfed for the past two days. Thugga looked at Boo, who was leaning against the frame of the door to the garage.

"He said fuck me, Boo," laughed Thugga.

"That's what he said, Slim," agreed Boo.

Boo was Thugga's older cousin from D.C. Thugga had brought him to Detroit because Boo was an official headhunter in the nation's capital. Boo had over fifty bodies under his belt. He didn't grow up looking up to the neighborhood hustlers, because there weren't many to name. In a city like D.C., the youth grew up looking up to the niggas who put the most work in and who had the most bodies.

Thugga's smile vanished. Besides Ed Bone, it was just Boo and Thugga inside the garage. No one could hear the torture session taking place because the entire block was filled with vacant houses waiting to be torn down by the city. Tacoma Street was the perfect place to murder someone because it would be forever before the corpse was discovered by anyone.

Thugga nodded, and his wicked smirk reappeared as he came up with the perfect torture tactic for Ed Bone, seeing that he didn't want to comply. Ed Bone owned a strip of apartment buildings down Chalmers Avenue that Thugga wanted, but Ed Bone refused to sign over the deeds. He wasn't about to be muscled into turning over his properties to the likes of Thugga so he could turn them into dope spots.

"Boo. Fuck this nigga," ordered Thugga.

What Ed Bone didn't know was that Boo went both ways, and he had no qualms about sticking dick to another man.

Ed Bone watched in horror as Boo unfastened his jeans and unearthed ten inches of uncircumcised, ashy dick. Boo began stroking himself to an erection as he closed the space between him and Ed Bone.

"What you finna do with that?" asked Ed Bone as Boo spit onto his hand for lubrication.

Boo pulled back a wicked grin, then pushed Ed Bone over onto the floor where he lay on his side still bound to the chair. "Get off me!" screamed Ed Bone as he fought to free himself from Boo's prying hands.

Boo snatched his pants down and spread his ass cheeks, then spat a glob of saliva against his ass crack. "Yeah," said Boo as he jammed the one finger inside Ed Bone.

"Ah! Get the fuck off me!" yelled Ed Bone, still trying to buck the inevitable.

Thugga had rolled a wrap of Cookie and was chiefing with a devilish smile on his face as he watched Boo ram inside of Ed Bone. Boo slapped Ed Bone hard across the ass as he fucked his back out.

"Fuck me, huh?" laughed Thugga. "Nah, fuck you."

Thugga wasn't into fucking other men like his cousin Boo, but he was just as twisted in his own way. It was a power trip for Thugga to have niggas submit to him. And if they didn't, he'd do something to degrade them, and then he'd kill them.

Thugga pulled out his phone and recorded the scene of Boo hitting Ed Bone from the back, and then he posted it to Facebook Live for all to see.

Thugga told himself that when it was all over with and he was in his grave paying for his sins, he wanted niggas to regard his name with fear and to say that he was a wild nigga.

Meanwhile, Maine had put together a team of young, crazy niggas who just didn't give a fuck like him and Thugga. None of them were any good at hustling, but they were naturals when it came to putting down the murder game. Maine had lots of work lined up for his young hittas.

Old man Cole worked downtown in the property and evidence room of the first precinct, known as Detroit Police Headquarters. Cole wasn't on the force. He was more like the station's janitor. He had access to the drugs sitting inside the evidence room, and for years he'd been switching out the coke and heroin with nothing but flour. Niggas who'd been caught with the real drugs would plead guilty, so it was never an issue. And for the ones who went to trial, the drugs would've already been tested before the start of the prosecution, so at trial the DA would be holding up a pure bag of flour instead of coke or heroin.

It was a perfect lick, one that had made Cole a wealthy old man. He was a janitor in the eyes of his coworkers, but what they didn't know was that Cole had millions put into real estate, and he was a trick master when it came to the younger broads.

Maine had respected the old nigga's play that he was putting down, except Cole wasn't playing by the G-code. Cole had become greedy over the years, so he picked up two partners who were detectives. Cole knew who was doing what in the game, and so did his two partners, so they started targeting specific drug dealers. Two detectives would seize the drugs, and Cole would steal them out of the evidence room, and within twenty-four hours the same drugs would be back on the streets.

Cole and his partners made the mistake of taking twenty-five kilos from one of Maine's stash houses on the east side. Their biggest mistake was when Cole's niece tried to sell the keys back to Maine, not knowing that they were his. Somewhere their wires got crossed, and Cole and his detectives thought the drugs belonged to another hustler.

Maine smiled when he looked over the twenty-five kilos because they all had his and Thugga's HUMMER stamp in the center of each kilo. Maine had met with Cole's niece, Brandi, at one of his apartments on Mt. Elliot.

"It's that A1," said Brandi, trying to sell Maine on the coke. She was a hustler at heart. She'd had her own bag, but she often got rid of work for her uncle.

"You say it's that A1, huh?" asked Maine as he picked up one of the kilos, examining it. "Where'd you get it?" he asked.

"Ah, you know my hand gets hit whenever something good is on the floor," said Brandi. She was a thick and pretty little something.

But it was too bad that she'd found herself caught up in the middle of the bullshit, because Maine wasn't into giving out passes. He set the kilo down on the table and nodded to his little man, Head, to lock the door.

Brandi's eyes darted to the door at the sound of the deadbolt clicking. Maine had unearthed a .50-cal Desert Eagle with a hole so big that Brandi could see the bullet straight through the barrel.

"Bitch, these is my keys. The police took 'em off me last night, so how'd you get 'em?" asked Maine.

"Uh . . ." stammered Brandi, because she'd been caught red-handed. She had known the play her uncle was running out of the evidence room, but she was in the blind about the other aspects of his operation, like purposely targeting drug dealers.

Maine had an idea for Brandi, seeing as she was having problems with her memory. He'd peeped the way his little hittas kept eyeing her fat ass and thick thighs since she'd gotten there.

Head, KD, and Pun were all posted up, just waiting for the word from Maine. Whatever the play was, they were going to run it.

"Y'all like this li'l bitch?" asked Maine as he cracked a smile.

"I like that ass," said Pun, breathing all hard. They called him Pun because he was light skinned and as big as Big Pun, the late rapper.

"Yeah, that pussy fat, too," added Head with a creep's smile.

Brandi saw where things were headed, and she promptly made the best choice of her life. "I'll tell you," she said.

"Bitch, you got about two seconds before I turn my young'uns loose on you," promised Maine.

"I got the work from my uncle, Cole."

Brandi gave Maine the rundown about her uncle. Then he still turned his pack of savages on Brandi, rewarding them for the work they'd put in later on killing her uncle.

Head, KD, and Pun circled Brandi like the predators they were, tearing her clothes off as they wrestled her to the floor. They took turns having her for hours until she begged that they just kill her. She would have rather died than to keep smelling the shitty stench of Pun's sweaty body as he went for thirds on pleasing himself with her body.

"You stink," spat Brandi as Pun lowered himself into her.

"You gon' stink too when I'm done, bitch," said Pun as he pushed himself back inside of her.

The city of Detroit had never before seen anything like Thugga and Maine and the ruthlessness they brought to the game. The only rules they were playing by were the ones they had written. Game on!

The End